"Christine Warren is amazingly talented and continues to show this in her latest novel . . . undisputedly a masterpiece of written talent and definitely a five hearts book!"
—*Night Owl Romance Book Reviews*

"Artfully realized tale with amazing characters and intriguing plots."
—*Fallen Angel Reviews*

Howl at the Moon

"Warren delivers a rapidly paced tale that pits duty against honor and love. Populated with intriguing characters who continue to grow and develop, it is fun to see familiar faces in new scenarios. This is a world that is always worth visiting!"
—*Romantic Times BOOKreviews*

"A fantastic addition to the world of The Others . . . grab a copy as soon as possible. Christine Warren does a wonderful job of writing a book that meshes perfectly with the storylines of the others in the series, yet stands alone perfectly."
—*Romance Reviews Today*

"Warren weaves a paranormal world of werewolves, shifters, witches, humans, demons, and a whole lot more with a unique hand for combining all the paranormal classes."
—*Night Owl Romance*

"*Howl at the Moon* will tug at a wide range of emotions from beginning to end . . . Engaging banter, a strong emotional connection, and steamy love scenes. This talented author delivers real emotion which results in delightful interactions . . . and the realistic dialogue is stimulating. Christine Warren knows how to write a winner!"

—*Romance Junkies*

The Demon You Know

"Explodes with sexy, devilish fun, exploring the further adventures of the Others. With a number of the gang from previous books back, there's an immediate familiarity about this world that makes it easy to dive right into. Warren's storytelling style makes these books remarkably entertaining."

—*Romantic Times BOOKreviews* (4 ½ stars)

She's No Faerie Princess

"Warren has fast become one of the premier authors of rich paranormal thrillers elaborately laced with scorching passion. When you want your adventure hot, Warren is the one for you!"

—*Romantic Times BOOKreviews*

"The dialogue is outrageous, funny, and clever. The characters are so engaging and well scripted . . . and the plot . . . is as scary as it is delicious!"
— *Romance Reader at Heart*

"Christine Warren has penned a story rich in fantastic characters and spellbinding plots."
— *Fallen Angel Reviews*

Wolf at the Door

"A great start to a unique paranormal series."
— *Fresh Fiction*

"This book is a fire-starter . . . a fast-paced, adrenaline- and hormonally-charged tale. The writing is fluid and fun, and makes the characters all take on life-like characteristics."
— *Romance Reader at Heart*

"Intrigue, adventure, and red-hot sexual tension."
— *USA Today* bestselling author Julie Kenner

St. Martin's Paperbacks Titles
By Christine Warren

Big Bad Wolf

You're So Vein

One Bite with a Stranger

Walk on the Wild Side

Howl at the Moon

The Demon You Know

She's No Faerie Princess

Wolf at the Door

BIG
BAD
WOLF

Christine Warren

St. Martin's Paperbacks

This is a work of fiction. All of the characters, organizations, and events portrayed in this novel are either products of the author's imagination or are used fictitiously.

BIG BAD WOLF

Copyright © 2009 by Christine Warren.

For information address St. Martin's Press, 175 Fifth Avenue, New York, NY 10010.

ISBN: 978-0-312-94795-8

Printed in the United States of America

St. Martin's Paperbacks edition / October 2009

St. Martin's Paperbacks are published by St. Martin's Press, 175 Fifth Avenue, New York, NY 10010.

10 9 8 7 6 5 4 3 2 1

CHAPTER ONE

Abstinence wouldn't be quite so bad, Graham decided, if not for the lack of sex.

Nursing his fifth scotch and wishing it were a fifth of scotch, the alpha of the Silverback Clan of New York City spent his Saturday night in a manner no self-respecting werewolf should ever have to endure—single and celibate.

At least he didn't have to spend it alone, he reflected, although the type of companionship he could expect to find at his friends' post-wedding engagement party left a lot to be desired. A bit long in the tooth for his taste. Graham preferred women who hadn't been painting the town red back when his ancestors still thought of the cotton gin as a newfangled contraption. Plus, seeing that he'd just broken off his on-again-off-again relationship with one particular vampire, he didn't feel any great compulsion to go start a new one. Immortal women all seemed to be just a little too demanding.

Why he bothered to sulk here in the corner,

rather than excusing himself and getting out there to meet the Lupine woman of his dreams, remained a mystery. He couldn't blame a fear of commitment like so many human men seemed to do. Werewolves relished the idea of a mate-bond and lived to beget lots of new generations of baby Lupines, and even Graham looked forward to the day when he would rear his own cubs in the traditions of his clan and his ancestors. Commitment sounded just fine to him. It wasn't fear that had him in this mood; it was boredom.

Graham suffered from a huge, honking case of the same old–same olds. Everywhere he looked, he saw the same faces, the same habits, heard the same gossip, and seduced the same women. Oh, their names and hair color might change, but deep down, they were all the same to him. The realization depressed him. What had happened to the carefree, rakish wolf he used to be? These days he acted more like a priest than a playboy.

He blamed the women, of course. What other reason was there for an attractive, healthy Lupine in his prime to suddenly go cold turkey from the pleasures of sex? He still enjoyed the act, after all, so his problem wasn't physical. Never in his life had he experienced any problem getting an erection when the situation called for one. He had no trouble getting it up, but lately he'd had a bitch of a time getting it back down, and that he blamed on his partners.

If he remained dissatisfied after a sweaty, breathless romp, he must be romping with the wrong woman, right? The conclusion sounded logical to him. As long as he ignored the fact that he'd been lucky enough to sample some pretty amazing women.

Take Natalie for instance. The blond vampire he'd recently broken off with made most supermodels look like sideshow freaks. With her pale hair, pale skin, and radiant blue eyes—not to mention the body of a Venus—she looked like an angel sent to earth to reward the truly righteous. The fact that she had the morals of an alley cat and the ruthless ambition of Napoléon Bonaparte explained why she'd spent the last three months writhing beneath Graham instead of singing in a heavenly choir. No one had ever accused him of being righteous, or even true.

The point was that he had no reason to be bored. Natalie knew sexual tricks to put a houri to shame and had the stamina of an undead Olympic athlete. She was willing to try anything, no matter how depraved, and if it got her off, she'd do it again until she could give lessons to the experts. How in God's name could he have gotten sick of that?

He didn't know, but he had.

He'd gotten sick of all the women, and all modesty aside, Graham Winters had had a lot of women. Some were little more than one-night stands, some recurrent companions, and some, like Natalie, had bordered on casual relationships, but none managed to hold his interest for more than a few weeks. The only reason Nat had lasted so long had more to do with his disinclination to deal with the fit he'd known she'd throw than with any real desire to keep her around. He'd tried just about anything he could think of to spice up their last few weeks together, but eventually even exotic tricks hadn't been able to keep his interest.

When he'd started leaving all-night orgies with his muscles trembling in exhaustion and his dick still hard as a pike, he had thrown in the towel. Now that he knew no woman could satisfy him, he saw no reason to keep torturing himself with sex that wore him out everywhere but where it counted. That had led to Natalie's dismissal, complete with the expected and unpleasant scene, and eventually to this— his thirteenth night of celibacy, spent in Dmitri's living room celebrating his friend's post-wedding engagement party.

Taking another sip of liquid fire, Graham glanced around the room and wondered how much longer etiquette required him to stay. He viewed Dmitri as a brother, and he genuinely liked Regina, so he was glad to share in the celebration, especially since he'd had to duck out on his best-man duties at their reception in order to deal with a fire in the kitchen of the nightclub he owned. What he wasn't so glad of was the speculative glances currently being aimed in his direction by a large number of the room's single— and some not-so-single—women. He worked at ignoring their interest, but he knew it was only a matter of time before one of them decided to lay off the staring and make a move.

"I vote for the redhead. She looks like the type

who's ready for anything. Plus I don't think she's wearing panties."

His friend and beta appeared at Graham's side, carrying a dark brown beer bottle and wearing a repressed smile. Logan Hunter knew all about Graham's predicament and seemed to find it amusing. Graham shot him a narrow look.

"She never does," he grumbled. "But I doubt Shelley is going to put the make on me, not after the last time we went out."

"Did you spill a drink on her dress or something?"

Graham shook his head. "I criticized her, um, technique."

Logan winced around a chuckle. "Ouch. Okay, maybe not the redhead then." He glanced back to where Shelley stood, whispering to a couple of other women. "Could be her friend, the one almost wearing the green dress. Do you think those are real?"

"On vampires, they're always real. They can't afford to bleed out during surgery just to get implants." He gave the other woman an assessing look. "Besides, not even silicone can make tits that firm. Hildie works out."

Raising his beer for a drink, Logan rolled his eyes. "And I'm sure you'd know. But you could at least make an effort. Lady knows you need to do something to lighten your mood. What the hell is up with you tonight anyway?"

"Three guesses," Graham muttered. "I'll even spot you the first two."

Logan grimaced. "Shit. Curtis."

"Right both times."

"What's he done now?"

"Same old, same old. This week he tried to get Bill Lakeland to take an interest in examining the validity of the challenge Dad and I fought when he decided to retire and leave the business of alpha to me."

Logan nearly choked on his beer. "You've got to be kidding me."

"I wish."

"I don't care how many packs consider Bill an expert of the traditional procedures for alpha challenges, you took that fight fair and square. Your father wouldn't even cut your *mother* any slack in a challenge ring, let alone the son he raised to continue his family dynasty!"

"You know that, and I know that . . ."

"And so does anyone who was there watching. You took that challenge fairly and by the skin of your teeth. For a few minutes, I wondered if both of you were going to leave the circle alive."

Graham's mouth twisted. "So did we."

"So how does he figure he can protest the outcome?"

"Beats me. I doubt he thought he'd really get anywhere with that kind of nonsense. Chances are he was just pulling my chain."

"And how long has that been his favorite hobby?"

"Let's see. I'm thirty-four and Curtis is seven years younger, so . . ." Graham pursed his lips and pretended to think. "About twenty-seven years, I think."

Logan nodded. "And you did what to set him off again?"

"Be born first, be my father's son, and be more of a Lupine than he'll ever be?"

"Right. So you're just going to go on ignoring him?"

"That's the plan." Graham saw the disgust in his friend's expression and smiled. "Trust me, it's easier to ignore him than it is to dignify his idiocy with a response. If I got worked up every time he pulled a stupid stunt just to piss me off, I'd be the first Lupine in recorded medical history to have to take blood pressure medication."

Logan sighed. "True enough." He took a long pull on his beer and gave the room another thorough glance. "Which means that you could definitely use a distraction tonight. So? Who's it going to be."

"No one."

"Excuse me?"

"I'm not in the mood for a woman."

"You know, you've been saying that with distressing regularity lately, my friend," Logan pointed out. "I don't know about your blood pressure, but you might want to talk to a doctor about your libido if this keeps up."

Graham glared at him. "There's nothing wrong with my libido. It's not me; it's the women. Haven't you noticed they're all the same?"

"Well, where it counts, I suppose. . . ."

"That's not what I mean. Or maybe it is. I don't know. I just know I'm . . . bored." He gestured around the room with his whiskey glass. "Not a fresh face in sight."

"Since when do you go for a fresh face? I thought you were an ass man."

"Since I realized I'd seen all of these faces a hundred times before."

"Come on," Logan chided. "There has to be a woman here you haven't slept with."

"Regina."

"She doesn't count. Dmitri would break your legs, wait a couple of hours for them to heal, then break them again. And after that, he might get cranky. I'm talking about the rest of them. The ones who aren't married to your best friend, and aren't from our pack, since they're all practically family."

Graham took a quick look around, followed by a longer look. On his third sweep of the assembled crowd, he stopped and pointed toward a grouping of furniture occupied by three very attractive females. "There," he said. "Those three. I haven't slept with a single one of them."

Logan followed his gesture and sighed. "Yeah. Regina's closest friends, who are probably the only human women here tonight, and we both know you don't do humans."

A grin flashed across Graham's face. "I thought about doing the one on the right. Ava. She's the one Dmitri had me staking out before he changed Regina. I came real close to watching her from the other side of a pillow, instead of from the front seat of my car. But she's human."

"According to anyone who's ever done business with her, that's just a front. She's really a shark."

Graham shrugged. "Anyway, you asked who I hadn't slept with. They're it."

"Just those three."

"I think so." Draining his glass, Graham scanned the room one last time, dismissing each of the women he passed. His eyes never seemed to pause more than half a second on any of them, no matter how attractive or how skimpily dressed, until they drifted over one curvaceous female bottom and skidded to a grinding halt.

He could almost smell rubber burning.

His eyes caressed the full, generous lines of her backside encased in a form-fitting skirt of some clingy black material. The fabric draped over that delectable tush, showing him each rounded curve in heart-stopping detail. To his surprise, he couldn't tell if she was wearing panties, but unlike Shelley's lack of lingerie, the idea of this woman bare beneath her dress aroused more than just his curiosity.

"And her," he growled, all his attention focused on the woman whose face he still hadn't seen. If it looked half as good as what he *had* seen, he'd be a very happy man. "I haven't had her. Yet."

Missy sidled into the party more than two hours late, but the way she figured it, Reggie was lucky she'd come at all. Especially in this dress.

She tugged surreptitiously at the hem, trying to make it fall more than four inches below her crotch. No dice. Every time she pulled, the hem sank, but so did the neckline. She could flash the world from either above or below, and neither held much appeal.

How in God's name did I let them talk me into this? she wondered for the gazillionth time. Not even threats and bribery should have induced her to put on this poor excuse for a dress and let her friends serve her to her latest fantasy fix on a silver platter. She'd barely escaped the last two rounds with her pride intact. She should have run screaming at the idea of round three. Unfortunately, it was way too late for that.

Missy supposed it had been too late the very minute the five friends had experienced their brainstorm during a particularly enthusiastic—and alcoholic—episode of their biweekly girls' night get-togethers. After much too much wine, one of them had made the fateful observation that despite their status as single women, they each had a decent-sized pool of male friends, family members, and co-workers who could be counted as potential dates. Just because one woman didn't find her dream man among her own male acquaintances didn't mean that one of her friends wouldn't. So they had come up with the brilliant idea of setting one another up on a series of blind dates called fantasy fixes; more than just regular dates, the fixes were supposed to be opportunities for each woman to live out her sexual fantasies with a man her friends had prescreened for safety and discretion.

It had sounded like a great idea at the time, filtered through about a bottle of sauvignon blanc, but as soon as she had sobered up, Missy had experienced some misgivings.

Translation: she had panicked.

Always the shyest and most conservative member of their clique, Missy wasn't the type to live out sexual fantasies with men she'd barely met. She was the kind to plant daffodils along the bottom of a white picket fence while her enormous brood of children were in school and her banker or lawyer or accountant husband was at his office winning the family bread.

Unfortunately, her friends had devious natures and insidious stubborn streaks, and with Missy's own compulsion to please on their side, they took ruthless advantage. They knew Missy harbored an intense reluctance to go on her fantasy fix dates, but she'd done the first two rounds because they'd asked her to, and because she didn't want them thinking she was an even bigger coward than they already believed.

But a soft heart and a latent sense of determination only went so far. Two rounds had been the limit of Missy's good nature, and they must have guessed that, because this time they had arranged for her to meet her fix at an event she couldn't avoid—Reggie's engagement party.

Never mind that Reggie's wedding had taken

place two weeks ago. It had all been arranged with so little notice that it had left the officiant with a bad case of whiplash, hence the post-ceremony engagement party to include all those left out of the wedding itself—which turned out to be most of the combined acquaintances of the bride and groom.

Missy had *not* been one of the people left out of the ceremony; she'd been the maid of honor. But that didn't mean she'd had even the slightest chance of wriggling out of attending tonight's function. Reggie and Missy had been best friends since high school, and Missy could never skip a party in her friend's honor. So here she was, dressed like a French whore and trying desperately to come up with a way to make this third fix turn out just like the other two, because she had the hideous feeling that this time luck would not be on her side.

She gave up tugging at the front of her dress and wormed her way into an alcove where she turned her back to the room and yanked the dress down over her ass. It pulled the neck down until her breasts threatened to fall out of the clingy material, but if she just kept her face to the wall, no one should be able to see that and what they could see would be almost decently covered.

She didn't think Ava, Danice, and Corinne had spotted her yet, but she knew it was only a matter of time. They would be keeping an eye out for her, since she was so late and had refused to answer any of their calls to her cell phone thanks to the blessing of caller ID. Once she realized she had arrived, her reprieve would be over and she would have to face her latest fix, whoever he happened to be.

The last two rounds, the gods themselves must have been looking out for her, because those fixes couldn't have gone better if she'd planned them herself. Her kidnapping mountain man had turned out to be her older sister's high school boyfriend, and the idea of being trapped with little Missy Roper in a secluded cabin for forty-eight hours with nothing to do but test out the huge old feather bed in the corner had turned him an interesting shade of green. He'd given her a pair of his sweats, encouraged her to change out of the flesh-baring clothes her friends had picked out for her, roasted her some marshmallows, and checked himself into a hotel room until it was time to deliver her back home. As he walked her to the door of her apartment building, he'd even made her promise not to tell Ava how their fix had really turned out. Like full disclosure had even been a possibility. She'd rather have told her parents she'd decided to become a leather-clad, bisexual dominatrix.

She'd rather have *become* a leather-clad, bisexual dominatrix.

Those same gods must have appreciated her prayers of thanks afterward, because they looked out for her on fix number two as well. In that one, the buff fireman who had rescued her from the deliberately stuck elevator at Ava's office building had been willing to give her the ol' college try—right up until he had pulled off her mitten-knit hat and seen the dull ash-blond color of her hair. That's when she started to remind him of his four-year-old daughter, which in turn reminded him of his ex-wife, and *that* reminded him of how much he wished he were still married.

Instead of a quickie in a stopped elevator, Missy had spent close to two hours listening to the tale of Bobby's broken heart and cooing over pictures of his high school sweetheart and their little girl. Little Mandy had looked like a real sweetheart, and even if Missy couldn't see the resemblance, she vowed to send the child a birthday card every year to show her gratitude for unknowingly rescuing Missy from her rescuer.

She hadn't even had to worry about Bobby spilling the beans on that one. The day after her rescue, he'd moved back to Boston to be near his daughter and try to persuade his ex-wife to take him back. All Missy needed to do was blush whenever anyone asked her what happened and she was home free. The way conversations with her friends usually went, blushing had been no problem at all.

Missy occasionally wondered if "friends" was really the right word to describe their little clique. Reggie seemed more like her sister than her friend— someone who loved her unconditionally but also delighted in tormenting her, who sometimes drove her crazy, and who would defend her to the death or the homicide. Corinne and Danice were more like drinking buddies. They had a great time together, despite the fact that they had less than nothing in common, and no one could make Missy laugh harder.

Then there was Ava.

Ava simply defied description. She presided over the lot of them like a temperamental bitch-goddess, dispensing gifts or torment, depending on her mood. Ava wasn't the sort of person you just "liked" or "got along with." She made you work too hard for that, but she was loyal and fierce, and Missy could easily picture her ripping the heart out of anyone stupid enough to hurt one of her friends. Missy loved her for that, which probably explained why she put up with all the crap Ava managed to put her through.

Like tonight.

Missy had dressed in this ridiculous pseudodress, taken a cab to the Upper East Side, and walked through Reggie and Dmitri's front door looking like a call girl on the clock, all because of Ava. If not for the other woman's meddling, Missy would have shown up looking like she usually did, in slightly baggy khakis and an oversized sweater, or in an ankle-length skirt and a diaphanous tunic top. Basically looking like a kindergarten teacher.

Since that's what she was, Missy saw nothing to be ashamed of. After all, where would the world be without kindergarten teachers? Lacking the basic skills of sharing and tying their shoelaces, that's where. Her friends could make fun of her profession all they wanted. Missy loved kids, and she refused to feel embarrassed that the innocence of her career mirrored the current innocence of her sex life. Besides, if her friends and this sad excuse for a dress had their way, that innocence wouldn't last the night.

Peering warily over her shoulder, she tried to locate the rest of her clique. At least then she'd know what parts of the room to avoid. She saw Reggie standing next to Dmitri—surprise, surprise—while they chatted with a distinguished-looking older gentleman with a shock of gray hair. He was the senator Missy had always thought looked like her Grandpa Harry. Well, except for his fangs. Grandpa Harry had a temper, but even he had never sucked a person's blood. Tonight, though, Missy didn't particularly care what the senator chose to suck as long as he kept Reggie engaged in conversation and away from Missy. One down, three to go.

She found the others all clustered together in a small conversational grouping near the fireplace. Ava lounged in an overstuffed armchair, making it look more like a throne, while Corinne and Danice sat on the sofa to her left. Each held a glass of champagne, and they all kept casting glances at their watches, the door, and one another, in that order. Ava appeared less than pleased.

It served her right, Missy thought, quickly facing the wall before they spotted her. It would have served them all right if she hadn't bothered to show up at all. No rational person could have blamed her. She had just walked into a room full of vampires and werewolves and God only knew what else, looking like chum at a shark convention, so she could be set up on a date she really didn't want to go on with a man she'd never met and whom she had no interest in dating, let alone sleeping with. Maybe she ought to rethink this whole "friends" thing.

Okay, now you're just being unfair, she scolded herself. A deep breath necessitated an immediate follow-up consisting of a tug to her neckline. She couldn't really blame her friends for not setting her up with the man she actually *was* interested in sleeping with, since his name remained a secret she intended to take to her grave. She knew her chances with him ranked somewhere below laughable and probably on par with her chances of bearing the next immaculate conception, because as the entire Other social world of New York knew, Graham Winters did not date humans.

Missy stared morosely into the leaves of a potted ficus while she absorbed the sharp sting of that knowledge. It wasn't news; she'd known it from their very first meeting, but even after six weeks, she still hadn't quite managed to work her way out of crushing disappointment and into grudging resignation. She still floundered in the morass of wishful thinking, thanks to her unruly hormones. The darn things put her on full alert every time she set eyes on his drool-inspiring body or knee-weakening gold-green eyes. That reaction gave her yet another reason to keep her face to the wall. The last thing she needed was to let him distract her. Since he was Dmitri's best friend and best man, she knew he was probably in the house somewhere, so she'd be wise to stick to the shadows and avert her eyes until she could make her escape.

But, Lord, wouldn't she just love to get her hands on him! She sighed wistfully and dismissed the mental image of running her fingertips over his broad, muscled chest, down his lean sides, over the rippled surface of his abdomen—

Christ! If she didn't cut this out, she'd leave herself open to attack. Her friends could spot her any minute, and when they did, she had no doubt they'd swoop down on her like a pack of attack dogs and drag her kicking and screaming to meet her fix. Now that she thought about it, such a scenario would explain the dress, too. They knew she couldn't struggle in the darn thing without it snapping like an overstretched rubber band. If she so much as threw a punch, her breasts would probably fall right out of the bodice. The idea of the dress's reaction to a swift kick made her shudder.

Her friends were even more devious than she had imagined, and frankly, instead of intimidating her, the idea made her that much madder. After all, she could appreciate that they wanted her to have a good time, but really, she was beginning to feel more like a john or a hooker than a date. While the idea of being fixed up with a man to fulfill all her fantasies had sounded like a good one at the time, sobriety and two failed attempts had brought her to her senses. There was only one man Missy could imagine hopping into bed with after having exchanged less than twenty words, and since he wasn't interested, she found that she wasn't, either.

When rebellion struck Missy, it struck with a vengeance. To hell with her friends and their fantasy fixes! Missy was a mature, independent woman capable of making her own decisions and getting her own dates. In fact, it would serve them all right if she thumbed her nose at their chosen match for her and picked up a sailor to take home! Hell, she should just pick some guy out of the assembled guests at random and take *him* home! If she couldn't have the man she wanted, she could at least have a man of her own choosing. That would show them that Melissa Jane Roper was not a woman to be trifled with.

Or at least, she was a woman who picked her own men to be the triflers.

Feeling brash and defiant, Missy spun around to face the room. She would pick up a man, one who was about as far from the fantasy fix—and from the object of her secret fantasies—as she could find, and she'd take him home and end her six years of semi-voluntary celibacy without the "help" of her interfering friends.

How about them apples?

Her defiance lasted all of three and a half seconds. That's when she saw Danice leap to her feet and heard her yell, "Melissa Jane Roper, where the *hell* have you been?"

At that point, bravado abandoned her, self-preservation instincts kicked in, and Missy did the smartest thing she could think of.

She turned tail and ran, just as fast as her three-inch heels would carry her.

She made it all the way across the living room, beating a path straight for the French doors that let out onto the side patio. She teetered on the very edge of making good her escape when a warm, solid object stepped into her path and blocked her exit. Missy slammed into it hard enough to knock her slightly silly, but the thing that really stunned her was feeling the immovable object wrap powerful arms around her and press her against the entire length of a very muscular and decidedly masculine body.

"Well, well, well," the object rumbled in a voice so low, she could feel the vibrations through the soles of her shoes. "Where do you think you're going in such a hurry, gorgeous? I was hoping you might decide to stay awhile. With me."

CHAPTER TWO

Graham had seen the object of his unexpected lust spin around and race toward him as if the fires of hell licked at her heels. Clearly, he must have done something very good to earn this kind of reward. He couldn't think what it might be, but he didn't care. When Miss Sexy Ass flung herself headlong into his arms, he offered up a quick prayer of thanks and decided to worry about the particulars later.

He initially wrapped his arms around her to keep her from falling, but he pressed her closer and held on for a slightly less noble cause. She smelled amazing—sweet and rich and edible—and she felt luscious pressed up against him, all soft and warm and deliciously rounded. The breasts flattened against his shirt were surprisingly delicate compared to the generous rear he'd already drooled over, but their nipples beaded on contact, nudging his chest, and he reminded himself that size didn't really matter. Not when he compared it to the importance of her killer ass, her mouthwatering scent, and the soft curve of her belly, which was currently pressed tight against his very appreciative groin. For all that, he could forgo the pleasures of a huge pair of tits and still consider himself a very lucky man.

He took a deep breath and felt the fit of his trousers tighten. God, no woman's scent had ever gone to his head like this. He appreciated a female's fragrance as much as the next Lupine, but normally, human women couldn't grab his attention with a pair of pliers. They tended to smell like artificial chemicals and sterile soaps to his kind. Even when it wasn't offensive, it wasn't exactly compelling, either. But this woman had him panting with nothing more than her luscious scent and her equally luscious curves.

"Well, well, well," he murmured, and he could hear the lust vibrating in his tone. He hoped she wouldn't be intimidated by it, because he doubted there was any way on earth he could have concealed it. "Where do you think you're going in such a hurry, gorgeous? I was hoping you might decide to stay awhile. With me."

He watched her head jerk up at his words and found himself looking into a pair of meltingly brown eyes the size and shape of china saucers. A man would have to be very careful not to get sucked down by the undertow he saw in those things. He ignored the vague sense of recognition he felt when he looked at her, because he felt certain they'd never met before. Graham was not the sort of man who forgot a figure like this woman sported. He'd been bored, not blind, but if he had his way, this woman would be relieving that boredom. At least for the night.

He smiled his most seductive smile, the one that made women melt and pant and compare him to a fallen angel, and loosened his grip enough to lean back. He looked down at her and patiently waited for her to respond to his pass. When she did respond, though, it wasn't precisely what he'd expected.

"Um, excuse me," she muttered, tearing her chocolaty gaze from his, ducking beneath his unsuspecting arms, and darting behind him to let herself out the French doors.

"What the hell?" He scowled. No woman had ever turned down that kind of invitation from him.

Beside him, Logan laughed. "Never thought I'd see the day." The other Lupine grinned. "The amazing Graham just struck out with a woman. And a human woman at that."

Graham scowled, both at Logan's taunting words and at the reminder that he'd gotten all tied up in knots over a woman from another species, no matter how good she smelled. What the hell was wrong with him?

He wasted about half a millisecond wondering about it before his instincts kicked him in the ass. He didn't care if this woman was from another planet. He still wanted inside her. Badly.

Shooting Logan a sharp glare, Graham caught the door before it could swing closed behind Miss No-Time-to-Chat.

"That was only the first pitch," he said. "Next one goes over the fence."

Ignoring his friend's snort, Graham disappeared through the doors and into the night, intent on pursuit and capture.

Hello, Twilight Zone, it looks like I've come to visit, Missy thought even as she jerked herself out of the arms of the man of her dreams and darted outside. She wondered if she had conjured the encounter just by fantasizing about him earlier. That was the sort of story line the Zoners really went for, right? And since she'd just finished reminding herself how entirely uninterested Graham had been in her before fifteen seconds ago, an alternate reality made the most sense of any explanation she could think of. Either that or she'd dreamed up the whole thing. Now, *that* explanation had logic and all sorts of other sensible possibilities going for it.

Jogging across the living room with lights blazing and civilized, carpet-covered hardwood had been tough enough in her strappy three-inch heels, but Missy quickly found jogging across the pitch-black patio to be impossible. Reggie and Dmitri must have assumed no one would want to go outside on this unseasonably cold spring night, because they hadn't left a single outside light burning. That might be fine for the other guests, but for Missy it threatened to break her ankles.

She stumbled to a halt on the uneven brick and debated kicking off her shoes and running barefoot. Then she noticed the cold of the masonry seeping up through the thin soles of her sandals and discarded the idea. All her friends wore heels as well, so the going wouldn't be any faster for them. If luck stayed with her, she might still be able to out-hobble them.

She peered into the darkness around her and blinked, trying to force her eyes to adjust to the dim light. The high garden walls blocked most of the streetlights, and since the moon was still not full, she couldn't rely on its pale light to illuminate her path. The day anyone could see stars in the night sky over New York City would be the day after it sank into the mouth of the Hudson.

Wishing for the enormous purse she usually carried, complete with a flashlight for just this sort of emergency, Missy cursed the tiny clutch that had been provided to go with the slinky black dress and began to pick her way slowly toward the courtyard gate and the street beyond. If she could just get a cab before her friends caught up with her, she could be back in her apartment and swathed in flannel PJs inside twenty minutes. Add a cup of cocoa laced with Baileys and she might once again resemble a happy camper.

The hand that clamped around her upper arm and dragged her to a halt dashed her hopes of happiness and startled her so badly, she squealed. Not screamed, not shrieked. Squealed, like one of her girlish students confronted with an inquisitive gerbil. Embarrassed, she spun around to face her pursuer and found herself looking up into Graham Winter's too-handsome face.

Oh, Lordy, she thought, swallowing hard past the knot in her throat. *I have just entered the Twilight Zone. Why else would he keep looking at me like that? Unless I died of embarrassment from wearing that dress and this is my eternal reward . . . .*

Now that would be a heaven worth dying for, she decided, even while her logical mind told her to get a grip and find out what he really wanted, because as much time as she had spent noticing the mouthwatering Lupine over the past six weeks, she felt positive he'd never even realized she existed. When he paid any attention to Reggie's friends at all, it usually consisted of circumspectly ogling Ava or casually bantering with Danice. He'd never bothered to give Missy a first—let alone a second—glance, so why was he now looking at her as if she were a particularly juicy soup bone?

"Um, hi," she ventured when he failed to say a word. "Did you want something?"

She saw a flash in his sexy green-gold eyes and realized she shouldn't have been able to see much of anything in the dark. Were his eyes *glowing*?

She tried to back up a step, but he held her firmly. She cleared her throat. "It's very nice to see you again, Graham, but I was just leaving. Maybe I'll see you around some other time. Buh-bye."

She twisted halfway toward freedom before his hand on her arm stopped her. Looking back at him, she saw his mouth turn down in a scowl.

"When have I seen you before?" he demanded, his tone of voice less than happy.

Now that was proof positive about how little attention Graham had ever paid to her. She'd been Reggie's maid of honor, and he'd been Dmitri's best man. They'd walked down the stinking aisle together, and he couldn't even remember where he'd seen her before?

Miffed, and more than a little hurt, she tugged at her arm and scowled back at him. "Around. I'm a friend of Reggie's."

"Where are you going?"

She gave up trying to yank her arm away and began trying to pry his fingers off of her one by one. They stayed stubbornly motionless. "I was going home," she grumped, "until you decided to go all Conan the Barbarian on me."

"Why were you in such a hurry? You ran right past me."

"Actually, I ran right into you, but that's neither here nor there," she said, looking around as if she could wish a crowbar into appearing close by. Nothing else seemed capable of breaking his grip. "Like I said, I need to get home. There are some people here I'd rather not see, if you must know."

Impossible as it seemed, his scowl deepened. "A man people?"

She started to shake her head, then caught herself. No need to appear quite as pathetic as she really was. "What business is it of yours?"

He responded to her defiance by tugging her body

closer and breathing in as if he were trying to inhale her, ridiculous heels and all. He planted his other hand on her behind, pressing her hips against him until she could feel the thick, shocking length of his erection prodding her through layers of cloth.

"I'd like to make it my business," he growled, and oh my God, was his hand *kneading her ass*? "I'd like to make everything about you my business. That means I want to know if I have to get rid of some moron before I can start convincing you to . . . spend some time with me."

Missy reeled at his answer. Of all the things he might have said to her, she couldn't imagine one that would shock her more. The man who had been so unimpressed with her for six weeks that he couldn't remember who she was, was now telling her he was willing to go through a potential rival in order to have her all to himself? Okay, where was Rod Serling?

She stiffened, because for a split second it occurred to her that maybe Graham was supposed to be her fix. She'd certainly fantasized about him enough lately, but the fantasy her friends had drawn for her third round had been about an intellectual type and playing doctor. Missy could no more picture Graham playing a detached medical professional than she could picture herself playing a whip-wielding dominatrix. Some things just exceeded the limits of her imagination.

There was no way Graham could be her fix, so why had he suddenly decided he wanted the woman he'd never bothered to notice? Maybe this wasn't *The Twilight Zone*; maybe she was on *Candid Camera*. She was about to look for a live TV audience when she heard the door from the living room open and the sound of a woman's high-heeled shoes tapping against the brick. Suddenly it didn't matter why Graham wanted to take her away from the party, just as long as he did. Now.

She stopped struggling to get away and instead let him press her up against his groin until she swore she could vouch for the fact that he'd been circumcised.

"No moron," she reassured him, struggling valiantly not to melt and run all over him like warm hollandaise sauce. If she could just get him to smuggle her away from the house before Ava found her, she could explain later about where they'd met before and why he couldn't really be interested in her. "No man at all. You know, it is too bad that we've never gotten a chance to get to know each other, isn't it? Since you brought it up, why don't we get out of here and really take the opportunity to get acquainted?"

Knowing she only had one chance to get him to rescue her before her friends reached them, she bit the bullet, took a deep breath, and slid her hand down his chest, over his taut abs, and down over the bulge beneath his fly until he went absolutely still and tense before her. "What do you say?"

He didn't say anything. He scooped her up in his brawny arms, tossed her over his shoulder, and sprinted for the patio gate. Two minutes later they were three blocks away and still flying, and Missy was trying to figure out how to explain to the werewolf she'd just teased that she really didn't intend to sleep with him.

Miracle, anyone?

He didn't set her down until he reached his second-floor bedroom. His house sat adjacent to Vircolac, the club he owned and operated for the Other population of New York, and on a Friday night like tonight the club was loud and boisterous, but his bedroom was quiet, private, and secluded. So secluded that Missy knew for certain no one would hear her if she screamed. She didn't particularly want to think about why she might decide to scream.

The minute her feet touched the floor, she scrambled backward, trying to put some distance between them. The difference between fantasizing about something and actually doing it had just hit home for her. With a sledgehammer.

Graham stalked after her, his chin lowered and canted forward in a predatory posture, his powerful body moving lithely and inexorably toward her. He looked tight and coiled, like a cat ready to pounce, or a wolf ready to leap to the kill. The expression in his glowing, greenish eyes made Missy feel a lot like lunch.

Or maybe a midnight snack.

"Um, Graham, I think we need to talk about this." She kept her eyes on him, afraid to blink when he had that look of intent etched across his angular features.

"No talking," he growled. His voice had lowered, becoming even rougher and deeper than she remembered, like honey-coated gravel. "Too late for talking. Time to mate."

She almost tripped over her own feet when she stepped off the edge of the carpet and met the bare wood floor where it disappeared beneath the door. She backed steadily toward the hall. If she could just make it that far . . .

She did, thumping back against the door with an awkward, "Oomf!" She'd been closer than she realized, but she hoped it had been close enough. Her trembling fingers closed over the cool metal doorknob and began to turn. Before her nerves finished processing the signal from her brain, Graham surged forward and pinned her against the unyielding wooden surface.

Missy yelped. Her purse flew into a dark corner. She tried to pull back, but caught between Graham's stony muscles and the closed hardwood door, she discovered a new appreciation for an old cliché.

Graham leaned forward and buried his face in her neck, his late-night stubble rasping against her skin. His hot breath scalded her, and the feel of his mouth against her flesh made her shiver. When his lips parted and his teeth closed delicately over the tendon that ran from neck to shoulder, her shiver turned into a shudder, and her panting turned into a whimper. His rough tongue rasped her skin, and he groaned.

"The way you taste," he growled, his hands gripping her and pulling her tight against an erection as surprising as it was intimidating. Restless fingers kneaded her hips. "So sweet. So hot. Want more."

Oh, God! Missy's head dipped back without her permission, baring her throat to Graham's hungry mouth. Her brain was telling her to scream, to run, to turn the damned doorknob and get the hell out of there. But her hormones were telling her to stay, to beg, to wrap her legs around his waist and hold on for the ride she might never be invited on again. Instead of doing either, she stood frozen against the door, trembling and panting, and felt an embarrassing dampness soaking through the thin cotton of her panties.

"Smell so good," Graham grunted, nuzzling around her neck to lap at the hollow at the base of her throat. He ran his tongue up the soft white curve, and her muscles spasmed in a convulsive swallow. "Wet, thick, creamy. Want it."

With every word, his voice became more guttural until she could barely understand what he was saying. Was he speaking English, or some Lupine language made up of rumbles and snarls? But in spite of herself, she understood the feel of his hands and his hardness and his hot, hungry mouth.

His weight pinned her lower body to the door, freeing his hands to explore her. She felt one glide over her ribs and close around her breast, roughly squeezing the soft mound. The other reached up to tangle in her hair, angling her head for his convenience before he swooped down and claimed her mouth in a kiss.

He ate at her, nibbling and tugging and sucking on her lips until they parted, then licking and teasing and taunting until they opened wider. His tongue plunged deep and took her. Missy moaned, and he stole the sound and swallowed it, taking it into himself as he forced himself inside. Truthfully, she didn't require much force. All Graham had to do was flick his tongue against the roof of her mouth and she opened wide and begged his tongue to enter her. He thrust it deep, over and over, in and out, in the primal rhythms of sex.

It drove her crazy, the way he seemed determined to taste every inch of her mouth without allowing her to do the same. She'd dreamed of this so many times, and in all of those dreams her favorite part had been when she'd gotten to touch and taste him for herself. Whimpering her displeasure, she waited until he thrust deep, then tangled her tongue with his and sucked.

His flavor amazed her, as rich and dark as Turkish coffee, as addictive as caffeine and twice as stimulating. Abandoning her grip on the doorknob, she wrapped both arms around his shoulders and pulled herself up against him.

Growling, either a threat or a promise, he wedged his foot between hers and forced her legs apart. His knee came up high between them until it shoved the hem of her clinging skirt up, high along the pale satin of her thighs. Already stressed beyond its design, the dress abandoned all pretense and rolled up like a window shade to settle in a narrow band around her waist.

Missy gasped in shock, but Graham just purred his satisfaction into her mouth and slid his hands down over her hips to cup the backs of her thighs. One after the other, he forced her legs to hitch up and wrap around his waist until he held her up with her arms around his shoulders and his hands beneath her ass and his groin pressed intimately against her.

Behind her closed lids, Missy felt her eyes roll back in her head. She'd never been so aroused in her life. If she'd had a weak heart, she felt sure this would have killed her. As it was, that overstressed organ raced and stammered with every new sensation he forced on her. His kiss consumed her, and as amazing as he tasted, she felt pretty sure she'd black out from lack of oxygen if he didn't let her catch her breath soon.

She pushed against his shoulders and turned her head to the side, succeeding only in making his mouth shift from her lips to her throat. He kissed her, lapped her, nibbled at her, drawing the flesh hard against his teeth in a rough love bite. Her head knocked hard against the door, but she barely felt it. Instead, she felt his hands slide from her bottom down the backs of her thighs to just above her ankles. He urged her legs higher against him and showed her how he wanted her to hook her ankles together behind his back to ride his hips more securely.

Immediately his hand shot back up her leg, this time traveling along the sensitive inner surface until he cupped her through the soaking crotch of her panties.

Missy hadn't worn hose, since Ava had forbidden anything so "common." Instead, she'd reluctantly donned a pair of sheer, silk thigh-highs that clung to her legs like perfume. Ava had also dictated that Missy should wear a lace bra so see-through it barely qualified as lingerie and a pair of matching thong panties. When she dressed for the party, Missy had strapped on the bra but drawn the line at the butt floss. She refused to spend an entire evening fighting the urge to tug the cloth out of there, so she pulled on a pair of her own white cotton bikinis instead. Now, she wished she'd worn a stainless-steel chastity belt, because the feel of Graham's hand cupping her through the thin layer of cotton almost killed her. She whimpered and pressed down onto his fingers.

"Graham, please!" she whimpered. She wasn't sure what she was begging for, but it didn't matter, not as long as he kept touching her. As long as he didn't think she was begging him to stop, everything would be okay. She got the impression a nuclear assault wouldn't stop him, though, so she figured it was safe to be non-specific.

He growled again, the sound even more animalistic than before. Instead of being frightened, Missy gloried in it. This was beyond her realm of experience but not beyond the realm of her fantasies. The idea of being wanted so badly by a man that his control threatened to fracture around them was at least as arousing as what his hands and mouth were doing to her. She felt drenched in her own fantasy world, felt like an entirely new, brazen creature, one she'd never known before. She gave in to this new side of herself, reveling in the freedom and adventure of it nearly as much as in Graham's hard body pressing against hers.

She buried her hands in his thick, dark hair and pressed his face closer against her. He lifted her higher against the door and lowered his head until he could catch the neckline of her stretchy dress in his teeth. One sharp tug and the thing disintegrated in his mouth. He turned his head, spat out the pieces, and when he looked back at her breasts, covered only by the sheer silken bra, his eyes glowed an even brighter green.

"Taste," he rumbled, and that was all the warning Missy got before he ripped open her bra and his hot, avid mouth closed over her left nipple.

He sucked greedily, forcing the ruched peak hard against the roof of his mouth, drinking from her as if she were his only source of nourishment. Missy moaned. She felt like he drew her soul out of her through her breast, but all she wanted was for him to pull harder, to take more of her into the wet furnace of his mouth.

He did. He sucked with bruising strength, then

pulled back until just the nipple remained inside his mouth. His straight, sharp teeth nipped at her, hard enough to sting but not hard enough to injure, and he leaned forward again, stretching his jaw wide and sucking at her flesh until almost her entire petite breast disappeared between his lips.

His free hand reached up and closed about the other peak, kneading with rough motions, pulling at her erect nipple with strong, lean fingers. She felt them tugging at her, making her crazy, and even as they moved, the hand between her legs went to work. He hooked his forefinger in the crotch of her panties and tore, ripping the panel right out from between her legs. Then his fingers were sliding through her slick folds and spreading the abundant moisture around her swollen lips and soft, hidden valleys.

Finger and thumb closed around the nub of her clitoris as if it were another nipple, tugging and pinching in a gentle mimicry of his hand on her breast. Missy cried out, her heels digging into the small of his back, her thighs clenching as she tried to lift herself away from his tormenting fingers.

Away? Toward? God, who knew?

His growl this time held as much menace as passion. His fingers abandoned her clit to tangle in her pubic hair and pull her back down where he wanted her. She moaned and settled into place even as her thighs tried to close against further sensory overload. His waist held her knees apart, keeping her spread and available, and he took shameless advantage. He tweaked her nipple again, making her yelp, then his hand shifted and smoothed, and he penetrated her with one long, unyielding finger.

She cried. Real, honest-to-God tears rolled down her face at the feel of him inside her, even only this much of him. She wanted more, but her long-neglected passage protested at even this small invasion. Missy hadn't had sex in six years, not since college, and then her partner had been nothing like Graham, the experience nothing like this rioting orgy of heat and pleasure and sweat. She wondered now how she would be able to take him if even his finger stretched her so uncomfortably. She felt his finger withdraw and press back a second later, followed quickly by another. Two strong digits pressed deep, tunneling through her body's resistance and showing her why it was much too late for doubt.

If he was going to pleasure her to death, she intended to enjoy as much of the experience as she could.

Using one hand to tug at his tousled hair, she dislodged his mouth from one breast just long enough to guide it to the other. He greeted her neglected nipple with a quick nip and a soothing pass of his rough velvet tongue before sucking it deep into his mouth. Missy felt every draw like a pulse between her legs, and knew Graham could feel it, too, when he began timing the thrusts of his fingers to the clenching of her inner muscles.

God, he was trying to kill her!

Desperate to feel more of him inside her, she slid one hand down between their bodies and into the waistband of his slacks.

The soft heat of her palm met his busy fingers between her legs, wringing from him a soft growl. One that morphed into a breathless curse when her fingers closed carefully around his eager erection.

Missy echoed the sound with a murmur of satisfaction, squeezing his thick shaft and savoring the smooth texture of his skin and the heavy, solid feel of his arousal. Her fingers couldn't quite close around him, because her hands were very small and Graham was very not. He filled her palm to overflowing, and Missy wanted to know if he would fill her body the same way.

She drew her hand away with the intent of finding out. Graham punished her desertion with a sharp nip to her breast and a deep, twisting thrust of his fingers. Missy cried out and bucked against him, but she remained determined. If he thought turning her on even more would make her change course, he could think again. She was having way too much fun to abandon her new toy just so he could catch his breath again. She quickly, if clumsily, unfastened the buttons of his trousers and tugged down the zipper, freeing his arousal from its confinement with a sigh of satisfaction. Graham's entire body stiffened, and he pulled his mouth and hands away from her heated flesh, grasping her hips and shaking her until her eyes met his.

"Now!" he bit out, and the harsh, spare urgency in his voice made her shudder. He lifted her hips higher until his erection parted her swollen flesh and pressed firmly against her entrance.

Missy saw the savage need in his eyes and felt a wash of excitement instead of the fear she had half-expected. Panting, she nodded with uneven, jerky motions and pressed her forehead to his.

"Now," she echoed, and had time for one shallow breath before her world tilted dizzily on its axis.

That breath ended on a scream as Graham's fingers bit hard into her hips, lifted her briefly above him, and then slammed her weight down to meet his violent thrust. His thick length tunneled endlessly into her, forcing her muscles to stretch wide to accommodate his girth. Sensations overwhelmed her. She couldn't decide if they consisted mainly of pleasure or pain. In that moment, it didn't matter. All that mattered was that he was inside her, thrusting hard and deep until he ground to a halt, nudging roughly at her cervix.

"Graham, wait!" she gasped, her mind whirling and her body protesting. She needed a minute, just a minute, to catch up with him, to adjust to his penetration and the unsettling feeling that something within her had changed in the instant that their bodies were joined.

Bracing her hands against his shoulders, Missy fought hard to regain her breath, her equilibrium, her identity. She felt like her entire self had boiled down to the rippling clasp of her body wrapping snugly around his. "Wait. Please."

Though her eyelids had turned to heavy weights, she struggled to meet his gaze, to maintain that connection to reality when everything around her had gone topsy-turvy. In the dim light of the bedroom, Graham's eyes flashed with an eerie glow.

"Too late," he growled, pressing her hard against the door as he began to move within her to a relentless, driving rhythm.

In her position, impaled on his thrusting length, held in place by the tenuous grasp of her watery legs around his waist and the biting grip of his fingers on her hips, Missy could do nothing else but cling to Graham's shoulders and let him conquer her like a foreign empire.

He pounded into her hard and fast, and she struggled to decide if she loved it or hated it. She'd thought she knew what sex was, but Graham Winters was showing her she had no clue. Lunging deeper inside her than she had thought possible, his corded muscles bunching and shifting against her, this man—this *werewolf*—seemed intent on teaching her that what she'd thought of as sex had as much in common with this urgent, primal act as a Chihuahua had in common with a Lupine.

His hands shifted to her ass and tugged. "More," he rumbled, his lips drawing back in a snarl. "Take more."

More? God, she could barely take what he was

already giving her! How could there possibly be more? She shook her head, unable to speak, fighting for each ragged breath she managed to draw into her starving lungs.

"More!" he insisted, and his demand became an order. The hand on her ass tightened and pushed, while the other moved to her stomach and thrust between their heaving bodies. One strong finger hooked beneath the soft flesh of her mound and pulled. The movement forced her to cant her hips upward, tilting her pelvis and changing the angle of their joining until she felt him slide impossibly deeper inside her.

Missy sobbed at the feel of another inch of silk-covered steel gliding home. His penetration butted against her cervix, nudged her darkest corners, and now she could feel his pelvis grinding between her legs, feel his hips against hers in a new, heavier impact. Finally he had buried his whole length inside her, and he filled her so deeply, she tasted his thrusts in the back of her throat.

"Graham!"

Her cry was a plea, a protest, and a demand for more. She had no idea which she meant most sincerely, but Graham answered only the last, ignoring the others completely. Pinning her against the door, now hot and slick from their sweaty bodies, he rode her hard, hilting inside her with each thrust, making her muscles ripple and contract on each entrance, collapse and yearn on each withdrawal.

She wanted desperately to thrust back against

him, but her position made it impossible. He controlled her every movement, holding her still and open for his powerful thrusts. She felt the constricting band of her tight dress where it had settled around her waist, felt the rasp of his dress shirt under her hands and against her breasts. She felt the rough fabric of the trousers he still wore low around his hips while he took her. She'd never felt anything so savage or so amazingly good.

The tension built inside her until she sobbed for release. He bent his knees for leverage, thrust high and hard inside her, and Missy's world dissolved in an endless, pulsing climax. Her body clamped tight around him, milking him with slick, wet muscles until Graham slammed her back against the door and roared.

Fingers gripping, muscles clenching, he crushed her between the hard wood and his hard body while he emptied himself inside her in hot, heavy spurts.

She melted around him, clinging to his waist and his shoulders with the last of her strength. Her breath sawed in and out of her lungs on ragged gasps. Her muscles felt like melted pudding, and they trembled under the least little exertion. If not for the solid door behind her and Graham's heavy weight in front of her, she would have trickled to the floor and lain there for at least a week.

Graham stirred, and Missy wondered where he got the strength. His hands cupped her bottom and held her in place while he crossed the room with three long strides. He tumbled her onto the bed with a thud. In the middle of the silk-covered mattress, Missy blinked and grunted while Graham settled his weight on top of her. He heaved a rough sigh and buried his face in the crook of her neck, his tongue lapping the salt from her skin with lazy strokes. She read more sleepy satisfaction than amorous intent in his actions and offered up a breathless prayer of thanks. She had just about enough energy left to close her eyelids and she'd be out like a light.

Her hands groped along the mattress, looking for a blanket to pull over them, but she found nothing. The only covering on the bed was the fitted silk sheet. In fact, she couldn't remember seeing sheets or blankets or even a bedspread pooled on the floor from a restless night's sleep. Too tired to wonder about it, she contented herself with Graham's body heat, which seemed more effective than an electric blanket anyway.

Tangling her legs with his, she shifted her hips and felt him still nestled half-hard inside her. She mulled it over for a moment, decided she liked the sensation, and wrapped her arms around him. Her last thought before she tumbled into unconsciousness was that no woman could possibly need a fantasy fix if she got to spend one night of her life with a lusty lycanthrope.

CHAPTER THREE

Honey and vanilla.

Graham's nose twitched, followed closely by his penis, as he slid gradually from sleep to waking. With his eyes still closed, he concentrated on the scent surrounding him, an intoxicating blend of honey and vanilla that reminded him of shortbread and sex and warm, melted ice cream. The thought made his stomach growl.

He nuzzled his face into a soft nest of hair and inhaled deeply to make sure he hadn't just dreamed up this woman with her mind-blowing scent and her passionate responses. Always before, her scent had been obscured by the environments they had met in, ones full of humans who used soaps and lotions and perfumes with such a heavy hand that Graham had learned long ago to block off his ultra-sensitive sense of smell in self-defense. If the woman beside him had applied any artificial scents last night, time and sweat had long since erased them. All that was left was the sweet, delicious scent of a woman he'd searched for all his life. Now that he'd found her, he'd be damned if he'd let her get away.

Unless he was very much mistaken, Graham Winters had just found his mate.

Normally, a new mating—especially for a pack alpha—was a cause for celebration. When your entire culture was based on the pack mentality, anything that led to the perpetuation of the pack won praise and respect, so he ought to be feeling just terrific at the idea that he'd finally found the one woman he could be happy with for the rest of his life. He just had two problems.

The significance of the first slammed into the back of his head like an iron pipe with a grudge the minute he looked down at her. With her hair soft and rumpled on the pillow, her makeup worn away by time and exertion, she looked completely different from the way he remembered her. Instead of the brazen, blond sexpot in the too-tight dress, she looked like a little girl, all fair skin and pink cheeks and child-like innocence. Her thick brown eyelashes lay in soft arcs against her cheeks, and her rosy lips were parted and slightly pouting. She looked like a china doll. A very human china doll.

Interspecies dating wasn't exactly verboten among Lupines, but it hardly represented the norm, either. His kind tended to view humans as amusing and occasionally useful, but hardly the sort of mates you brought home to Mother. After all, Lupine instincts still dictated that the strongest, the fastest, and the most dominant were the ones most likely to survive and most likely to reproduce. Humans, in contrast, could barely compete with newly whelped pups, let alone with mature wolves.

Graham knew all that, but it didn't seem to be doing him any good. Every time he tried to picture getting on with his life without this woman, his inner beast raised its furry head and growled, long and low and menacing. He expected to drool at any minute, but those instincts certainly made it clear that giving her up, human or no, was not an option.

And that led him neatly to dilemma number two.

The woman lying unconscious in the middle of his bed wasn't an anonymous and interchangeable human. She was Melissa Jane Roper, Regina McNeill Vidâme's best friend and pseudo little sister.

Already, the consequences of last night loomed large in his mind.

First of all, Regina would try to kill him. He'd only known his friend Dmitri's new wife for a few weeks, but that was plenty of time for Graham to learn how protective she felt toward her quiet, wallflower friend. Missy had been Regina's maid of honor, and though she'd faded into the background for him until last night, he clearly remembered the things Regina had told him about her.

"Missy is a sweetheart. Probably too sweet," Regina had explained at the rehearsal dinner while he'd sat, politely bored, beside her. "Don't be offended if she doesn't talk to you much, even if you are the best man. She's always been kind of quiet, especially around men. That doesn't mean she's some sort of

Pollyanna or a nun or anything. It just means she's more likely to listen than to talk. And she almost never says anything bad about anyone, but I just don't want you to think she's ignoring you or anything."

Graham hadn't noticed the woman enough to know whether she was ignoring him or not. With her hair in a neat, subdued braid and her body-camouflaging clothes, he'd paid her about as much attention as the flower arrangements on the tables at the restaurant. Even when he'd practiced escorting her away from the altar, he'd barely realized she was with him. Her grip on his sleeve had been so light, and she'd held herself so far away from him, that he might as well have been alone.

"Ava is trying to corrupt her, though," Regina had continued. "Now that I'm settled down, Missy is Ava's next project. If she has her way, Ava will turn the poor thing into a man-eater."

Something in him rebelled at the idea of Missy being shaped into some sort of femme fatale and then set loose on unsuspecting males. It had to be the fact that she was his mate, because pack leader or no, he'd never exhibited much of a possessive streak before, especially not when it came to women. To him, they made an interesting diversion but could be easily exchanged for the flavor of the week. Missy was the first woman he'd ever wanted to possess so completely that no other man would even dare to look at her. That, as much as his obsession with her sugar cookie fragrance, convinced him she really was his mate, no matter how inconvenient that might be.

He sighed, and Missy reacted to the small sound, frowning and shifting in her sleep. She rolled over to face him and burrowed into his furry chest. The tip of her cold nose brushed his nipple, and she nuzzled it sleepily, pressing a small kiss to the tight surface before snuggling back into sleep.

He fought hard against the urge to hook her leg over his hip and slide gently into her sleepy-soft warmth. After last night, he knew how quickly she could be aroused and readied for him. If only the knowledge didn't make his mouth water, he wouldn't be in this predicament.

That wasn't precisely true, he admitted grudgingly as he tried to keep his hands from straying down the silky-smooth skin of her back to caress her amazing ass. Graham had the distinct feeling that he'd been doomed from the moment he'd first noticed that particular feature of hers. Her scent this morning had only clinched the deal, but he couldn't pretend to understand why. Why should the smell of warm cookies stir him to previously unknown possessiveness when hideously expensive French perfumes only made him want to sneeze? He'd heard about the sort of instant knowledge other Lupines had when they met their mates, but he'd never expected it to hit him on an air current that smelled like tea biscuits and warm woman.

Just like he'd never expected to see the ass of his dreams on the back of a woman whose front he hadn't even given a second look.

If he could draw her fragrance permanently inside himself and smell her every time he breathed, he would be a very happy man. As it was, he was a hungry man with a hard-on.

Frowning, he eased his arms from around Missy's sleeping form and slid off the bed. The loss of his body heat made her shiver. His bed had no blankets on it, because he never used them. He generated enough body heat to keep warm in anything short of a blizzard, but his human guest didn't. He dug through his closet and found a spare blanket he kept around for moving furniture. Lucky for him, he'd washed it after the last trip, so it was clean and would serve to keep her warm.

He wrapped it around her, trying not to notice the way she curled up into a little ball beneath it, one hand resting under her cheek, the other tucked between her legs just above her knees. The urge to slide his own hand in beside hers, only higher, gripped him, but he shook it off and pulled on a pair of jeans before he padded barefoot down to his kitchen.

The pitch-blackness outside the windows told him it was still the middle of the night, and the clock on the microwave read 4:02. A little late for a midnight snack, but it was either food or sex, and he figured option two had already gotten him in enough trouble. He needed a few minutes to get his equilibrium back. Finding his mate apparently knocked a wolf for a bigger loop than he'd thought.

He rummaged through the refrigerator for a minute, dropping a hunk of roast beef to the counter and only looking up when he heard a knock. He darted out of the kitchen and down the hall to answer the door before the sound could wake Missy. Not until he had the door halfway open did he remember she was human and asleep and unlikely to have heard the soft knock even if it had been on the bedroom door, let alone a floor down and a few rooms away.

"You busy?" Logan asked as he stepped inside and closed the door after him. "I didn't want to interrupt anything. . . ."

Graham scowled at the other man. "Save the meaningful glances," he grumbled. "I was just grabbing something to eat."

He stalked back into the kitchen with Logan prowling after him. Graham didn't bother to worry that there was an emergency. When you ran a twenty-four-hour nightclub that catered to vampires, lycanthropes, and other assorted supernatural types, you got used to working at four in the morning.

"So what is it?" he asked, slicing off some chunks of raw beef. He dipped one in horseradish before popping it in his mouth. "Did Lourdes get blood on the carpet in the dining room again? I swear, I'm going to make that slob wear a bib next time he wants to eat in."

Logan shook his head. "It's not the vamp. The club's fine. This is pack business."

"At four A.M.?" Graham couldn't keep the surprise from his voice, but as his beta, Logan knew the pack almost as well as Graham did. If it was important to his second in command, it had better be important to him, too. That philosophy had saved him a lot of trouble over the years. "What's up?"

Logan snagged a piece of beef and looked around the room. "Are you sure you want to get into this with her still upstairs?"

Graham didn't ask how his friend knew Missy hadn't left. Her scent permeated the air, too fresh and intense to be just a remnant. It made Graham's balls tighten, and he reminded himself to breathe through his mouth. The urge to force Logan to do the same, by breaking the other man's nose, surprised him.

"She's none of your business," he dismissed, trying to be civilized but unable to stifle the instinct to stake a claim. "Forget about her. She'll stay put. Now what's going on?"

Logan gave him an odd look but shrugged, licking a smear of horseradish from his thumb. "Curtis."

"Shit." Graham's reaction was pithy but appropriate, since his cousin and chief headache, Curtis MacAlpin, had a lot in common with the stuff. Both were composed chiefly of waste and bile, both tended to turn up underfoot at the least opportune moments, and both stank to the high heavens. Only in Curtis's case, the stink was more of a moral one than a physical one. "What's he done this time?"

"He's been grumbling for months. You know that, right?"

"Logan, what has he done?"

The beta sighed. "He's sent up a Howl for the next Moon Night."

Graham cursed, long and creatively, and clenched his fist so hard that beef blood oozed out of the meat and trickled from between his fingers.

Howls were the Lupine equivalent of town meetings. Packs had them occasionally when there was trouble brewing, or when one of the members had big news to announce, like the formation of a new pack or the birth of an alpha's new pup.

"And what the hell made him think he had any right to do that?" Graham growled. "He's mid-pack. He's got no right to lead a Howl. I'm alpha. That's for me to do."

Logan settled his long frame onto one of the stools that butted against the island counter and raised his eyebrows. "We all know that, Graham. The problem is that Curtis doesn't care."

"He'll start caring once I rip a bloody stripe out of his hide. He needs to learn his place."

"I disagree. The problem is that Curtis knows his place; he just doesn't like it. He wants your place instead."

Graham's eyes narrowed. "He's thinking of challenging me? That puny little cub? He's barely twenty-seven, and scrawny to boot." Graham's scowl stretched into a savage grin. "In that case, let him at it. It'll take me five minutes to knock him back down to size, and we can forget all about this."

"It's not going to be that easy."

Graham raised his brow. "Are you implying he's strong enough to fight me?"

Logan rolled his eyes. "He's not strong enough to fight most of our infants. But he's clever, and that could be more dangerous. If Curtis were planning to issue a traditional challenge, he'd have been taken down months ago. Remember, he has to go through the entire rank before he gets to you. Even if someone like Tobias or Ethan didn't manage to take him out, he'd never get by me."

Graham acknowledged that with a nod. Logan had earned his place as beta a long time ago with a combination of intelligence and brute strength. The only pack member he'd never taken down was Graham himself, partly because of the loyalty between the two men and partly because neither of them could be absolutely positive who would win, and they weren't sure they wanted to know.

"True enough," Graham acknowledged, "but if Curtis isn't going to challenge me, what are you all worked up about? There's only one road to alpha, and you just said he's not taking it."

"See, that's where you're wrong," Logan said, his gaze level and intense. "Curtis isn't going to challenge you because he thinks he won't have to. He's going to call for you to step down."

Graham snorted. "He can call until he's too

hoarse to howl for all the good it'll do him. I'm alpha of this pack, and I mean to stay that way."

Logan grimaced. "You might not have a choice."

"What are you talking about?"

"I think Curtis is going to call on Breeder's Rights."

The term sounded vaguely familiar, but Graham couldn't place it. Lupine society overflowed with so many old traditions and rights and laws and customs that only an anal-retentive history professor could keep track of them all. As alpha of the Silverback Clan, Graham had more important things to worry about than whether or not someone had forbade the eating of deer meat on Tuesdays in all Februaries with blue moons.

"Old Lupine Common Law," Logan explained when Graham just scowled and shook his head. "It started back in the Dark Ages, as far as I know, when the humans were hunting us down just a little too successfully. In order to ensure our survival as a species, the elders made it a law that the alpha of any pack must be a member of a proven breeding pair. That way, each pack was guaranteed to produce a next generation strong enough to do the same. An alpha without cubs didn't do them any good."

The information left a sour taste in Graham's mouth, like rotten meat. He pushed the rest of his snack aside. "And Curtis thinks that because he fucked a brick-stupid omega and got her pregnant, he's suddenly the big wolf on campus?"

"Brick-stupid omega or not, Frannie whelped a healthy pup," Logan pointed out. "According to Common Law, that means something."

"Fuck Common Law!" Graham snarled. "I'm not stepping down so my cousin can feed his megalomaniacal delusions of grandeur, especially not when he hasn't got the balls to challenge me to dispute like a real alpha contender."

"Hey, I'm on your side," Logan said, leaning forward to meet Graham's furious gaze. "But Common Law still holds a lot of weight with the pack, especially with the elders and the conservatives. You and I know there's a lot more to being alpha than getting cubs, but traditions die hard for Lupines. In case you hadn't noticed."

"What do you suggest? I just step aside and let Cousin Curtis take over my pack and lead them all to hell in a handbasket? Should I wave to them on the way down?"

"You can take your sarcasm and shove it up your ass," Logan barked. "I'm trying to help you here. All I'm saying is that you're going to need to tread pretty carefully if you want to get around Curtis's argument. It would be a lot easier if you'd at least taken a mate, whether or not you had a cub yet."

Graham stilled, not sure he felt quite ready to share the news of his new mate, not even with his beta. Logan would have to know eventually, though, and the knowledge rankled. It felt almost like sharing her, and Graham still didn't have this possessive streak quite under control. He forced his mind away from the sleepy, sexy blonde in his bed and gritted his teeth.

"Even if you were newly mated and didn't have cubs yet, they'd have to give you one season of moon cycles to prove your fertility as a breeding pair," the beta continued. "If she got pregnant, the challenge would be thrown out and things could go back to normal."

Shit. Graham knew it would be hard enough to explain to Missy about their mate-bond. How was he supposed to break the news that he needed to knock her up as soon as possible? And it was all her fault. If she hadn't been wearing that ass-flaunting dress, he'd never have noticed her and never have gotten her alone and close enough to smell her above every other competing odor. Damn her and her sugar cookie scent.

Logan stared at him, brows knitting together and head tilting to the side. "What are you thinking?" he asked. "You've got a really weird look on your face, and if you inhale any harder, I think your face might cave in. Not that I don't agree she smells fabulous, but—"

"Keep your nose to yourself, Hunter." The possessive warning lashed, jagged and sharp, between them.

Logan eyed his alpha's feral snarl, and his eyebrows shot toward his hairline. "Tell me you're not thinking what I think you're thinking."

"It's none of your damn business what I'm thinking," Graham growled, scooping up the remains of his snack and dumping the lot into the garbage. He needed to get back upstairs to Missy.

"It is if you're thinking about taking someone you just met last night to mate. And it's doubly my business if that someone happens to be human!" Logan grasped Graham by the arm to keep him from leaving the kitchen. "That makes it pack business, Graham, and the pack will not appreciate having a human as its alpha female."

Graham ripped his arm out of the other Lupine's grasp and growled a warning. "I don't care what the pack wants, Hunter. The pack will do what I tell it to do, or it will face the consequences." His snarl held a world of menace and more than a hint of frustration. "If it's so important that I take a mate, then let the others live with my choice of one."

Logan's hands curled into fists, as if he had to fight to keep them to himself, a wise move if he wanted to leave the alpha's house with both intact. "They would be able to live with any choice you made if it was one of our own kind. Silverback alphas have been bred by your family for the last seven generations, but you won't breed the eighth if you insist on getting your cubs on a human."

"It's not like it's never happened before. We've been interbreeding with the humans from the first, and our genes are always dominant. Our pups are still Lupine."

"But they're not full-bloods. They're mongrels, and none of the pack are going to be willing to submit to a mongrel alpha."

"They'll submit if he's strong enough to make them," Graham proclaimed, arrogant and unyielding in the knowledge that Fate had already made the decision sometime when he wasn't looking. It was irrevocable. Missy was his mate. Case closed. "Alpha isn't a matter of heredity anyway. It's a matter of power. If my pup isn't strong enough to lead the pack, someone who is ought to have the job."

"And give up seven generations of tradition?" The confusion in Logan's tone drained away some of Graham's anger. If his beta didn't get it, he ought to get used to no one else getting it, either.

"Traditions can be broken and new ones founded, but a mate is permanent." Logan pointed out, switching tactics. "Lupines may mate for life, but humans don't always do it, no matter what they claim. What happens if she changes her mind?"

Graham's eyes narrowed dangerously. "She won't."

"It's been known to happen."

"Not this time."

Logan was silent for a moment. "It really doesn't matter to you what I say, does it?"

"No."

Graham knew it to be absolutely true. Missy was his mate. Whether he would have admitted that after one night if not for the challenge from Curtis was a moot point. Graham needed a mate, and his instincts wouldn't let him have any mate but Missy. He met his friend's gaze with a steady one of his own.

Logan sighed. "Does it matter what she says, then?"

Graham thought of the things she'd said when he'd had her pinned against his bedroom door, and the things she'd said when he'd woken her an hour later with his tongue buried in the sweet honey between her thighs. His lips curved into a smile, and he hardened beneath his jeans.

"No," he said, heading for the stairs and beating back the niggling feeling that maybe he was taking one or two things for granted here. "It doesn't matter at all."

CHAPTER FOUR

I could always say I was drunk.

Missy lay in the unfamiliar bed, curled up beneath a nubby cotton blanket that didn't quite combat the chill of the room, and practiced the fine art of not panicking.

He didn't spend much time talking to me, so he probably won't remember if I was slurring my speech. Wait, he can probably smell stuff like that, and I know I didn't smell like a brewery. Darn it.

She'd woken up when Graham left the bed. Sleeping in a sixty-degree bedroom was fine when you had a werewolf radiator cranking out heat beside you, but once he got up, the cold brought awareness back in a hurry. Not that she hadn't pretended to still be unconscious. Until she figured out how to handle this situation, she had every intention of playing possum.

Except you can't stay here forever, unfortunately, her inner voice told her. *So that really isn't an option. Better go to Plan B.*

There is no Plan B.

There should always be a Plan B. Didn't you learn that in Girl Scouts?

Squeezing her eyes shut, Missy groaned and yanked the blanket up over her head. The movement let some of the icy air seep into her cocoon, and she felt her skin pucker into gooseflesh. She doubted even God himself could deliver her from the situation she'd managed to get herself into. Even she couldn't quite grasp the reality of having been kidnapped and screwed senseless by the wickedly sexy werewolf of her dreams. The same one who had never been able to remember her name before last night.

To be precise, he couldn't remember it last night, either.

In fact, I'm not quite sure he's managed to figure it out yet. You may still just be slut du jour.

And that's what was turning her stomach into a knot. Missy was not the slut type. She was a kindergarten teacher, for heaven's sake! Kindergarten teachers were not sluts. They were plain and kind and boring and wore sensible shoes and unflattering clothes. Missy had been living with those guiding principles for the entire four years of her teaching career and had even gotten in some practice while she was still in college. After her disastrous experience with Jim from her child psychology practicum, she had pretty much resigned herself to the whole frumpy-spinster-with-cats scenario, and she was okay with that. After all, someone had to be the frumpy spinster. Cliché preservation could be an admirable cause, and Missy had been serving dutifully until some twisted instrument of Fate had decided to step in and make her fantasies come true.

How the heck was she supposed to deal with that? She wasn't the type of woman who lived fantasies, not even when her friends handed them to her with great big bows on top. This one night had managed to set her entire world tipping into surrealism. The only thing that kept her from convincing herself that she had dreamed the whole thing was the irrefutable physical evidence.

Like the fact that she was lying in a strange bed, under a strange blanket, in a strange room.

Naked.

Whisker-burned.

And sore in some really uncomfortable places.

Missy winced and sat up, then immediately shifted her weight onto one hip, pulling the blanket with her to wrap it around her like a cape. Apparently, sitting normally wouldn't be happening for a while yet. An estimate of when it might eluded her. Which was when she realized she had no idea what to do next.

The problem with abstinence, she decided, was that once you got out of practice, picking up on the ritual behaviors of sex stopped being second nature. Once upon a time—back in college when the term "sex life" had actually applied to her—the idea of what to do the morning after had seemed like second nature. But now, as she sat in the strange bed, the language of bedroom etiquette made about as much sense to her as the things Dmitri mumbled in Russian when Reggie exasperated him.

Was she supposed to stay where she was? Maybe she should throw off the blanket and pose across the sheets or something, so she'd be ready when Graham came back to bed. Or maybe she should feign sleep, so she could pretend that he'd woken her when he crawled back in. That way she could take her cues from him. If he seemed like he wanted to talk, she could do that, or if he seemed like he wanted more sex . . . well, maybe she could suffer through that, too. After all, Graham might get to sleep with women four times prettier than her every day, but she knew what the chances were of her ever again getting the opportunity to snuggle up to a man half as gorgeous as Graham Winters: precisely nil.

But oh no! What if the reason he had disappeared was because he realized who he'd gone to bed with and he just wanted to get away from her? Maybe he'd woken up and had a coyote moment—the kind where a man would rather chew off his own arm than wake up the woman beside him—and he'd really left to give her the chance to be gone before he came back? What the heck was she supposed to do?

"Okay, first, calm down," she told herself, closing her eyes and taking a couple of slow, deep breaths. "No need to panic. Everything's okay. Just breathe."

That worked for about fifteen seconds before the demons of embarrassment and low self-esteem made themselves known by raking icy fingers down her back and urging her to get while the getting was good. No matter how remote the possibility, there was no way she'd survive it if Graham came back and really was disappointed to see her. She'd rather cut and run now, before he left her heart and her ego in shreds on his bedroom floor.

She eased carefully to the side of the bed and slid to the floor. The boards chilled the bottoms of her feet, but she ignored the discomfort while she hurried around the dimly lit room in search of her belongings. If she could get dressed and sneak out before Graham returned, she might actually get to preserve her illusions and treasure this as the best night of her life instead of the stage for her most humiliating experience. But where the heck was her left shoe?

She found it tossed into the corner between a dresser and the wall, along with her purse. She grabbed both, then nearly jumped out of her skin when her purse chimed at her. Terrified Graham would hear the noise, she grabbed her cell phone and flipped it open before the first ring had ended.

"Hello?" She kept her voice low and cast a wary eye toward the bedroom door. It remained closed.

"What is the matter with my friends? Do none of them have the least little trace of manners in their stubborn bodies? What is it about them that compels them to run out on prearranged meetings with perfectly luscious men, who are then left wondering what the hell is going on, while I am forced to explain that it isn't them? It's my lamebrained, flaky, irresponsible, and uncivilized friends."

"Don't start with me, Av," Missy hissed, gathering up her ruined panties and bra and the balled-up wad of black fabric she assumed was her dress. "I've had a really bad morning so far, and I don't need you adding to it. I think you've done enough already."

"It's only four twenty-two. There hasn't been a morning yet," Ava dismissed. "Besides, you deserve everything you get for running out like that. Do you have any idea how hard it is to explain to a man why his blind date took one look at him and ran from the party? Do you?"

"That's not why I ran. I didn't even see the guy. And why the heck are you calling my cell phone at four thirty in the morning?"

"Why the hell are you answering?"

Missy froze. "Um . . . I asked first."

"Oh, that's very mature, darling," Ava drawled. "If you must know, I'm calling your cell phone to try and find out where you are in the middle of the night, since you didn't go back to your apartment."

"How do you know I'm not at my apartment? Where else would I go?"

"If you're at your apartment, why don't you roll over and tell Stephen I said hello, since I gave him the spare key you left with me and told him to wait for you."

The silky tone made Missy blanch almost as pale as did the idea of a strange man waiting in her apartment for sex, because if this Stephen guy was her fantasy fix, he wasn't planning on discussing the finer points of macramé with her. "I can't believe you sent a man to my apartment to wait for me to come home and have sex with him. Don't you realize how creepy that is? Ava, I gave you that key so you could water my plants when I went away to visit my parents, not so you could let strangers into my apartment. How do you know he hasn't emptied it out and pawned my stuff?"

"Really, Melissa, a successful vascular surgeon at Mount Sinai is hardly likely to hock your television, now is he?" Ava dismissed. "Besides, I've known Stephen for years, and he's perfectly harmless. You'll love him. If you'll get your butt back to your apartment and let him introduce himself."

Missy risked taking her eyes off the door and crossed to the other side of the bed. She knelt and stuck her head underneath, looking for her right shoe this time. Any second now she might have a complete outfit. Or as close to one as she could come with that ridiculous dress and a handful of tattered lingerie. She grabbed the high heel and struggled to hang on to the tact and diplomacy that usually came to her a lot more easily.

"Okay, I think we need to communicate a little better here," she began, rocking back onto her knees behind Graham's massive mattress. "I didn't run away because I realized I had left my iron on. I'm just not interested in being fixed, Ava. I admit, I should have mentioned this before, but there it is. I'm sorry."

"I don't care if you're interested. I care that this is the best thing for you. I didn't lay off of Regina, and I'm not about to lay off of you, darling. You will get fixed, like it or not."

"Ava, we're getting into the realm of creepy again.

This is sex we're talking about. 'Like it or not' seems a little harsh."

She could practically hear the other woman setting her jaw.

"You know what I meant, Melissa. You will like the fix if you'll just cooperate and give it a chance. Now go home."

"While there's some strange man probably sitting naked on my sofa? I'd really rather not."

"Stephen will wait all weekend if he has to, Melissa. He's very anxious to meet you. Besides, what else are you planning to do? The others all know I'll kill them if they harbor you."

"So now I'm the Fugitive?"

Ava swore in exasperation.

"For your information," Missy informed her, "I was on my way home when you called, but there's no way I'm going there now. As soon as I sneak out of here—"

A large, masculine hand reached down and plucked the cell phone from her hand, powering it down, and tossing it onto the bed in front of her. "I'm afraid you're not leaving anytime soon. I'm not nearly finished with you yet."

The sound of the rich, gravelly voice froze Missy right where she was, on her knees in the middle of a strange man's bedroom floor. She hadn't even heard him come in, let alone heard him cross the room. Why hadn't the stairs creaked, or something? It was just plain unnatural for a set of stairs in a house as old as this one not to creak.

She risked a glance over her shoulder and found herself staring straight at the fly of his blue jeans—which was unfastened—and the intriguing shadows that filled it. She swallowed hard and tried to pretend her legs hadn't gone all liquid. She clutched her clothes to her chest and yanked her gaze away from his groin, dragging it up over his well-muscled and beautifully furred chest. That did nothing for the liquid problem. In fact, it only compounded it. She could feel her body softening and growing damp, despite the raw, sore feeling it had protested about only a few minutes ago.

Darn thing doesn't know what's good for it.

When her eyes finally made it as high as his face, she saw the look of amusement there and stiffened. "That was rude. I was talking to someone."

He folded his arms across his chest and gave her a stern look. "You were planning on leaving without saying good-bye. I consider that to be pretty rude."

The challenge of maintaining her dignity while stark naked and kneeling at the feet of a gorgeous hunk of a werewolf made Missy fidgety.

It also made her lie.

"I never planned on not saying good-bye. I was just going to—"

" 'Sneak out of here.' I heard."

She was thoroughly sick of staring up at him, but until she figured out how to distribute her pathetic bundle of clothes to cover all vital areas, she thought she'd stay put. " 'Sneak' is just an expression."

"Which means to move stealthily in an attempt

to avoid detection." He prowled a step closer to her, and she scooted a few inches farther away. In a minute she'd have rug burn to go along with her whisker burn. "That sounds rude to me, Missy."

She halted in mid-scoot. "What did you call me?"

"Missy. Why? Did you change your name recently? You prefer 'Melissa' now?"

She ignored the sarcasm latched on to his words like a barnacle to the bottom of a boat. Stress, she liked to think, made her snap things she never normally would have said. "Oh, so now you remember my name? Last night you didn't even remember meeting me before."

He scowled. "I was . . . distracted."

"I don't care if you were struck temporarily brain-dead. You don't forget someone you walked down a church aisle with!"

"It's not like it was at *our* wedding. I was there for about fifteen minutes before I got the call that the club's kitchen was on fire, so I'm sorry if I didn't—" He cut himself off. "Wait a minute; what the hell am I doing? This is completely not the point. The point is that you are not going anywhere right now."

Missy stopped inching toward the door and bit her lower lip. "Well, you can't keep me here."

"Wanna bet?"

Before she could manage a properly outraged response, he grabbed her by the upper arms and tossed her gently down onto the bed. She bounced twice, which made it difficult to scramble away before he coiled his muscles and leapt up after her. At that point, the fact that she had two hundred pounds of grinning werewolf lying on top of her made it impossible. Either way, he had her trapped.

She stared up at him with her mouth hanging open and her eyes practically popping out of her skull.

His grin widened. "You were saying?"

Something made rather irrelevant by her present position.

"Okay, poor choice of words, since you obviously can keep me wherever you want me. But it's still illegal and immoral. And really mean."

He shrugged. "What can I say? I'm a werewolf. Haven't you heard? We're monsters."

"You are not," she retorted, wriggling experimentally beneath him. "So if you're done showing off and acting all big and bad, would you mind getting off me?"

Her wiggling brought her hips up against the pronounced swelling of his erection, concealed by his jeans, and he growled softly, his eyes going all glowy and aroused again.

"As a matter of fact, I would," he said, lowering his head to flick his tongue against the turned-down corner of her pouting mouth. "I think I like it right here."

Her traitorous body responded that it liked him right there, too. In fact, it would like him even more if he took off his jeans and shifted his hips just a tad to the right, but her mind had the good sense to be outraged and indignant. If only it weren't also struck temporarily dumb by the heavy, masculine, hot, sexy, orgasm-inducing feel of him.

She swallowed hard.

He traced the motion in her throat with his tongue, which made her swallow again, which made him trace again, and she figured she had maybe five more seconds of this before he reduced her to a quivering mass of goo.

She cleared her throat and moaned when the sound made him stutter his tongue against the sensitive skin. Her hands pressed against his shoulders, and she mustered one last coherent protest. "Um, I really do need to be going. I have things I need to do."

He reached up and locked both of her wrists in one of his big hands. Then he used his tongue to investigate the hollow at the base of her throat and the smooth curves of her collarbone.

"At four thirty in the morning? I don't think so."

"Maybe I'm an early riser."

"I know I am. Wanna see?" He ground his erection against her and wriggled his eyebrows suggestively.

It took some doing not to be charmed by his sense of humor and his blatant sexuality. "No!"

He grinned. "Liar."

She felt the blush rising in her cheeks. "What I want is for you to let me go."

"Why?"

"Why?"

"Yes. Why do you want me to let you go?"

He looked down at her with his disconcerting green eyes, and Missy suddenly realized she really couldn't remember why she felt so determined to leave when she still had fantasies he could be fulfilling. And he certainly wasn't helping matters by rubbing his thumb gently against the wrists that he still held pinned above her head in an unbreakable grip.

She shrugged. "Why do you want to keep me?"

The smile spreading across his face reminded her of sunrise and fallen angels and wicked, wicked intentions.

"Silly question," he rumbled, a sound half a step away from a purr, as he brushed her crumpled clothes aside and bared her body once more to his gaze. She saw the light of appreciation in them and fought not to show how much she liked that he enjoyed looking at her.

She tried to mold her expression into a scowl, but she knew it probably looked as forced as it felt. "Silly answer. I doubt very much that you can't get sex any time and from anyone you want."

He leaned down to lap at her nipple, wetting the tip and making it stand out from her breast. He pursed his lips and blew, watching as the crest tightened further. "But I don't want it from anyone. I want it from you."

Missy squirmed and fought to keep her breathing from turning into panting as he left one breast and moved to the other. She wanted to concentrate on what he was saying, especially since it seemed more likely to be a product of wishful thinking than hard-core reality. But she defied anyone to concentrate while Graham played with their tender bits. It couldn't be done.

He scraped his teeth over her skin, then lifted his head to survey his handiwork. "In fact," he purred, "I think I only want it from you from now on."

"But why?" she moaned.

His mouth closed over her neglected nipple, drawing the aching peak inside and sucking rhythmically. He pressed it firmly against the roof of his mouth, and she could feel his tongue rubbing in tiny strokes against the underside. The sensation made her want to cry out, and when he pulled away, she nearly did.

"Because you taste so good," he murmured, shifting until he could slide his tongue down the center of her chest and dip teasingly into her navel.

Her muscles clenched, from her abdomen to her ankles and everywhere in between. He breathed warm currents against her skin and ruffled her pubic hair with the tips of his fingers. Her hips arched reflexively into his hand, and she bit back a moan when his hand slid lower and eased her gently open. Her moan changed to a gasp when he buried his face in her curls and inhaled deeply.

"And you smell even better." His murmur had become a growl, and when he slid his tongue along the path of his fingers, Missy echoed it with a breathless cry. His tongue circled in a wave of hot, moist sensation before dipping into her center and drinking her wetness. Her free hands slid into his hair and cradled him to her while his tongue drove her crazy. Her nerve endings seesawed between pleasure and pain for a brief second until his head came up.

"You're hurt," he said, the growl back in his voice. "Why didn't you say anything?"

"About what?" She barely recognized her voice, as breathless and soft and drugged as it sounded.

"About the fact that I hurt you," he grumbled, pulling back from her and sliding off the bed. "From now on, I expect you to tell me."

He scooped her up in his arms and stalked into the bathroom while she was still trying to reconnect the synapses he'd blown with his clever tongue. As soon as the darned things got back into working order, she was going to get mad. The man was snarling at her because of something he had done! Logic, anyone?

She glared up at him from the edge of the bathtub where he set her down. "As I recall, you weren't real interested in anything I had to say at the time you were making me sore, Conan."

Graham scowled at her and turned on the faucet, testing the temperature before plugging up the drain and letting the tub fill with steaming water. "Next time, say it louder."

She crossed her arms over her chest to still the hopeful flutter inside. "Is there going to be a next time?"

"Damn straight," he retorted. "It's just a matter of how soon before it happens."

He turned his back and rummaged under the sink,

coming back with a paper milk-carton-looking container labeled: "Epsom Salts." He dumped a handful into the tub and stirred to dissolve the crystals.

Missy watched and brooded. "Are you always this dictatorial?" she finally ventured.

Graham twisted off the taps with a grunt. "I am now, so get used to it."

Without waiting for an invitation, Missy eased herself down into the water. Naked underwater, even clear water, was better than naked in plain sight. She winced when the heat stung her raw skin. "What's that supposed to mean?"

The werewolf looked down at her with a hard expression. "That you'll be spending quite a lot of time with me, so you'd better get used to my foibles."

Her eyes widened, but she couldn't tell if they did it because of his abrupt declaration or because he punctuated his words by stripping off his jeans and sliding into the tub with her.

The oversized old claw-foot was plenty big enough for the both of them, as long as they didn't mind touching. Graham obviously didn't. He settled his large frame into the opposite end of the tub and stretched out his legs on either side of hers until his feet rested beside her hips. He draped his arms over the sides of the tub and pinned her with a probing stare. "How does this feel?"

Missy wrenched her gaze from his damp chest, complete with its rough-smooth mat of hair and the flat brown nipples that made her mouth water. "How does what feel?"

His expression softened infinitesimally, and his mouth quirked up at one corner. "The bath. Is it helping any?"

Hoping her blush could be blamed on the heat, she nodded and sank up to her chin. "It's lovely. Thanks."

"Good."

They soaked in silence for a few minutes while Missy tried to figure out what event had landed her in this alternate universe, because she didn't want to accidentally repeat it and get herself tossed back into reality. She much preferred the existence where sexy, charming werewolves fell head over heels in love/lust with plain, average kindergarten teachers to the one where she couldn't get a date unless her friends arranged it, and the last two men she'd gone out with had both decided they'd rather be celibate than have sex with her. She intended to cling to this little fantasy until it shriveled up and died. Then they could try to pry it from her clutching fingers.

The hot, salted water began to work its magic on her, easing her sore muscles and soothing the raw feeling between her legs. Too bad it couldn't soothe the raw feelings of confusion and fear and doubt that lurked under her blustering declarations. She draped her hair over the back of the tub to keep it dry and let her head rest against the cool, enameled iron. Her eyes drifted shut of their own accord, and she stifled a yawn. With the adrenaline of the evening fading from her system, Missy began to realize just how short her nap in Graham's bed had really been. She felt like she could sleep for a week, but she didn't want to miss a second of her fantasy fulfilled.

God, what wouldn't she give if this one encounter really could go on forever? She couldn't imagine anything more heavenly than to have Graham so enamored of her that he never stopped touching her. All the sexual exertion might kill her, but boy, would she enjoy the trip to the cemetery!

When he picked up her feet and began to massage the arches with firm pressure, she sighed in pleasure.

"You're welcome to do that for the rest of my life," she murmured, and drifted into that cloudy, peaceful state between sleeping and waking where the sound of the lapping water and their quiet breathing faded into a soothing metronome in the back of her mind. She felt like she just might sleep for a week. Or at least until the water began to cool.

"I'd be happy to do it for the rest of our lives," Graham murmured, his voice distinct and warm and rumbling through her sleepy haze. "So why don't you make it easy for me and move in with me?"

CHAPTER FIVE

Graham wasn't quite sure where the words came from. He could only think to blame it on instinct and the relaxation caused by the hot water and the soft woman that let such instinct overwhelm his normally well-developed internal sensors at such a critical moment.

He had intended to ease Missy into the idea of being his mate, of becoming a permanent and tangible part of his life. He knew that knocking her over the head with the reality of the situation the first time he opened his mouth wouldn't do any good. He knew she wouldn't be able to understand his point of view. Not yet. He needed time for her to get to know him, for her to become well acquainted enough with the Lupine mentality to give him a fighting chance at chasing away her doubts. The few short hours they'd been together so far weren't nearly enough.

Missy, he reminded himself very deliberately, was human, and as such, she would require very special handling of the sort that did not come like second nature to a Lupine. Humans always wanted to "take things slow" and let romances "develop" over weeks or months. Or even years. Lupine relationships didn't work that way. Fate decided on each Lupine's mate, and their young learned from an early age that the only way to deal with Fate was to accept it. When a Lupine found a mate, he didn't waste any time in claiming her. But Graham also knew that attempting to claim Missy in the Lupine style would just as likely earn him a kick to the balls as a partner in his bed.

He needed to start playing things cool. Or as cool as possible for a single, horny Lupine who had just found the woman of his dreams.

"Very funny."

Missy's grumble emerged from between the wry curves of her lips, and Graham had to concentrate to keep from leaping across the length of the tub to prove exactly how serious his hasty words had been. Fortunately, Missy failed to open her eyes or even lift her head from the back of the tub, which gave him the chance to scramble for a little control and come up with a new plan for winning her over.

"You don't know what you're missing," he said, this time making his voice deliberately teasing. "You'd get foot rubs on demand, I generally pick up all my own socks, and in case you hadn't noticed, I'm really spectacular in bed."

He watched her warm, brown eyes open and fix on him. They looked soft and a little bit hurt. She stared at him for a long minute before she spoke beneath a skeptically arching eyebrow. "It's not nice to tease a woman while you're rubbing her feet. We're too vulnerable. Be serious, okay?"

"Didn't I sound serious?"

"No man sounds serious when he asks a woman to move in with him on their first date."

"Technically, this wasn't a date. For it to be a date, we'd have to go out somewhere and do something other than have mind-blowing sex."

She blushed at that, and he found the bright rise of color beneath her pale skin to be charming. Infinitely more charming than the way she started to shake her head.

"If you were serious, then you're also insane." She pulled her feet from his lap and started to sit up straighter until the movement brought her breasts above the waterline. She quickly sank deeper and pulled her knees to her chest and her feet out of his reach. The expression she wore now looked upset and a little sad. "I really wish you hadn't shattered my illusions quite so soon. I should be going. Can I have a towel please?"

"No."

She looked over at him, her eyebrows lifted high and her eyes wide and startled. "No?"

"No, you can't have a towel. If I give you one, you'll dry off and go home, and I'm not ready to let you leave yet. And no, I'm not crazy. Just Lupine."

"Haven't we already been through this once?" She frowned and crossed her arms over her chest. "You really can't keep me here."

His instincts urged him to demonstrate to her how wrong she really was about that, but he beat them into submission. If he wanted this woman to be at ease with him, he'd have to go slowly. More slowly. With all the rush and hurry of a glacier. He was learning she wasn't quite as delicate as she looked, but he knew he could still spook her if he wasn't careful.

Damn it. Maybe he should have relaxed his rules earlier and dated a few humans before. Then he might have had a little more practice in how to deal with them. It felt like such a struggle to watch their foot-dragging, instinct-ignoring way of doing things. They all seemed to take their long, safe lives for granted. They thought they could live according to the rules of logic, and Graham was too Lupine to even make such an attempt.

He had thought limiting himself to asking her to move in with him, rather than informing her that she would marry him and bear his pups, like he wanted to do—like he would *already* have done if she were Lupine—was pretty restrained. But apparently the situation called for even greater delicacy. He struggled fiercely to adjust from warp speed to wuss speed.

"I have no intention of holding you prisoner," he said, even as he squashed those very impulses. "But let's be logical about this. What do you plan to do when you leave here?"

"I'll go home."

"To the naked stranger sitting on your sofa?"

Graham remembered the parts of her phone conversation he'd overheard. He had to clench his jaw to keep from expressing exactly how he felt about any man other than him being in Missy's apartment, let alone being naked and lying in wait for her. He might be able to make visitation exceptions for a father or a brother, but it would be a near thing. And everyone who ever got within fifty feet of her again had damn well better be wearing a full set of clothes.

"You didn't sound very happy about that idea on the phone," Graham continued. "Have you changed your mind?"

He watched her shoulders droop briefly before she squared them again with visible determination and lifted her little chin defiantly. "I can go to a friend's house," she said.

"You mean to one of the people who got you into this situation? The ones you were running from last night when you bumped into me?" He almost regretted pointing that out when he saw her chin sink and her expression fall into regretful lines, but he had goals to remember. Everything he was doing would be for the best in the end, for him and for his mate. "Is that really what you want to do?"

He heard her sigh, saw her shrug. "There isn't much else I can do. Except maybe call the police, and I don't want the poor man arrested. I just want him out of my apartment."

"You can stay here." He held up a hand when she started to protest. "Wait, calm down. I'm not talking about kidnapping you and holding you here against your will; I'm just offering you a place to crash." He mentally crossed his fingers. "Just spend the weekend. Once it's safe and whatshisname is gone, you can go back to your apartment, and I'll wait until after we've had a few real dates before I bring up our next step."

In reality, he had no intention of ever asking her to move in with him again. She'd figure it out for herself after their first cub was born.

He saw her start to waiver and pressed his case. "It's just a couple of days. You can be home in time for work on Monday morning."

"I don't have to work on Monday," she murmured, chewing on her lower lip until he wanted to sink his own teeth into the pink flesh. "Next week is spring break."

He filed away that useful tidbit and kept up the pressure while she debated with herself. "That's even better. In case the loser doesn't clear out until he goes to work Monday. It gives you a buffer. You won't have to feel pressured to go back until you're sure he's gone. Besides, you didn't tell Ava where you were, did you?"

She shook her head. "How did you know I was talking to Ava?"

"I've met all of the women Regina calls close friends," he said as he buried his face in Missy's neck. "None of the others are that intimidating. So if you didn't tell Ava where to find you, you're safe.

No one would ever think to look here, would they? They have no reason to. Why not take advantage of that? You get to keep them out of your hair for two whole days. Doesn't that sound pretty good?"

She tapped one slender finger against her shoulder while she thought, and he tried to focus on that instead of on her luscious mouth. It didn't cool him off any, but he did manage to stay on his end of the tub.

"Won't my being here mess up your plans for the weekend?"

He tried not to grin triumphantly. "I don't have any plans for the weekend," he assured her. Other than keeping her as naked as possible. "You wouldn't be messing up a thing."

She pursed her lips. "And where exactly would I sleep?"

"Was the bed not comfortable?"

She eyed him with an odd expression, and Graham couldn't tell if she was offended or intrigued or disgusted or overcome with lust. This was why humans should have tails. Or at least bigger ears. A wolf's ears made reading expressions so much easier.

"You could be a gentleman and offer me your guest room," she finally said, watching him intently.

"I'm not that much of a gentleman. Or a masochist," he said, flashing her a grin. "And it would feel a lot like padlocking the door to the empty barn. Besides, if we're going to be spending the weekend together, don't you think we should take advantage of the opportunity to get to know each other better?"

"I think talking would be a perfectly adequate way to accomplish that, don't you?"

"We can do both. Haven't you ever heard of pillow talk?"

Missy blushed, which he found adorable, and Graham fought to keep from drooling. He doubted she would appreciate the Lupine compliment, no matter how sincerely meant. "You really want me to go back to bed with you?"

"Right now, if you're willing."

She shook her head like she couldn't believe what she was hearing. "There's no reason for you to act like this. You could have any woman you wanted just by giving her one of those killer smiles of yours. Why should you want me? I'm still surprised that you could even see me last night over all those tall supermodel types throwing themselves at your head."

He couldn't have stifled his grin if his life depended on it. "You're jealous."

Missy laughed, still shaking her head. "No," she denied, "just confused."

He saw gooseflesh on her skin and realized the water must be getting cold. He climbed out of the tub and grabbed a towel from the cabinet. "You don't have to worry. I'm not interested in any other woman."

Ignoring the water dripping off of him to the

tile floor, he wrapped the towel around Missy and rubbed the terry cloth gently against her soft, pale skin. He debated telling her *why* he wasn't interested in any other women but then reminded himself again that she was human. His chances of keeping her in his house were a lot better if he didn't bring up the term "mate-bond" for another day or so. As a human, she would probably need a little time to get used to him before tackling the whole fated-to-spend-eternity-together thing.

Graham hunkered down in front of his petite, delicate mate and continued to dry her legs and feet. He'd bet she didn't wear above a size 6 shoe; her feet were just that tiny, with high arches and toes polished a blushing shade of pink almost the exact color of her skin when he pushed inside her. The thought made him harden instantly, and he fought not to lean forward and bury his face in the thatch of light brown curls that shielded her sex. Having it so close and convenient didn't seem to be helping his willpower any.

He forced his eyes back to her feet until he could feel her gaze on the top of his head.

He looked up. "What?"

She shook her head. "I was just wondering something. . . ."

He stood and finally took pity on her, wrapping the towel around her body so she could unclamp her arms from in front of her breasts. He hoped she realized exactly what the show of chivalry cost him. "What were you wondering?"

Missy hugged the cloth against her like a security blanket and tucked her hair behind her ears. Then she looked down at the floor and shrugged. "Why you're acting like you're so interested in me."

"Um, because I am?" Graham wondered where these ridiculous doubts were coming from. How could she doubt how badly he wanted her? Had she gone blind? He thought about grabbing her hand and wrapping it around his aching cock, just to give her a tactile demonstration of exactly how interested he really was, but there was that whole problem with her being likely to run from him, screaming.

"Yeah, right."

He frowned. "What's that supposed to mean?"

"It means that I have a little trouble believing that I'm all of a sudden irresistible," she said, her chin lifting again as she forced her eyes to meet his eyes with obvious effort. The way she could turn from bashful flower to rebellious firebrand fascinated him. "You've known me for six weeks and tonight is the first time you've looked at me like I was more than an extension of the wallpaper."

"I've obviously been a moron," he countered, enjoying the way her brown eyes had gone warm and were sparking at him. And he had been. Clearly. How could he not have noticed how amazing she was before this? "What else were you expecting? I'm a man. We're morons by birth, or so my female cousins tell me."

"Some of you are more moronic than others,"

she agreed. "But I'd really prefer it if you didn't act as if you've suddenly realized that I'm utterly gorgeous and sexy and everything a man has ever dreamed of."

"But you are."

Missy shook her head, her expression taking on a hint of anger. "Just because I teach kindergarten does not make me a simpleton. Don't lie to me, please."

The way her skin flushed and her breasts rose and fell with her angry breathing made his beast sit up at attention. Her indignation turned her scent sharper, more bitter, more heavily spiced. He wanted to lick the pique from her skin until it turned to lust, and then he wanted to lick it from between her thighs until it turned to satiation.

"I'm not lying." He had to force himself to concentrate on the conversation. "I really *am* a moron, and I really *do* think you're utterly gorgeous and sexy. Didn't you figure that out when you had me so hard and hot that I devolved into a monosyllabic cretin just because I couldn't wait to get inside you?" He shook his head. "That's not the kind of thing I can fake."

"From what I understand, you don't have to fake a thing," she snapped. "You've got quite a reputation, Graham. I hear there's not more than a handful of women you've ever met that you haven't ended up in bed with. So forgive me if I don't think it's an accomplishment that I gave you an erection."

An unexpected spear of hurt coursed through

him. He had enjoyed every single one of the women he'd taken and had no reason to regret a single one, but somehow his mate made him want to wash away his past. He raked a hand through his hair and frowned.

"You're making it sound like I only wanted you because you were there. Like I would have just as soon had someone else."

"Exactly."

Frustration made him want to howl. It succeeded in making him pace.

"It's not like that," he snapped, trying to think of a way to make her understand his need without terrifying her so badly she'd run. "I want *you*, Missy, not just another female body."

"Yeah, right."

"I mean it. I've had plenty of female bodies. You were right about that," he admitted, and had to grit his teeth against the hurt he saw flicker in her eyes. "But that means I know the difference between them and you. I don't want another woman. I didn't invite another woman to spend the weekend with me."

He saw her shake her head and strode back to her side, grasping her by the arms and forcing her to meet his gaze. He needed to impress her with the truth, and he hoped she'd be able to read it in his face.

"I didn't invite another woman to move in with me. I've never invited a woman to do that. Just you."

"But that's what I don't get," she whispered, her

eyes wide and confused as she gazed up at him. "Tonight is the first time you've ever spoken more than five words to me, and all of a sudden you're crazy about me? More than a few hours and a few rolls across the mattress crazy? That doesn't make any sense."

For the first time in his life, Graham regretted being a werewolf. If he were a vampire like Dmitri, he could just read her thoughts and figure out exactly how to reassure her, but instead he floundered for a way to make her trust him without also making her see him as an even weirder creature than she already did.

Unable to resist, he reached up to stroke her silky hair, remembering the way it looked spread out on his silk sheet. He wanted to see it there again, now, but he wanted more than that. If he was going to convince this woman to be his mate, he'd have to move more slowly than he ever had in his life. Slower than he knew it was possible to move. And if that wasn't a matter of teaching an old dog new tricks, he didn't know what was.

"Why don't you stop thinking about it so hard and give me a chance?" he suggested. "You've already agreed to stay here this weekend, so let me use it to convince you that I'm serious."

"Sex is not going to—"

"He chuckled and gave in to the urge to hug her until she squawked a protest. "I promise sex will only be part of it," he teased, loosening his grip only slightly. "We'll do other things, too. Things people do when they want to get to know each other. Like talk . . . and watch movies . . . and play games . . . and order Chinese food. What do you say?"

She met his gaze in silence, and he could see her searching for some clue. He hoped what she found would reassure her. He knew how serious he was; he just had to convince her. Finally she drew a deep breath and nodded once.

"All right," she agreed. "Since I'm stuck here anyway, there's not much I can do to avoid you, I suppose."

"Perfect!" He laughed triumphantly and hugged her again, planting a great big kiss on her surprised mouth before pulling away and heading for the bedroom door. "Hang on a second and I'll dig up something for you to wear. Then I'll take you out for breakfast. I don't know about you, but I'm starving."

He couldn't quite contain the spring in his step as he left her staring after him. As soon as she got dressed, he'd take her out to his favorite diner and feed her. With the things he had planned for their weekend together, she'd need to keep up her energy.

CHAPTER SIX

Missy pulled on the black slacks Graham had provided and silently thanked whatever employee at his club had provided them. The idea of putting on her super-short dress from last night made her shudder, especially considering she lacked any sort of underwear to put on beneath it. The scraps left after Graham had torn her lingerie off last night now graced the trash can in the bathroom, and she struggled not to wriggle at the unfamiliar feel of going pantyless.

She didn't worry so much about the bra. Being a long way from a D-cup, she could get away without one, especially since the shirt she wore was one of Graham's and could have fit three of her. She had to roll the sleeves up almost to the shoulders and tie the bulk of the material at her waist to keep from being overwhelmed by the thing, but it was comfortable, and the roomy fit hid the fact that her breasts were bare beneath it. All she really needed now was a layer of cloth to hide her feelings.

Having the man of her dreams devoted to fulfilling all of her wildest fantasies could definitely go to a girl's head, and Missy could only pray it wouldn't go to her heart as well. Graham had just offered her the opportunity to spend an entire weekend living out her dreams, and she'd seized it with both hands. As much as she wanted to protect her feelings, she'd never be able to forgive herself if she didn't do everything she could to have this one interlude with the man she'd been mooning over for the past six weeks. She knew perfectly well it couldn't last forever.

No matter what level of lust and curiosity Graham felt for her now, she knew it was only temporary. She just hoped she could be satisfied with her memories of this weekend when it ended. She couldn't bear it if she spent the rest of her life in love with a man who had gotten bored with her.

Graham stuck his head through the open bedroom door just as she was contemplating her bare feet. Somehow her stiletto pumps from the night before just didn't go with the outfit.

"You almost ready?"

"As ready as I can be," she answered, dragging her attention back to the outside world and wiggling her toes, "but I think I fall in the 'no shoes, no service' category."

He pushed the door open and held out a pair of white tennis shoes. "I looked at your heels. No one on my staff wears a five and a half, but I got a pair of sevens and two pairs of thick socks."

"Thanks." She took the shoes and sat on the edge of the mattress to pull them on. "I feel like I've taken rotten advantage of your waitresses, stealing all their clothes."

"You didn't have to steal; they were donated. Besides, the shoes came from my secretary. She had the smallest feet."

He tapped his own booted foot against the floor while she laced the sneakers tightly and tested the fit. A little loose, but the socks would keep her from feeling like she wore clown shoes.

"Okay," she announced, sliding to the floor. "I'm ready."

Graham grinned. "Great. I just need to let the staff know where we're going and we can leave. Come on."

He took her hand and tugged her toward the door. Missy followed, trying to pretend she had a choice.

She hadn't gotten a chance to see much of anything the night before, what with making the trip to his house and up to his bedroom face down over his shoulder in the pitch-dark, but now she got a chance to look around.

The old town house had the elegant sort of grace that nineteenth-century architecture naturally seemed to impart. The dark woodwork gleamed with the richness of age, and the soothing, earth-toned décor had a masculine and comfortable feel to it. It wasn't the type of place she would have pictured Graham living in, but maybe he had facets to his personality that she hadn't seen yet.

The only facets he'd been interested in showing her so far were protuberant and demanding.

Expecting to be led out the front and around to the entrance of Vircolac next door, she was surprised when he made a left turn into a large study and walked up to a well-stocked section of built-in bookshelves. He reached out and pressed a button, then took hold of the shelving and pulled it toward them to reveal a well-lit and entirely un-dusty hallway.

"It's not quite like I always imagined a secret passageway," she said.

Graham smiled. "I could add some cobwebs and dirt, if you want." He put his hand on the small of her back and ushered her in ahead of him. "It's not really secret, though. My staff and I use it when we need to go back and forth between the buildings. Saves time. And it keeps us dry when the weather's bad."

The short corridor was papered and lit like a regular interior hallway and ended at a handsome six-panel door. They stepped through into another hallway and turned right, emerging from behind a grand staircase into the front hall of the club.

It looked like Missy's image of the foyer of a grand London town house for some rich aristocrat. It had that look of age and wealth and power seemingly oozing from its wainscoted walls. The décor seemed more like someone's home, rather than a club, but she imagined there weren't a lot of people's homes that experienced this much activity before 6:00 A.M.

She could hear the sound of voices and the tapping of footsteps beyond the open doors that lined the hall, and staff members passed back and forth fetching and carrying in their crisp black and white uniforms. Several of them greeted Graham and gave her some curious stares as their boss led her toward the front of the building and one of the few closed doors in the hall. Missy tried to ignore the glances and busied herself taking in the club she'd been wanting to get a look at.

"I just need to talk to my assistant for a sec," Graham explained when Graham paused outside the door with his hand on the polished brass knob. "Plus, she made my introducing you to her a condition of lending you her shoes."

Missy raised her eyebrows at that but allowed Graham to usher her into the room in front of him. They stepped into an office, which Missy identified from the filing cabinets, note boards, and desk inside. A second door in the right-hand wall behind the desk opened into an inner office.

The generous workstation sported a neat and organized surface, a casually dressed woman sitting behind it, her long brown hair pulled back into a ponytail. The woman looked up and smiled when they entered. She looked to Graham first, but when her blue eyes fastened on Missy, they did so with evident curiosity.

"Good morning!" She practically bounced up from her chair and hurriedly crossed in front of the desk to stand before the couple. "I'm so happy to meet you! I was so excited when Graham told me about you."

Missy offered the other woman a friendly smile. At least, she tried to, but the brunette seemed determined to stare at someplace near Missy's right elbow. Her smile turned into a puzzled look, and Graham stepped forward to make the introduction.

"Missy, this is my assistant, Samantha Cartwright."

Trying again with a smile, Missy extended her hand. "It's nice to meet you."

Samantha took her hand and leaned forward to kiss her lightly on the mouth. Surprise made Missy jump back a little, and Samantha's eyes opened wide, meeting hers for the first time.

"What's the matter? Did I do something wrong? Luna, I apologize—"

Graham cut her off. "It's no problem, Sam. I think you just surprised Missy."

Which was true, for what it was worth, but Missy found Graham pretty surprising, too. She had figured out all on her own that the kiss had served as some kind of formal Lupine greeting, not a pass. But what was up with this "Luna" thing?

"There's nothing to apologize for," she told Samantha with another smile. "Actually, I wanted to thank you for loaning me the shoes. That was really sweet of you."

"Oh, it's nothing!" Samantha rushed to assure her. "I'm just sorry they're not really your size."

"Well it's not like I expect your feet to shrink for my convenience," she laughed. "With the socks, these are just fine."

Graham laid a hand on her arm and smiled down at her. "Let me just tell Samantha what's going on with the club business and we can go, okay?"

Missy gave him an odd look but nodded. "Sure. Take your time."

He smiled at her, and she turned away to keep from going all mushy at the sheer adorableness of the expression. The man's appeal made things way not fair.

While he talked to Samantha about suppliers, accounts, and correspondence, Missy wandered around the room and checked out the working environment of the man she'd just agreed to spend the weekend with. She fought the urge to peek into the inner sanctum, since Graham hadn't bothered to point it out, but it was a struggle. She wanted to see where he worked, so she could picture what he might be doing once their time together was over.

The outer office was comfortable and casual and a little bit cluttered to flesh out its *Architectural Digest* bones. Utilitarian file cabinets lined up against a beautifully paneled wall just beneath a stretch of individually paned windows. The desk looked like a combination of antique and contemporary sections, but it was covered with ultra-modern computer equipment and reams of paper. Samantha looked comfortable and at home in a pair of faded blue jeans and a battered NYU sweatshirt. Missy felt slightly less comfortable with the fact that the other woman couldn't seem to stop staring at her.

Finally, she gave up wandering around and pretending not to pay attention to them. She leaned up against a filing cabinet to wait. Samantha looked away as soon as Missy met her eyes, making Missy frown. Did she have a stain on her shirt? Was her hair sticking up at odd angles? Did she have a huge hickey on her neck? Missy was starting to feel like a sideshow freak or something, with all the sideways looks and tension.

The possible explanation for the odd behavior struck Missy as Graham finished signing a sheaf of paperwork and said good-bye to Samantha before leading Missy out the door.

As soon as the office door closed behind them, Missy brought up her suspicions as subtly as she could manage.

"Do you have something going with your secretary?"

Graham paused with his hand on the knob of another door and cast Missy an incredulous look. "With *Sam*? Of course not. What the hell made you think that?"

Missy shrugged. His reaction seemed perfectly innocent, but she couldn't think of any other way to explain the other woman's odd behavior. "I don't know. I just thought she seemed kind of . . . uncomfortable around me. Like she was expecting me to turn into some kind of Wicked Witch of the West, or something."

He opened the door and pulled two jackets out of the large hall closet, helping her slip one on.

"You're imagining things," he said, tucking his own jacket under one arm while he rolled up the sleeves of the one she wore until her hands finally poked out of the bottom. Thankfully the old denim was soft and pliable, so she didn't feel like a two-year-old in a snowsuit by the time he'd finished.

"I wasn't imagining the fact that she could barely stand to look me in the eye. I'm not totally clueless, you know."

"I never said you were." He shrugged into his coat and pulled open the club's main entrance door to let her outside. "That had nothing to do with you. Well, not directly, anyway. It's just Samantha."

"But—"

He cut her off with a sigh. "It's a little more complicated than a one-word answer, so can we wait until I get some coffee in me? The diner's only a couple of blocks from here."

Reluctantly, Missy nodded. "I guess so, but I do want to know."

"And I promise to answer all your questions, okay?" He smiled down at her and reached out to hold her hand in his. "For now, let's just enjoy the fresh air and the company."

Missy found herself smiling. "Is that your suavely polite way of telling me to shut up?"

He nodded, flashing his charming grin. "At least until after the coffee. Is it working?"

She shrugged and smiled, letting him guide her north along the quiet street.

It wasn't even 6:00 A.M., but already the city was grumbling awake. She could hear the sound of traffic seeping in from the edges of the neighborhood, smell the faint tinge of exhaust in the crisp morning air. The cold made her cheeks and nose tingle, and she stuffed her right hand in her pocket, but her left, held firmly in Graham's, stayed toasty warm.

She kept her questions to herself and just enjoyed the morning walk until a magenta-haired waitress seated them in a window-side booth with thick ceramic coffee mugs and plastic-covered menus. Once they were alone again, Missy gave in to her curiosity.

"All right. So what's up with you and Samantha?"

Graham tossed back half his coffee like a slug of whiskey, never mind the steam that curled up from the rim of the cup. He didn't seem to register the heat, but Missy couldn't help wincing. Even after adding four little creamer cups to her own mug, she still had to set it aside for a few minutes to let it cool.

"I told you, there's nothing 'up' with me and Samantha," he said. "She's an employee and a member of the pack. That's it."

"She's a werewolf, too, then?" Missy asked, but his nod just confused her further. "Then why did she look like she was afraid I'd jump her? She could probably spin me on one finger like a basketball."

He got a couple minutes of reprieve while the waitress came back to take their order, and Missy could almost see him sorting through explanations in his head while he looked for the best one. He sighed when the waitress took their menus and headed back toward the kitchen. "She probably wasn't exactly afraid of you. She was just being cautious."

Missy gave him a look over her coffee cup. "Cautious? Of what? Unless she has a mortal fear of 'The Alphabet Song,' I doubt she has much to fear from me."

"Like I said, it's . . . complicated."

"'Mary Had a Little Lamb'?"

"It's a Lupine thing," he began, pausing when she rolled her eyes.

"And I wouldn't understand? I thought you wanted us to get to know each other better. How will we do that if we avoid anything complicated? I mean, I'm going to go out on a limb here, but I'm pretty sure complicated is a given when members of two different species start dating."

He tapped his fingers on the scratched Formica and frowned. "You don't sound a lot like a kindergarten teacher at the moment."

"Somehow I don't think you've associated with many since you were five," she said. "And don't change the subject. Just because I teach five-year-olds doesn't mean I'm okay with being treated like one. What is this big werewolf secret I wouldn't understand?"

"It's not a secret, just a point of culture."

She leaned back when the waitress set their orders down, but she didn't look away. She wanted to know what was going on.

"And?"

He studied her, and she set her shoulders and lifted her chin, determined to make clear her refusal to back down.

When he spoke, he sounded matter-of-fact and just a little bit cautious. "You're her new alpha. She was being cautious around you as a sign of respect. That's what the kiss was about, too."

"Alpha? I'm not even Lupine. *You're* her alpha, not me."

"Alphas come in pairs, male and female. I'm alpha male of the pack, but Samantha acknowledged you as alpha female, and Lupines call alpha females Luna because they're as influential as the moon."

Missy wondered if the world would ever shift back onto its axis, because it had been off-kilter since he'd first touched her the night before.

"I'm not Lupine," she repeated. "I'm not even a member of the pack. I can't be a leader of it."

Graham swallowed a mouthful of bacon. "Samantha obviously disagrees."

"She can't just decide to do that, can she? I mean—"

Missy's protest sputtered to a halt when Graham slid a forkful of fluffy eggs into her open mouth and leveled a stern glance at her.

"Can we not talk about Samantha, please?" He looked a little impatient, but at least he tried to be polite. "You're only giving me a weekend to win you over, and this particular conversation is cutting into my time."

Missy nodded reluctantly—since she couldn't do much else with her mouth full—and he withdrew his fork.

"Good. Now finish your breakfast. We're going to have a busy day."

Graham turned his attention right back to his meal, and Missy tried to pretend she didn't interpret that comment in an entirely sexual manner. But she still had to cross her legs and press her thighs together to ease the ache her imagination and his husky voice inspired.

She looked down at her plate and began spreading blackberry jam on her toast, more to keep her hands occupied than because she wanted to eat it. Somehow, the strain of the night had her craving protein, not toast. She forked up a bite of her asparagus and cheddar omelet and tried to behave as if the idea of keeping busy in his bedroom all day had never crossed her mind.

"What are we planning to do?" She met his gaze with the most casual expression she could muster, but she still ended up blushing at the devilish glint in his eyes.

"Well, you said we needed to get to know each other better," he said, polishing off his eggs and digging his fork into a stack of pancakes. "So today, you're going to show me everything there is to know about you. Then tomorrow, I'll show you everything there is to know about me. Monday, we can revisit the moving thing. I'll even help you pack."

Missy rolled her eyes and laughed, but she couldn't quite suppress the little voice inside her that wailed at the injustice of the fact that by Monday he'd be sick of her and moving on to the next woman who caught his attention. That moment of truth was still two days away, and she sure didn't plan to waste this opportunity brooding about the way it would end. In fact, she didn't plan to waste a minute sharing all the boring details of her life just so he could get sick of her that much quicker. She planned to milk every drop of enjoyment out of their time together that she possibly could, and that did not mean letting him watch while she did her laundry or finished her grocery shopping. If she only had this one weekend with him, she wanted to spend it touching him. Preferably naked. And, even more preferably, horizontal.

Then, she'd spend next week holed up in her apartment, crying her way through box after box of tissues.

"Letting you know everything there is to know about me is not going to take all day," she said, pushing away her half-eaten meal, hoping the gesture looked more like she was preparing for something and less like her stomach had knotted up so hard she couldn't swallow. "In fact, I can tell you all about me in just a few short sentences."

The voice inside her head shrieked in protest, but Missy ignored it. She ignored her pounding heart, her shaking fingers, and her suddenly dry mouth and prayed for the strength to seize what she knew would be the two best days of her life.

Okay, she thought, taking a deep, trembling breath. *Here goes. Just don't let me look like an idiot. That's all I ask.*

Missy leaned back in the vinyl booth and stretched out her legs until she could hook her ankle around his calf and pull him closer. Then she gave him what she hoped was a seductive smile and lowered her not-quite-steady hands to her borrowed shirt, unfastening the first two buttons with slow, teasing motions.

She saw him still, saw his eyes drop and fix on the pale skin newly bared by the partially unfastened shirt, and she felt a sense of power that made her smile widen.

"I just turned twenty-seven years old," she said, slipping her hand into the open placket of the shirt she wore and trailing her fingers along the pale skin from her throat to her modest cleavage and back again. His eyes followed the motion as if they were glued to it. "Only child. Born in Brooklyn, raised in Westchester County. Went to Sarah Lawrence. Degree in early childhood education. Never broken a bone, but once sprained my wrist playing tennis. Haven't picked up a racket since."

She continued speaking, opening another button every few words. By the time she started telling him about her parents and the fact that she was mortally afraid of jellyfish, the dimple of her belly button was just visible in the opening of her shirt. She saw his jaw clench and circled her fingertip around the last remaining button. It and the knot in the shirttails were the only things standing between her and her very first arrest for indecent exposure.

"Allergic to shellfish, but adore catfish, especially blackened. Favorite musicians include Stevie Ray Vaughan, Sarah McLachlan, and the Indigo Girls."

She paid no attention to anyone around her, since none of them paid any attention to her. They lived in Manhattan, which meant one woman in a diner with her shirt hanging open but still covering all her vital parts didn't make front-page news. In fact, it probably wouldn't even make a blip on their radar.

Licking her lips, she rubbed her foot against his leg under the table and slowly, slowly unfastened that last button.

"I like long walks in the park, breakfast in bed on Sunday mornings, and watching old musicals on DVD. Biggest turn-ons are confident men who know what they want, have a sense of humor, and turn furry once a month."

She shifted slightly, baring the center plane of her pale, smooth torso to his avid gaze. A low growl rumbled in his chest and he clutched the tabletop in a white-knuckled grip, but she couldn't resist pressing just a little further.

Her eyes on his face, she pushed her shirt aside just far enough for him to see the inside curves of her breasts, then ran her hands between them and down to the fastening of her slacks.

"Think you know enough about me yet?" she asked, her voice husky and purring and as taunting as her subtle striptease. "Or did you need something else?"

Her fingers flexed and the top button on her slacks popped open. Almost instantly, Graham's eyes blazed a vivid, glowing green and his arm shot into the air.

"Check, please!"

CHAPTER SEVEN

They made it back to his house in seven minutes flat, including calculating the waitress's tip, though Graham didn't so much calculate as throw her a wad of cash and drag Missy out the door before she could utter another word. After that stunt, she'd better not open her mouth again until she was ready for him to put something in it.

He managed to refrain from slinging her over his shoulder again only because they were already so close to home. But lest she think he wasn't impatient for her, he fell on her like an attacking pit bull the minute the front door closed behind them.

She landed on the entry carpet with a hard thump, and he heard the hiss when the impact managed to knock most of the air out of her lungs. Whatever she had left, he stole from her in a kiss so hot and wet and mind-blowing he almost came just from the feel of her mouth under his. His lips moved against hers, firm and avid, while his tongue plunged deep to tangle with hers. She tasted of coffee and woman and the sweet, wild flavor of Missy, and he wanted to devour her. He swore she tasted even better than she had the night before. Richer. More intense.

Maybe he was imagining it, but in the interest of accuracy he figured he'd better make sure by conducting a few more tests.

Taste tests.

Naked taste tests.

Growling in anticipation, he closed his hands over the knot holding her shirt closed and ripped it apart. Never mind he'd just reduced his own shirt to dust rags, because the treasure that lay under it was a hell of a lot more important to him. His hands clenched into fists as he spread the sides of the shirt and bared her breasts to his hungry gaze. Her nipples beaded even before he touched them, stabbing into the air like little pebbles and making his mouth water. He popped one between his lips quickly, before he started drooling in his enthusiasm.

She murmured and shifted beneath him, creating a distracting friction against the demanding inhabitant of his jeans. A growl rumbled deep in his chest, and he reached down to tug open her zipper. Somehow the black fabric of her trousers disintegrated under his hands. He hadn't intended to be that rough, but apparently his instincts couldn't care less about his intentions.

Missy didn't seem to mind, judging by the way her breathing sped up and her hands slid from his hair to his shoulders and then down his back. Slim fingers grabbed handfuls of fabric and pulled his shirttails from his waistband. He levered some of his weight off of her, bracing his palms against the Oriental carpet that covered the hardwood floor. He gave her nipple a last, fond lick and began to nuzzle his way across her chest to her other breast.

He was right—her taste had gotten richer, sweeter, hotter since the night before, but he knew he'd have to taste another few select spots before he could confirm that theory. Her neglected nipple was only next on a very long list.

Halfway across her chest, when his nose hit that heated patch of flesh between her breasts where her scent had pooled, Graham froze. In that moment all doubts fled and he knew for certain that her scent had gotten stronger. He also knew why.

Missy was fertile.

He held himself over her, poised and still and trembling with the effort of restraint. His beast howled in protest, and Graham had to fight to keep it far enough under wraps not to hurt her or rush her or send her screaming from his house in terror. His nostrils flared, and he inhaled deeply, unable to control the need to drink in her fragrance, even though every drop made it more difficult to restrain his impulses. He stood on a precipice, and he knew that if he didn't pull away from her now, this minute, and get as far out of range of her scent as possible, he would make her pregnant. When that happened, their mate-bond would go from theoretical to irrevocable. After that, it wouldn't matter what she wanted, because Graham would never be able to let her go.

Missy whimpered beneath him. Her hands tore at his shirt, but the sturdy material held fast, and her hands had to detour between their bodies to attack his buttons. One after the other, she slid them from their moorings until she could push the shirt off his shoulders and out of her way. Then she bowed her body upward and ran her warm, pink tongue over one of his flat nipples, and Graham knew he'd passed the irrevocable stage of their bond a long, long time ago. She was his, and now he would make sure that never changed.

With a fierce snarl, he reared back onto his knees, pulling away from her just long enough to rid himself of his clothes, tossing them away and falling on hers. He shredded the fabric with fingers whose tips had sharpened into claws and scattered them across the hall floor. When all of her skin lay bared to him, he crouched back on his heels and licked his lips.

Missy stared up at him, her eyes glassy and narrowed, her lips parted to make way for panting breaths. "Graham. I want you," she breathed, reaching up and twining her fingers in the silky-rough pelt of hair on his chest. She tugged, and he grunted at the sharp sting of pulled hair but didn't move.

She frowned up at him. "Now," she said, her voice louder and firmer. "That wasn't a generalization; it was an invitation. So get moving."

His beast leapt forward at that, clearly intent on fucking her senseless, knocking her up, and then howling his triumph to the waxing moon. Fortunately, Graham grabbed it by the throat before it could pounce and wrestled it into temporary submission. If he frightened her now, he risked a lot more than sexual frustration. He risked a lifetime of misery, because an unhappy mate did not bode well for their relationship.

"Do I have to make it an order?" Her eyes narrowed at his hesitation, and her hand slid down the slowly spreading patch of fur on his chest, down his quivering abdomen until her fingers curled around his shaft and squeezed firmly.

He nearly did howl at that. Her soft fingers felt so cool and silky wrapped around his heated skin, and when he looked down, he became transfixed by the sight of her small, pale hand against his flushed shaft and the deep brown of the fur he couldn't keep from spreading.

His jaw clenched so tightly, he thought it might snap. Desperately he fought for control, fought to keep his beast pinned inside, while it screamed and wailed and struggled for freedom. Graham knew that as surprisingly bold as his mate was turning out to be, she was still too human and too new to be faced with certain reminders of his Lupine nature. He figured he could pick a much better time to change in front of her for the first time than when she had her thighs spread and her hand wrapped around him. Now was *not* the right moment.

When her other hand slipped from his chest to his thigh and then darted low to cup him, his beast made another lunge. Graham had to resort to a full-body tackle and to making a certain number of compromises just to keep it in check. His beast agreed to stay beneath the surface of his skin if Graham agreed to give up the internal debate and take Missy now. When her slick, clinging muscles wrapped around him, his beast would content itself with that and stop with the foaming-at-the-mouth bit. It was a truce Graham could definitely get behind.

Before he could reach for her, Missy's patience ran out. She dropped her hands, pushed herself up from the floor, and glared straight into his eyes. "Did you break all those land speed records so you could admire my fine eyes, or could we get on with the more interesting stuff?"

His beast growled, and the smile he gave her felt feral. When his tongue darted out to lick his lips, it rubbed against the edge of his fangs, and he smiled wider.

"Interesting," he growled. "Very interesting."

Then he lunged.

He dove for her like a wolf diving for the jugular of its prey. She jerked with the gracelessness of instinct and rolled away. He feigned a pounce and grinned when she scrambled to her knees to eye him warily.

"What the heck are you doing?" she demanded.

"You said you liked men who get furry. I'm letting you see my furry side."

Her eyes widened, and he watched as her posture shifted from aggressive to wary. He sniffed, testing the air, but he couldn't smell any of the bitter taint of fear marring her rich, sweet scent.

In fact, he thought, sniffing again, *the vanilla's stronger. She's excited.*

The idea made his body tighten—in some places more than in others—and he began to prowl slowly toward her. He kept his eyes on hers and paced closer, carnal intent in every motion. She scooted backward, but the fact that she was still kneeling hampered her movements. He saw how she never took her eyes off him, but he also saw when her muscles began to bunch and tense as she prepared to get to her feet.

She never made it.

Before she could even get one sole on the carpet, he leapt and brought her down in a gentle flying tackle. Wrapping his arms around her and hugging her against his chest, he twisted in midair and landed beneath her, absorbing the impact on his shoulders and back. He had her back on the floor before she could even gasp her surprise, but she was gasping the very next minute when he flipped her onto her stomach, pulled her legs apart, and wedged his knees between her spread thighs.

She reared beneath him, pushing up on her hands and craning her neck around to stare at him with wary eyes. "What are you doing?"

His answer consisted of a feral grin and his hands gripping her hips, jerking them up off the floor until she knelt on all fours in front of him. Then he leaned over her, blanketing her body with his until he could nip gently at her earlobe, then slide past to nuzzle his cheek against hers. She shivered, and he followed it up with a lick that drew his tongue from her jaw all the way to her hairline.

"You said you liked me furry," he repeated, placing his hands over hers and pinning them to the floor when she would have tried to scramble away. "You said you wanted me. Did you change your mind?"

He closed his teeth around the nape of her neck and held on when a shiver raced down her spine. His tongue darted out to taste the warm skin, and her scent rose to tease him, filling his senses with her sweet, heavy perfume. Every time they touched, her fragrance got stronger, more filled with honey and vanilla and the indescribable richness of her fertility. It told him how much she wanted him, but more than that, it identified her as his mate, because no other woman had ever affected him like this. No Lupine, and certainly no human.

He'd never experienced a scent like hers, one that told him how ripe she was and how welcome his seed would be inside her womb. The idea of his pup growing beneath the soft curve of her belly stretched his cock to the point of pain, and he knew he needed to be inside her soon.

"Did you change your mind?" he demanded, scraping his teeth along the sensitive column of her spine. She quaked beneath him, and her head dropped forward in a submissive gesture that made the beast within him roar in triumph. He had to fight not to bite harder, sink his teeth deeper. His beast wanted to mark her pretty skin, and lust had his mind so clouded he could barely remember why that was such a bad idea.

"No," she whimpered, snapping him out of his fog with a surge of triumph. "I want you, Graham. Please."

Her words whispered faintly, even to his keen senses, but he still heard, and he still snarled in satisfaction.

"Then take me," he growled. And thrust.

She screamed, but the sound didn't faze him. He barely heard her over the deafening pleasure of feeling her slick heat close tight around him. He grunted when she thrust back against him, savoring the smooth curve of her back as it arched into his blanketing chest. Her hands twisted beneath his, trying to pull free, but he pinned her easily. Holding her still for his ravenous thrusts.

Leaning forward, he closed his teeth over her shoulder, pinning her in place the way his beast demanded, barely refraining from marking her. He ground his hips hard against her cushioning bottom, pushing so deeply into her he could feel her womb at the bottom of each hard glide. The echo of her scream had died, fading into the gasps and pleading murmurs that drove him deeper into his possessive frenzy. His beast may have agreed to remain under his skin, but it hadn't promised not to control his actions.

Growling low in his chest, he closed his teeth harder against her skin, warning her, commanding her to stay still for his pleasure. His hands lifted and hovered for a moment, waiting to slam hers back into place, but she never moved them. She simply locked her elbows and used the leverage to thrust harder back against him.

Greedily his hands took advantage of their freedom, sliding up to squeeze her breasts and tease the firm nipples with twisting pinches. Missy moaned and trembled beneath him. Her arms collapsed under her, and she landed on her elbows with a gasping cry. The position thrust her hips higher into the air, canted her pelvis to a new angle, and allowed him to slide even deeper with every pounding thrust. Rearing back from her, he grabbed her hips in his hands, careful not to pierce her skin with the claws he couldn't keep from emerging. His firm grip held her in place and held her up when her knees, too, would have slid out from under her.

Pinning her in place, he took her with hard, ruthless digs. His beast gloried in the tight clasp of her moisture-slicked muscles, in the whimpers and yelps that tore from her throat and echoed in the empty hall. Her noises sounded like mate cries in his ears. They made his muscles tighten, made his spine tingle and his fingers clench until they bruised her soft flesh. He rammed his pelvis against her gorgeous ass and listened to the sound of his mate approaching orgasm. He felt her body tensing and trembling, felt her temperature soar, felt the rippling of her inner muscles grow more intense. He inhaled deeply, and her hot vanilla scent exploded in his head just as a scream exploded from her lips.

Bucking beneath him, she ground her hips against his as her body clenched hard around his, milking it with powerful, ecstatic ripples. Graham threw back his head and howled, driving into her with even greater force. He felt himself scraping the mouth of her womb as she pulsed down to meet him. The rich fragrance of her musk advertised her ripe fertility, and he burst apart, pouring her full of his seed while the image of his child making her stomach jut out before her flashed behind his eyes.

With a satisfied growl, he relaxed and let his weight carry them both to the carpet. She sprawled bonelessly beneath him, panting for air even as her body continued to shiver around his softening length. He growled, a soft, satisfied sound, and laid his hands over hers, lacing their fingers together in an intimate knot. She murmured something unintelligible and shifted beneath him, rubbing her skin along his as if savoring the sensation.

Graham hummed his approval and nuzzled her neck, licking her salty-sweet skin and nipping gently at her earlobe.

"Mine," he whispered, squeezing her hands gently in his.

Her muscles tensed briefly against his, and he rolled his hips against her, emphasizing the connection of his semi-erect shaft still clasped tight inside her. He felt the shiver that raced down her spine, and nipped again, a little harder this time.

"Mine." And this time it was more growl than whisper.

She turned her head and opened her eyes to meet his, which he knew were probably glowing green and possessive above her. She licked her dry lips.

"Yours." She agreed so softly it barely qualified as a whisper.

"Damn it. He always gets the good ones."

Graham didn't think he'd ever seen a human move so fast. Logan's words had brought Missy's head up like a deer scenting gunpowder, and it hadn't taken a mind reader to pick up on her horror at being caught in flagrante delicto on his hallway carpet. A quick bark had sent Logan back behind the door to the club long enough for Graham's mate to scramble out from beneath him, grab her clothes, and sprint for the stairs as if the hounds of hell nipped at her heels.

Swallowing a curse, Graham reached for his jeans and tugged them back over his hips. Not that he hadn't appreciated the view of his mate's retreating derriere, but he'd have appreciated it more if he'd been following her up the stairs in anticipation of another round of the passion they'd just shared.

"Is it safe to come out now?"

Graham looked from the door to his discarded shoe and back. He considered scooping the thing up and letting it fly at the wall or Logan's head, whichever got in the way, but dismissed the temptation. With his luck, he'd knock his beta unconscious and have to haul his sorry ass to the sofa and let him stay until he regained consciousness. Instead, he jerked the door open and glared at his former friend.

"What the hell do you want now?"

The beta stepped into the hall with an innocent shrug. "Well, a minute ago, I wanted to tell you about an interesting piece of news I got this morning. But now I'm thinking I want one of what you just had. With a cherry on top."

Graham's lip curled. "Come within six feet of my woman and I'll strangle you with your own intestines."

Through a foggy red film the alpha saw his oldest friend's eyebrows shoot up, followed by a pair of hands raised in a universal gesture of surrender.

"I meant no disrespect, Alpha," Logan offered, carefully dropping his gaze and turning his head to the side. "Only a compliment on your choice of mate. Of course, I would never think to touch your woman."

Intense effort drew a lungful of air into Graham's chest, followed by another, then another. By his fifth breath, the red haze covering his vision had faded to a soft pink and he could no longer feel his heart beating in the vein at his left temple. He grasped shakily at the thin strands of his self-control and fixed Logan with a baleful glare. It took another few breaths before Graham finally regained the ability to form words rather than the howl of a death challenge, and even he could hear the remnants of rage floating below the surface.

"In the interest of our continued friendship and your continued heartbeat, Hunter," Graham snarled, "I suggest you not make any other stupid comments along that line in the future."

"No, Alpha."

Logan's respectful tone and deferent posture finally had their desired effect, signaling to Graham's wolfish subconscious that no challenge would be offered to his authority. Considering how long the two men had known each other (since about five hours after Logan's birth) and how rarely the beta deferred to anyone (never), the message sank through the alpha's thick skull and smoothed his hackles back into place. Graham's mate was safe and his sanity could once again take its rightful place in guiding his actions.

Shaking off the lingering hostility like a retriever shaking off the salt water, Graham blew out a deep breath and focused on his beta without a film of violence clouding his vision. "Right. Now, I think you'd better share what it was you came here to tell me."

Logan kept his gaze fixed on a point just below and to the left of Graham's shoulder. "My apologies for interrupting you, Alpha, but I tried to page you. You didn't answer your intercom. If I had known why you failed to pick up—"

"Oh, cut the crap and look at me," Graham growled. "I already feel like an idiot for jumping down your throat. You don't need to make me feel like the damned Lupine Hitler with the subservient routine."

The beta lifted one eyebrow and shifted his gaze cautiously to Graham's. "You sure? Because to be honest, I think if I were you, I'd have been pretty POed by my interruption, too."

Graham snorted and lifted a hand to rub at the lingering muscle tenseness at the back of his neck. "You could do with a lesson or two in timing."

"Honestly, I had no idea she was still here. I figured you'd have packed her off home by now."

"Did we not have a conversation about this in my kitchen last night?" Graham frowned. "Did I dream that?"

"No, we had it. I just didn't get how much you meant it, I guess. I figured, you know, heat of the moment. It *is* kind of a big decision."

"Since when has a Lupine 'decided' anything having to do with a mate-bond?"

Logan heard the sardonic tone and grimaced. "Right. Fate just smacks us upside the head, and we get in line with her plans like good little wolves. Doesn't that ever kind of piss you off?"

"You saw what she has planned for me," Graham said, his grin sudden and wide and wolfish. "How hard would you fight it?"

"You may have a point."

"Right. And since I'd really rather be spending the next three or four hours with my Fate, as opposed to with you, no offense—"

"None taken."

"—how about you spill your big news so I can get back to spilling something of my own."

Logan rolled his eyes. "Charming. No wonder the human fell for you and your smooth-talking ways."

Graham just waited.

"You've received an invitation," the beta continued. "For this evening."

"I think I'm going to be busy tonight. Tell whoever it is that I'm washing my hair."

"It's from the elders."

A curse, long and comprehensive and equally foul in both English and Lupine, colored the air of the hallway. Logan didn't even blink. Which hardly surprised Graham. If he was ever called upon to appear before the Silverback Clan's oldest and most well-respected—and well-feared—members, the beta would likely have much the same reaction.

While technically the elders were expected to function as counsel to the sitting alpha of the pack, in reality Graham hardly ever acknowledged them. He'd never been the sort of leader to question his own abilities or his own decisions, and the idea of weighing three extra opinions before he did whatever he'd originally planned to do anyway had always seemed to him to be nothing more than a colossal waste of time.

So far, his strategy had worked out well. He'd pretty much ignored the elders, and they had blessed his tenure as alpha with the tacit approval that came from staying out of his face. Why they would want to stick their noses into things now could only have one explanation.

"Curtis," Graham ground out with all the elocution of a wolf spitting nails.

"That would be my guess."

The only reason either Lupine could come up with to explain why the elders would choose now to begin giving Graham the advice he'd never before needed or wanted had to be linked to his troublemaking cousin. Anything else was just too big a coincidence to be believed.

"What the hell did he say to them to make them interfere now?"

Logan pursed his lips. "You want me to tell you what I think?"

"Of course."

"You're not going to like it."

"No shit."

The beta shrugged. "I think he's stirred them up over the subject of you being mateless. If he does really mean to challenge you on the basis of Breeder's Rights, it can't hurt him to have the elders on his side."

"Maybe, but how much can it really help him? They're advisors, but no one has to take their advice. They don't have any real power."

"No, but they do have a significant amount of influence. Ninety percent of the pack is related to them, one way or the other."

Graham made an impatient sound and began to

pace down the long hallway. "My cousin has the timing of a defective jack-in-the-box."

"He always has. Remember his first change?"

"Remember? It was right in the middle of my high school graduation speech. At four in the afternoon. Our mothers had to cover him in my dad's suit jacket and Aunt Vivian's sun hat and hustle him out of the bleachers with some story about seizures brought on by photosensitivity. By the time they got him turned over to Uncle Glenn, Mom had missed half my graduation party."

"Exactly. And think of all the years he's had since then to plan this little inconvenience."

Graham rolled his eyes. "I suppose I should consider myself lucky he didn't catch me twenty minutes ago. Like some people."

"Hey, if you're going to mate in the hallway in the middle of the day, it's not like an interruption should come as all that big a surprise."

The alpha sighed. "I guess I wasn't thinking all that clearly."

"Not from what I saw," Logan agreed. "Didn't look to me like much thinking was involved at all."

"I can't help it. I take one look at her and my palms start to itch." Graham made the admission with a sheepish expression and a clenching of his fists. Actually, all he had to do was *think* about Missy and his hands ached for the feel of her soft, warm skin. "It's the damnedest thing. She's the only woman who's ever gotten to me this way."

"Maybe you should tell that to the elders," Logan

said. "You'd put a hell of a hole in Curtis's strategy if they knew you had found a mate. Even if she is human."

"I thought about that, but it's just a bad idea."

"Why?"

"The human thing."

"I don't think that's such a big problem. Not an insurmountable one, anyway. There have been one or two human mates in the clan before. Yours wouldn't be the first. A few of the pack might grumble, but none of them would be stupid enough to do it to your face."

"Sure, there have been a couple of human mates before in the pack. But how many of them have been Luna?"

"None."

"Right. And in the past, how long has it taken to convince a human that they were the Fated mate of a Lupine?"

Logan winced. "A while."

"Which is time I don't have." Graham swore again. "I've barely got her convinced to spend the weekend with me. What happens if I tell the elders I've found a mate and it turns out that I end up having to chase that mate across three state lines when she tries to make a break for it?"

"You think she will?"

"I think it's too early for me to be taking for granted that she won't."

"Have you considered filling her in on the situation? Maybe if you explained about Curtis, she'd be willing to work with you. At least put up a united front until the challenge thing blows over."

"First, 'the challenge thing' isn't going to blow over as long as Curtis is alive," Graham said. "And second, Missy is currently about as skittish as a November turkey. She'd hear the words 'mate' and 'breeders' and 'challenge' and go to ground so fast I'd need a were-terrier to find her again."

Logan stared at his friend for a moment in silence. Then he shook his head. "Wow. I guess you're just screwed then."

Graham growled. "Thanks."

"No problem." The beta shifted and turned back toward the door to the club. "What do you want me to tell the elders, though? I'm thinking they expect you to treat their invitation as a summons. They seem to look at it that way."

Graham thought about the woman upstairs who had last seen him as she scrambled out from under him in embarrassment, glowing the color of cherry syrup and making small noises of distress, and then about the three pack elders who were likely to give him a hard time about something he wouldn't change just because they thought they could. Both situations smacked of duty, but there was only one of them that he really cared about.

He turned toward the stairs. "Find out when the elders want to meet and then let me know. And call before you come over. I'll keep an eye out for voice mail if I don't pick up."

Logan nodded. "All right. I'll ask them when they can come back, and I'll let you know."

Graham made it up three stairs before the words registered. He spun to face his beta's retreating back. "*What* did you say?"

"I'll go ask the elders if they can come back to talk to you at another time."

"You mean they're here now?"

"In your office."

Closing his eyes, Graham prayed for patience, but the Moon offered no answers. She probably thought this whole thing was funny. Judging by the scent wafting down the stairs from his bedroom, though, his mate currently wasn't seeing the humor in anything. At all.

"Wait," Graham sighed. He turned and stepped back down into the hall. "I'll see them now. If they've come here without sending any warning, they must be worked up. In that case, it would be a bad idea to let them stew over it."

And his decision had nothing to do with wanting to let Missy calm down before he faced her again, he assured himself.

Nothing at all.

"Right. Of course." A grin kicked up one corner of Logan's mouth in an expression far too knowing for Graham's taste.

"Shut up." He scowled and stomped through the door to the sound of his beta's echoing chuckle.

CHAPTER EIGHT

Graham knew the instant he saw Samantha's worried expression that something far worse than the pack elders was waiting in his office. And if that wasn't the frosting on the cake . . .

"What?" he barked.

"I'm sorry, Alpha, but he said the elders were expecting him to join you." Samantha frowned, her skin giving off the distinct odor of nerves.

To her credit, she looked directly at him, despite her unease, her eyes averted only slightly toward his temple as a mark of her respect. His pretty, sensible assistant had never lacked for balls.

"Him, who?"

"Curtis MacAlpin."

Graham was the one who averted his eyes at that, raising them to the ceiling while he counted to ten and attempted to rein in his temper. Then he counted to twenty.

When he reached ninety-seven with no improvement, he looked back down at Samantha and breathed very evenly. "He's in with the others?"

She nodded. "Grey, Hawkins, and Fleet."

The most well-respected elders of the clan, each of the three men Samantha named had reached his seventieth year, an age not unheard of but considerably less common in Lupines than in the human population. The pack's lifestyle, system of social advancement, and feeling of invincibility among young male Lupines all conspired to make the average life span of Graham's peers somewhere around sixty-five.

The only consolation was that Fate had balanced things out. Lupines healed remarkably fast, potentially fixing a broken bone in a matter of a few hours and cuts and slashes within minutes. They also benefited from an immune system that protected them from many of the diseases that plagued humans, making them impervious to most infections. Once a male Lupine reached the age of fifty-five, chances were he could survive well past his hundredth birthday. The problem was that only about 5 to 10 percent of the males ever made it that far.

Female Lupines had it slightly better. Because they tended to fight fewer challenges for advancement within the pack and took far fewer stupid risks in their youth, their average life expectancy put them well into their late eighties, with many living to celebrate their centennials.

Graham himself was thirty-four. If he survived another twenty years, it would not be thanks to his cousin Curtis.

The door behind Samantha's desk opened and a

rough, age-shaken voice called out, "Winters. We can hear you out there. Our ears aren't gone yet. Come inside. We want to talk to you."

Samantha saw him wince and asked, "Do you want me to page you in fifteen minutes? I could make up an emergency only you can handle."

"Not that I'm not tempted"—and oh, how he was!—"but I'm hoping this won't take that long."

She shot him a skeptical glance but said nothing. She just watched while Graham straightened his shoulders and entered what should have been his private sanctum but had instead turned into a den of hungry lions.

They had taken over the comfortable sitting area at the far end of his office, three elder statesmen of the Lupine race and one spoiled brat with delusions of grandeur. Jonathan Grey, Nathaniel Hawkins, and Edward Fleet sat relaxed and sharp-eyed on a dark leather sofa and matching club chair, while Curtis MacAlpin lounged in the corner between them, arms crossed over his chest and one shoulder propped against the wall in a pose Graham instinctively recognized and vowed never again to consciously adopt.

Especially not if I look like that big of a prick when I do.

Curtis looked as well-groomed and useless as always, his brown hair carefully and expensively styled, his clothes a veritable billboard for the latest hot designer. Worst of all, his nails shone with the careful buffing of a recent manicure. He had the kind of hands that had never done an honest day's work in their lives. Hell, not an honest hour's. Curtis felt as if he deserved to have what he wanted handed to him on a silver platter, and when he didn't get it, he got mean.

Graham dismissed Curtis the way he always did, with a glance.

"Gentlemen," he said, nodding to the elders and closing the office door softly behind him. "To what do I owe this unexpected pleasure?"

Fleet snorted. "No need to charm us, pup. No one here thinks pleasure would be your first reaction to seeing us turn up on your doorstep."

Graham felt his mouth twitch. Edward Fleet was reputed to be almost 80 years old, but he looked more like 120. His jowls sagged and his shoulders drooped with age, and the hand that rested on his elegant ebony cane bore a road map of protruding veins and discolored age spots. His hair, though, was thick and lush and the color of stainless steel, and his eyes still glinted sharp and golden beneath the snarling thickets of his brows.

Lupine eyes.

He'd always respected Fleet, Graham acknowledged silently, so his response contained more self-control than he might otherwise have bothered with.

"Maybe not," he said, "but curiosity was right up there. I don't think I've seen the three of you in one place since my breaking year was up."

Every alpha served the first year of his term under the close scrutiny of the elders. The Lupines might expect a leader who claimed power by force, but they wouldn't tolerate him for long if he proved incompetent at the job. Even though he'd taken power with a ceremonial challenge match at the age of twenty-five when his father had decided it was time to retire, Graham hadn't even needed the year. He'd been born and bred to rule his people.

"We thought you might be able to smooth things out better with less interference from the peanut gallery," Fleet acknowledged.

"Yes, and look where that's gotten us," Hawkins grumbled.

Hawkins was always grumbling. Graham had long ago decided the elder had swallowed something bitter during his whelping and the taste of it lingered with him still.

Graham clung to his diplomatic skills with carefully sheathed claws. "One of the most peaceful and stable periods in pack history since the time of my great-grandfather?"

Jonathan Grey scowled. "If you want to look at it that way."

"How else would you suggest I look at it?"

"I think what the gentlemen are trying to say, Cousin, is that they have developed some . . . concerns regarding your leadership style." Curtis spoke from the corner, his voice carefully serious, his muddy yellow eyes glinting with mockery and malice.

Graham couldn't stop his lip from curling. After

all, when a man smelled something rotten, he couldn't exactly pretend everything was rosy sweet, could he?

"And I think that if anyone wants to criticize my methods, he can do so for himself," the alpha said, his tone a clear warning rumble. "From his own lips and in his own words."

"Oh, I wouldn't call them criticisms, Winters," Fleet broke in. His eyes stayed on Graham, sharp and steady. "They're more like a few issues we thought you might want to be paying a bit more attention to. Suggestions, like."

What the hell was going on with the universe lately? Graham wondered as he frowned at his unwelcome guests. First he finds the woman of his dreams, only to discover she's human. Then his new mate has the gall to try to run from him before her skin had fully cooled from his touch. And now his cousin—because Graham hadn't needed Curtis's presence in the room to know what this was all about—had set the pack elders on him to grade his performance as alpha of the Silverback Clan. Had everyone in the world suddenly forgotten what being alpha *meant*?

Clinging desperately to his rapidly fraying temper, Graham raised an eyebrow and attempted a look of mild inquiry. If it managed not to come across as blind, murderous rage, he figured his luck might be changing.

"Oh?" he drawled.

"Absolutely. We've discussed a number of problems we'd like to see you put right." Nathaniel Hawkins reached into the breast pocket of his conservative—some might say funereal—suit and pulled out a folded sheet of paper. "It is, after all, your duty to guide the pack in the proper direction."

Blessed Mother Moon, Graham thought. *He's got a freakin' list.*

"Not only that, he's got to lead the pack without disregarding tradition," Grey added, leaning forward as if to emphasize his point. "Lupines have never recorded their history and laws and customs in books like the humans do. It's always been too dangerous. What if a human got their hands on that kind of library? Ours is an oral tradition, but that means we need to be especially diligent at making sure nothing gets lost."

"And the only way to do that is to carry on those traditions the way we've always done," Hawkins concluded. "Which brings us nicely to our first point."

"Does it?" Graham ground out. "And what, pray tell, *is* your point?"

"There are some members of the pack who are upset that you've never gotten around to appointing a new *guthi* after old Hank Chase passed away," Curtis pointed out.

Graham turned and pinned him with a stare. "Are there? And I suppose you're one of them."

The alpha's sarcasm was obvious. The idea that Curtis cared one iota about keeping filled the largely ceremonial position of pack storyteller when most of the progressive packs in the Western Hemisphere had abandoned it a generation ago was ridiculous. Graham knew it and Curtis knew it, and the fact that such a lame opening salvo in their private little war for supremacy was the best the other man had to offer made Graham frankly uneasy.

His cousin shrugged. "I'm not without concern, but I wouldn't say your failure to appoint a *guthi* was my number one concern."

"No? So what is?"

"We'll get to that," Hawkins snapped. "We're just getting started here, pup."

Graham had been willing to let Edward Fleet get away with the casual form of address because he respected that old man and had detected no trace of mockery in his words. Hawkins's, though, had been clearly laced with contempt.

"I'll hear every item on your list, old man," Graham said softly, his quiet, intent voice more fierce than the wildest howl, "but it will happen a whole lot neater if you remember how to address me. You might be old enough to be my grandfather, but I'm still your alpha."

Hawkins stiffened, his gaze meeting Graham's for a long, tense moment before he dropped his eyes to his list with a dismissive sniff. "We've got more important things to do here today than argue."

Graham unclenched his fists slowly. "Can't prove it by me," he muttered under his breath.

"Some members of the pack think the lack of a *guthi* is just a symptom of your lack of respect for our traditions," Grey jumped in to say. He carefully kept his tone free of Hawkins's antagonism, but the message came through clearly. "People have noticed your ignorance of Common Law. Any time an issue with a Common precedence has been brought to you, you've had to confer with advisors to learn what the proper ruling should be."

Lady, please grant me patience, Graham prayed. He took a deep breath.

"First of all, I have a deep and abiding respect for the traditions of our race and of this pack," he said evenly. "I would never have sought to become alpha if I didn't. When Chase died, no one stepped up to express a desire to take on his responsibilities as *guthi*. It's not an easy job, so I don't blame our younger members for not champing at the bit for the chance to do it. But we do have other choices available to us that weren't when the role of *guthi* was created, and I availed myself of those. In the five years we've been without a storyteller, I have hired—at my own expense, I'll add—a university-trained and highly respected anthropologist from California to make a complete record of the Silverback history and mythology. He's Lupine, so he's familiar with our basic culture, but he's also an outsider, so every story he hears has been recorded faithfully, without the bias of someone who has heard some of them a hundred times. If that's not respecting our traditions, I don't know what is.

"And," he continued, "I know for a fact that my father was no more versed in Common Law when he took over as alpha than I was. If that were a requirement of the position, we'd give it to the pack's best lawyer instead of the pack's best leader."

Graham didn't even bother to try to gauge the reactions of his audience. He was too disgusted. He couldn't think of a more colossal waste of his time than to stand here defending his spotless record as the Silverback alpha to a bunch of interfering busybodies his cousin had dragged out of their rocking chairs to grill him like Torquemada wannabes. He could care less what they thought. He knew he had been a good alpha to his pack, and history would bear him out. And they could all suck his left—

"There is also the more serious matter of your relationships outside the pack," Fleet said, interrupting Graham's mental tirade and focusing the alpha's attention back on the matter at hand.

For a minute Graham thought the elders meant to take him to task for his choice of Missy as a mate, and he was already making a mental note to have Sam call upholstery cleaners for quotes on how much it would cost to get the blood and other bodily fluids cleaned out of the carpet and leather sofa cushions.

No one had better try to come between him and his mate.

"Before you took over, the pack's involvement with the Council of Others was always kept to a minimum." Curtis took on an air of concern while insincerity dripped like poison off his tongue. "We heard what they had to say, but all decisions about the pack were made within the pack. We didn't allow any outside entities to tell us what to do with our own lawbreakers, or how to keep our own veil of secrecy intact."

"And you think someone is doing that now?" Graham said incredulously. "You honestly think I am taking orders from the Council on how to run my pack?"

His cousin shrugged. "You've have a very close relationship with both the past and current heads of the Council. No one likes to speculate, of course, but given that fact, it is difficult to ignore how often you and the Council seem to find yourselves in perfect agreement."

No one likes to speculate, my ass!

"Did it ever occur to you that I might agree with the decisions of the Council because I felt those decisions were reasonable, well thought out, and in the best interests of the pack?"

"Dmitri Vidâme and Rafael De Santos are not members of the pack."

"No? And here I thought vampires and Felix were now eligible for junior memberships and the basic version of our super-secret decoder ring."

"Gentlemen!" Fleet held up a hand. "Let's not turn this into an argument."

"I think it's a little late for that," Graham snarled. "I've just been accused of putting the bonds of my personal friendships over the needs of my pack! And I'll be damned if I'll take that kind of insult from anyone, elder, cousin, or the Lady of the Moon herself!"

"No one is accusing you of anything." Jonathan Grey was beginning to sound nervous, shifting his weight and licking his lips, and he fixed his glance on the alpha's shoes. "We just thought these were matters of concern that should be brought to your attention. Perhaps if you put certain limits on your involvement with people outside of the pack, it might reassure those who worry about your loyalties."

Graham thought again of the woman upstairs, the delicate blonde with the warm cocoa eyes and the luscious figure and the heart as sweet as cotton candy, and felt his jaw tighten. The first one to suggest he limit his involvement with her would learn what it felt like to wear their lungs as a backpack.

"My loyalties are exactly where they need to be," he said, his voice as hard as his expression, "with my pack, my family, and my future. Anyone who has a problem with that—"

"I think the problem is that none of us know where that future is going," Fleet interrupted, pushing to his feet and straightening as far as his osteoporotic bones would allow. "What kind of future does an alpha Lupine have without a mate? Hm?"

"I don't know. Want me to ask him when I find one?"

Out of the corner of his eye, Graham saw Curtis stiffen.

"What is that supposed to mean?" he demanded. "Are you trying to tell us that you've found a mate all of a sudden? That seems awfully convenient for you. Who is she?"

Graham heard the anger and unease in Curtis's voice and cursed himself for his outburst. The last person he wanted to talk to about Missy was his cousin. The second through the fourth to last were also currently staring at him with avid curiosity.

"Well, boy, out with it," Fleet urged. "This is big news. An alpha needs a mate, and I'm not afraid to tell you it would ease a lot of minds if you had one of those to introduce to the pack. You need to send up a Howl to make the announcement. Hasn't been one of those in too long, either, if you ask me."

The alpha slid a glare toward his cousin. "I believe Curtis has taken care of that for me. Isn't there going to be one next weekend?"

Fleet waved a hand dismissively. "Bah, that can be rescheduled. Howls are your responsibility, and if you override the one your cousin sent up, no one will even bat an eyelash." The old man leaned in close to Graham and lowered his voice to keep from being overheard. "In fact, anyone who thought about throwing their hat in with him will be happy enough to come back to your side, Winters, no matter what promises Curtis made to them."

"Promises?" Graham murmured, his fingers itching for the opportunity to close around his cousin's disloyal little throat. Just because Graham had believed Curtis had been plotting against him for a while now didn't make having it confirmed any more palatable.

"He's offered to make us elders members of an official 'privy council,' to be consulted on all major decisions. Privy council," Fleet snorted. "Probably the best name for it, since the idea stinks like the inside of an outhouse to me. You mark my words, Winters, that pup is up to no good. He fancies himself the next king, and he doesn't care if he needs to cut your head from your shoulders to get his hands on the crown."

Graham grimaced. "Tell me something I don't know."

"What's that?"

"Nothing. But I'm not ready to introduce my mate to the rest of the pack just yet," Graham said, deliberately raising his voice so that the others could hear.

Jonathan Grey frowned. "I'm not sure that's in your best interest, Alpha. The pack will want to see her. You know how folks are. The longer you make them wait, the more they're going to start speculating about what's wrong with her."

"There is *nothing* wrong with my mate, and anyone who speculates otherwise will owe me a few explanations." The alpha turned back to Fleet with a deliberately conspiratorial grin. "You know how females are today. They all want to be 'dated,' not mated. They think things should be like what they see the humans do on television, pretty words and 'pretty please' and all of that."

Fleet snorted and shook his head. "I tell you, things were a whole lot easier back in my day. When we saw the girl we wanted, we threw her down and crawled on top, and if we managed to stay there long enough for a little hide-and-seek, we called it a wedding!"

The three older men chuckled at the crude joke and Graham smiled along. Only Curtis looked less than pleased.

"You take my advice," Edward Fleet said as he slapped Graham on the back with a surprisingly firm hand. "Give the girl a day or two to come to her senses. Then, if she doesn't fall into line, you take her down and do a little hiding and seeking. Once she's got a cub on the way, she'll fall into line."

Somehow, Graham wasn't sure how likely that was to be true with his skittish, stubborn mate. Still, he maintained his smile and shook hands with all three elders as they made their way out of his office and into Sam's. He was very aware of Curtis's brooding presence as he was swept along toward the front of the club.

The old men each stopped to flirt with Graham's assistant on their way out, and Sam handled them with the naughty, breezy charm of a favorite grand-daughter, leaving them grinning and chuckling on their way out the door. As it closed behind them, only Curtis looked back over his shoulder for a moment before he, too, departed into the late-afternoon sunshine.

"Wow," Sam breathed as she waved away the

club's butler and closed the front door herself. "You might want to pat yourself down for holes, boss. I know looks can't really kill, but I'm not so sure the ones your cousin was giving you couldn't at least leave a puncture wound or two."

Graham snorted and shoved his hands in the front pockets of his jeans. It was either that or punch a hole in the club wall, and he didn't want to deal with the hassle of finding a plasterer to rush out here on a Saturday evening to do the repair work.

"I've survived worse," Graham said.

"True. But I wonder what got him so stirred up."

Graham eyed his assistant with amusement. "Doing a little fishing, are you?"

Sam grinned up at him. "If I don't dip my line in now and again, I'll never catch anything."

"I'm just surprised you didn't have a glass pressed up against the door so you could hear it all for yourself."

"Just poured myself fresh coffee. I didn't want to waste it."

"Hm, that's rough."

Graham turned toward the rear of the hall and the door that led back to his own home. Behind him, Samantha sighed gustily.

"You're not going to tell me anything, are you?"

After twenty-something years of teasing Samantha like the little sister he'd never had, it was hard to ignore the reflex. Still, there was no reason he couldn't tell her the basic truth.

"There's nothing to tell that you haven't heard

before. Curtis is just playing another round of The Boy Who Would Be King."

The woman squished her face up in disgust. "Ick. Well, if he ever wins that game, at least you'll get to see my impression of the girl who would be gone. I swear, I'd run from here to Connecticut so fast the drivers on the Merritt Parkway would be jealous."

Technically, the pack in Connecticut that Samantha would be running to owed fealty to the Silverback, so it wouldn't get her completely away from Curtis's influence, but Graham could appreciate the metaphor. But not the possibility she might ever need to act it out.

"Actually," he corrected her as he strolled toward the connecting hallway, "I wouldn't get to see your impression."

"Why not?"

He flashed her a grin that owed all of its character to fangs and none of it to humor.

"Because the only way Curtis gets to be alpha of this pack is over my dead body."

CHAPTER NINE

Glancing at the alarm clock on the side of the bed, Missy calculated that it had been a hour since she'd raced up to this room bare-assed naked in an attempt to avoid the avid stare of a tall, dark-haired man whose name she still didn't know.

"God, what is happening to me?" she muttered aloud. Well, semi-aloud. It came out slightly muffled due to having her flaming-red face buried in her hands. "Less than twenty-four hours ago I was afraid someone might catch a glimpse of the tops of my stockings under that ridiculous dress. Now, a strange man has stared at my naked ass after catching me having sex in a front hallway in broad daylight."

She shook her head.

"My mother would kill me if she ever found out. I've become a total slut."

Sighing, Missy dropped her hands and pushed to her feet. Her original plan, formed while doing approximately 24 miles per hour toward the sanctuary of Graham's bedroom, had been to shower, dress, and hide in said sanctuary until the red stain of embarrassment faded from her skin or the beautiful antique rug sprouted a hole and swallowed her alive. Apparently, the carpet around here had no mercy, and she knew from experience that her blush wasn't likely to fade until she stopped remembering the scene in the hall with a mixture of humiliation and horror. Which meant she could be dead of old age long before her skin returned to its normal fair tone.

Since she was again fully dressed—in a second set of borrowed clothing—Missy decided to bite the bullet and head back downstairs. She padded down to the first floor and peered cautiously into Graham's study. His assistant had come over a few minutes after Missy had gone upstairs to tell her Graham had some urgent business to take care of but that she should wait for him in this room until he finished. She tried to ignore the knot in her stomach that insisted he wanted to make sure she didn't disappear before he had the chance to tell her how disgusting he thought she was for behaving so shamelessly in a location where anyone could stumble in on them at any moment. Obviously. He wanted to tell her he'd changed his mind about having her stay this weekend and he'd call her a cab, but she had to get out of his house before she made him sick.

Okay, calm down, she urged herself, pausing outside the door and taking a deep breath. *I doubt he's going to tell you he's disgusted by something he started, so don't panic. Whatever happens, happens. You knew going in that this wasn't permanent, so don't whine about it ending sooner than you hoped. Just think about the memories he's leaving you with. You're lucky to have those. No sense in getting greedy and wanting the real thing, too.*

Her inner voice made a lot of sense, but that didn't mean Missy liked what it had to say. She knew very well that her arrangement with Graham was never destined to go beyond the weekend, but that hadn't kept her from hoping. She knew she was a closet romantic, but even she had a hard time believing there would ever be a chance for something more. They had great sex together, but nothing would convince her that a man like Graham couldn't have great sex any time he wanted, with anyone he wanted. He certainly didn't need her around.

Tugging the hem of her donated shirt, Missy pushed the depressing thoughts from her mind and stepped into the study, surprised to see Graham already returned from the club. Her shower must have taken longer than she'd thought.

He glanced up from a pile of papers and looked her over with a penetrating gaze. Her T-shirt was a little too snug and the jeans a pack member had lent her were a size too big everywhere except around her butt, so the waist had an alarming tendency to slip down and let her navel play peekaboo with the outside world. Before today, none of Missy's parts had ever played peekaboo with anyone.

She tugged at the shirt hem and knew Graham's eyes followed the movement. She felt his gaze like fingers on her skin, and even before she looked up to see them glowing, she felt the heat they radiated.

"Thank—" Missy broke off on a squeak, cleared her throat, and tried again. "Um, thanks for finding me something else to wear. I feel like I'm raiding the closets of every woman you know."

Then it occurred to her just how many women he knew, and she quickly changed the subject.

"Catching up on paperwork?" She nodded to the documents he'd been looking over and played nonchalant. His expression told her how obvious her ploys were, but he went along with it.

"No. My manager is handling the club for the rest of the weekend. This was just a time killer until you came back downstairs."

Missy shrugged and buried her hands in the front pockets of her jeans, then quickly pulled them out again. Pushing down on that particular garment was a bad idea, though the look in Graham's eyes when they followed the movement said he approved.

Heartily.

"Well, I'm dressed. What's next? I'm not hungry enough to order Chinese, but didn't you say something about watching movies? I really want to see the new haunted-house movie that just came out."

Graham rose from his seat behind the desk and took her hand, leading her away from the door and tugging her to sit beside him on the sofa. When he didn't say anything, she started to get nervous.

Okay, *more* nervous.

"Oh, wait. Something came up, right? Wasn't that why your . . . friend, um . . . dropped in?" She winced at the memory. Maybe he really did think she was a slut. "So that means you're going to be really busy for the rest of the weekend and you have to cancel on getting to know me better. It's okay. I understand. You'll call when you get free to reschedule, so I should just wait to hear from you. Okay. Let me just grab my purse—"

She made it almost off the sofa before Graham closed one strong hand around her elbow and tugged her back down, straight onto his lap. This time he pinned her in place.

"You aren't going anywhere," he grumbled, and Missy saw the glowy green thing was happening to his eyes again. "I am going to be busy this weekend, but you're going to be busy with me. We're not nearly done yet."

Missy thought about her sore thigh muscles and the ache between her legs that for once was not caused by lust—at least, not by a *resurgence* of lust—and her eyes widened.

"We've got a whole bunch of things to talk about, and not a lot of time, so you get the *Reader's Digest* condensed version. Listen up."

She couldn't quite decipher the reaction she felt to having him clarify that "we're not done yet" had meant they weren't done talking, rather than that they weren't done with sex. If the idea of more sex aroused her, she'd be a masochist, because walking had already become an interesting challenge, but if it didn't disappoint her just a little, she figured she wouldn't be female.

"All right. Fine. But can I get off your lap first?"

He tightened his arms and shook his head. "No. So, I know you ran off before you got to hear any of what Logan had to tell me—"

Missy blinked, scowled, and crossed her arms over her chest as she felt the crimson tide of her blush returning. This time she guessed it would be a rather unique shade of crimson. "Do we have to talk about that?"

Graham looked puzzled. "Well, yes. Why wouldn't we?"

Rolling her eyes and wishing she lived in the alternate reality her Lupine lover seemed to inhabit, Missy fixed her gaze on the rich brown leather of the sofa and gritted her teeth around her answer.

"Because I find it a little humiliating to remember being seen fully naked on a hallway carpet, obviously having recently concluded having sex with a man I just met, by *another* man to whom I have never been introduced." She paused to glare at him. "But maybe I'm just funny that way."

His chuckle made her eyes narrow and her fist swing, but he caught the blow before it could impact against his chest. "Ah. I understand."

He raised her hand to his mouth and nibbled the backs of her knuckles, which only succeeded in making her angrier. Damn him for still being able to arouse her even with the memory of that embarrassment fresh in her mind.

"You're not being funny, just human." He grinned. "Sorry, but I forgot about that little quirk of yours."

"Quirk?"

He ignored her yelp and freed her hand so he could pull aside her shirt collar and examine the reddened bruise where he'd bitten her. She'd seen it when she changed and had wiped away the faint traces of blood that had dried there, only to find that he had barely broken the skin. All in all, it looked worse than it actually was.

"Quirk," he repeated, tracing the faint marks left by his teeth. "It's easy for me to forget you're human when you smell so damned good, but then you get all embarrassed about something perfectly natural, like nudity or sex, and it all comes back to me. You people are so weird about that."

"Weird!?"

"Weird," he repeated, leaning forward to lave the bruise with his tongue and nearly making her swallow her own. "Lupines aren't embarrassed by our bodies. We come into this world naked, and the only reason most of us wear clothes is because it gets damned cold for part of the year, if we're not planning to spend that whole time sporting fur."

"Also, there are laws," Missy pointed out.

"Sure. Human laws, but the practicality argument trumps those. And as for sex, it would just be silly to be embarrassed about that. It's natural and healthy, not to mention a hell of a lot of fun. We all know everyone does it. At least, they do when they have the opportunity—otherwise how did the rest of us get here? How will the species survive? When you look at it that way, it's hard to see reason for the kind of inhibitions you humans like to wrap yourselves in."

"I am not wrapped in inhibitions," Missy protested, struggling for dignity while her bare toes curled and her belly launched its newly familiar tumbling routine. The man's tongue was *talented*. "I'm not ashamed of sex, but that doesn't mean I want strangers to come face-to-face with the evidence that I've just had it."

Graham's hand slid under the loose waistband of her jeans and cupped her warm mound. His fingertip briefly tickled her dark curls before sliding between her lips and finding the moisture hidden there.

"That's okay, baby," he purred as he closed his teeth around her earlobe and tugged delicately. "I don't mind being private with you. In fact, I like the idea of keeping you all to myself."

His blatantly possessive tone sent arousal trembling through her. But hadn't he said they needed to talk? Because there was no way on God's green earth she'd be able to concentrate on what he had to say if he kept touching her like this.

She wrapped her fingers around his wrist and pulled hard, but his hand stayed buried between her legs, and he slid one finger deeper to press against her opening.

"Shhh. Hush, hush." His finger penetrated, sliding deep, the rough, callused surface abrading her already tender interior walls. "Just let me touch you, baby. It's been so long since I touched you."

She bit back a moan, her nails digging into the leather upholstery. Two or three hours was his idea of a long time to go without sex? Holy Mary, she'd be dead of exhaustion before the end of the day. "H-h-has it?"

"Um-hm, it has. And you were so tight for me last time. I'm afraid I might hurt you if I don't keep you nice and relaxed and open for me." His finger withdrew in a reluctant glide and suddenly thrust back, three fingers this time that stretched and filled her. Her head fell back on a moan even as her muscles clamped around him. "No, no, sweetheart. I said relax." One nail lightly scraped inside her, and she gasped. "Let go for me, Melissa." His fingers worked forward and backward in a relentless sawing motion that brought tears to her eyes and set her pussy on fire for him. "Trust me. I'll take care of you."

"Graham!"

His fingers thrust hard, his thumb teasing her most sensitive nerves as he drove her closer and closer to insanity. She shuddered and whined helplessly.

He bent over her until she felt his breath against the mark he'd made on her shoulder, and his voice sounded in her ear like the voice of temptation itself.

"I'll always take care of you, baby. I'll always make sure you're safe and secure and so deliciously wet."

She whimpered a protest, even as her hips lifted toward him, pressing against his clever fingers in a blatant demand for more.

"My sweet Melissa." His voice was a growl and a purr, and it caressed her hot skin with puffs of humid air. "Such a pretty girl to have fallen into the clutches of the big bad wolf."

His hand closed around her thigh in a grip just short of bruising and shifted it to the side, spreading her. Against her ear, his tone went from teasing to very, very serious. Something more than arousal drove him now. Missy could feel it, but there was no way her overloaded senses would let her concentrate long enough to puzzle out what it was.

"Like Little Red Riding Hood, you didn't know what you were in for when you left home, did you?" His fingers moved in some arcane pattern that had her eyes rolling back in her head and her body begging for release. "That's too bad, because once the wolf has ahold of a pretty girl, he doesn't ever let her go."

The tension inside her built to the breaking point, to the point where she was ready to shove her own hand down her jeans just to finish herself off. He caught her wrists in his free hand and held them captive as if he sensed her thoughts. She moaned and pressed herself harder onto his thrusting fingers.

"A wolf never shares," he growled. "No one else will ever touch you the way I'm touching you. I'll kill anyone who tries." She heard the violence in his tone, but he kept her too hot to care.

"And the reason for that, Melissa Jane," he continued turning his head so that his lips brushed hers and his luminescent eyes burned as they met her heavy-lidded brown gaze, "is because. You. Are. My. Mate!"

He shoved his three fingers deeply inside, and held them there while her orgasm consumed her. She broke apart, raining down on him in tiny little fragments, each of which pulsed with the heavy rush of blood between her legs. She sobbed and curled her hands into fists and moaned her pleasure into his mouth when he caught hers for a hungry, possessive kiss.

She tore her lips from his after a few seconds, desperate to catch her breath. His shoulder offered her a hiding place and a refuge while she tried to put her scattered wits back together. He cradled her there tenderly. He released her wrists, and she curled her trembling arms around his neck, feeling his hand slip from between her legs, ruffle affectionately through her curls, and then slide around her waist to cuddle her close.

He petted her like a kitten, and she found it soothing. At least, until her brain kicked back into gear.

"I'm your what?"

Her head spun around so fast that she knocked him in the nose with her forehead.

Graham winced.

"My—ow!—mate. Hey! Hold still before you cause any permanent damage." He pinned her arms to her sides and scowled down at her. "Like I was saying—"

"I don't want you to say anything else, since you aren't making the slightest bit of sense. What I want—"

It was his turn to interrupt, so he shook her gently. "What do you think I'm trying to do? But you need to stop arguing long enough for me to get a word in edgewise, okay?"

Her teeth clicked shut, and he glared at her for another minute before he seemed satisfied that she intended to behave.

"If you'd let me explain what Logan came in to tell me—"

"Let you explain?" Her disbelief mixed with embarrassment and exploded into something that looked a lot like anger. "Who stuck whose hand down whose pants, buster?"

Graham clamped his hand over her mouth and gave her a reprimanding look.

"As I was saying," he continued, arching the cup of his hand to avoid her sharp teeth, "Logan needed to tell me about some trouble that's been brewing in the pack. Normally, I wouldn't worry you with it, but I can't predict what might happen next, and

I don't want to take the chance of you being caught off guard."

Since when was she supposed to be on guard? Missy wondered. And against what?

She crossed her arms over her chest and arched an eyebrow over his fingers.

"Logan has been keeping me up-to-date on some trouble a lesser member of the pack is causing. Unfortunately, the upstart gamma in question is my cousin Curtis."

Missy subsided from fulminating into listening. Damn it, she seemed constitutionally unable to not give anyone the benefit of the doubt. It was an inherent weakness. Like porous bones. She inclined her head for him to go on.

"It turns out that Curtis thinks he'd make a better alpha than I do."

She snorted, and Graham grinned.

"Thanks. That's what I think, too. Anyway, alphas aren't like elected presidents or anything. Our packs operate a lot like wolf packs. Alphas earn their position by being the strongest, and if another Lupine wants to be alpha, he has to prove worthiness by beating the current alpha in a fight. Even though my father was alpha before me and he had offered to retire so I could take his place, I still had to fight him to prove I was capable of leading the pack. But there's no way my cousin could beat me, and he knows it."

She rolled her eyes at Graham's arrogance, but

inside she admitted she couldn't really picture anyone beating him in a fight, fair or foul.

"So like the spineless little coward he is," Graham continued, "Curtis has been trying to come at the issue from the side of manipulation and treachery instead of issuing a good, honest challenge. Lately, he seems to be experimenting with turning the pack's opinion against me, in hopes of having me ousted. If I were to be overthrown by a popular uprising of the pack, there would be a power vacuum while every young male with more balls than brains challenged anything that breathed for my position."

Missy frowned. That sounded chaotic. Not to mention violent.

And potentially messy.

Graham read her expression and nodded. "It wouldn't be good for anyone involved. Obviously, not for me, but not for the pack, either. That kind of infighting drains time, energy, and resources away from what we should really be focusing on, like building unity with the other non-humans in the city in preparation for the Unveiling."

She tilted her head in inquiry.

"'The Unveiling' is a term most Others use to describe a public announcement of who we are to the human world. It's a pretty contentious idea, but there are a lot of Others out there who think it's only a matter of time before it has to happen, and I'm one of them. We can't go on hiding forever, and there's no reason we should want to. We can't outrun science forever, and if the human world has to find out about us, I'd rather it be on our terms, so that *we're* the ones in control of the spin."

Missy thought about that and nodded. She could understand what he meant and saw the merit in his thinking. But she was getting really tired of not being able to talk. She muttered something under his palm, but he ignored her.

"Logan came over here earlier to tell me that Curtis had gathered up the three most well-respected elders in our pack to point out to me all the things I'm doing wrong as alpha. I think he wanted me to be afraid that he had already marshaled their support, and therefore the support of the whole pack, behind the idea of him taking over as alpha. It didn't work that way, but I'm guessing that's what he intended. And he was none too pleased when he saw that it had failed. But because of his plotting, I had to give everyone some news a bit prematurely."

He glanced down at her ruefully. "And this is where you come in." He sighed. "There's an old Lupine tradition that says only Lupines with mates can be alphas of their pack. My cousin thinks he can use the fact I hadn't chosen a mate against me. It's the one area where people aren't going to think it's okay not to be old-fashioned. There's nothing in our culture that's as important as finding a mate and having cubs. If Curtis spins that hard enough, he just might be able to win enough support for himself to make my life so miserable, I'll almost *want* to step down."

Missy snorted.

"I said 'almost,'" he clarified. "Anyway, he brought up that issue today, in front of the elders. Frankly, he made it impossible for me to keep the news to myself."

His eyes, deep and green and glowing, locked onto her and made Missy's stomach clench. They made some lower things clench, too.

"I hadn't meant to make any kind of announcement so soon," Graham said, leaning toward her until his forehead rested against hers and she could feel his breath tickling her face where it wasn't covered by his hand. "I knew you'd need some more time to get used to the idea, and I didn't want you to feel pressured. Then it slipped out and I realized that it shouldn't make that much difference whether I waited a few more days or not. Timing can't change the truth, right?"

Missy had no idea what Graham was talking about, but something in his tone or in her own mysterious female intuition was making her feel very uneasy anyway.

"And the truth is that the news was a big blow to Curtis. It shot his current plan all to hell, which probably pissed him off, and I don't want you getting caught in the crossfire, so I needed to warn you. You need to be prepared for anything, because the pack is probably already talking, and you deserve to hear the news directly from me."

If he didn't stop being cryptic, Missy was going

to take a chunk out of his hand if she had to dislocate her jaw to do it.

"What news?!" she shouted, although with his hand over her mouth it came out more as an indistinct grumble.

"Curtis will have to come up with a new reason why I shouldn't be alpha of the Silverback Clan, because his old one no longer applies. I have a mate now. I have you."

It took a moment for the rumble of his voice to vibrate through her eardrums and hit her brain so that his meaning could penetrate. That's when she bit him.

Hard.

"Shit!" Graham jerked his hand from her mouth and shook it, staring in disbelief at the delicate teeth marks she'd left in the fleshy part of his palm. "What the hell was that for, you little savage?"

Missy pushed herself off his lap, planted her hands on her hips, and glared at him. With him still on the sofa and her standing on the ground, she was almost taller than him. Now she wouldn't have to crane her neck while she chewed him out.

"Don't call me a savage, you barbarian!" she countered. "I'm not the one who figuratively just whacked someone over the head with a mastodon bone and dragged her by her hair all the way back to his cave. What do you mean you 'have' me? Did I miss the part where I get to have a say in whose 'mate' I am?"

Graham rubbed the marks in his hand with the

opposite thumb and frowned. "I'm Lupine, not libertarian. It's not like being the mate of a were-wolf comes up for a vote."

"And *that* is just the point. I am *not* the mate of a werewolf. I don't remember being anything of the sort."

His eyes glinted. "If you want me to ruin another set of clothes, I could refresh your memory."

"Don't be an ass," she dismissed. "That was sex. Your definition of 'mate' seems to include a lot more than that, buster. You aren't talking about the verb anymore. You're getting all noun-y here."

Missy watched while his mouth tightened and he crossed his arms over his broad chest. "And what if I am?"

"Then we need to talk about it," she said. "You can't just *announce* that I'm your mate. That's like just announcing that we're married. It doesn't work like that. You have to ask first."

Graham had the nerve to look genuinely puzzled. "Ask? Why would I ask? What does asking have to do with it? That's not how a mate-bond works. No Lupine has ever been asked if he or she wanted to be someone's mate; it just happens."

How dare he be baffled while she was in a huff?

"Yes, well, in case it has escaped your notice, *I* am *not* Lupine." She glared at him, drawing herself up to her full height, which wasn't much, but which made her feel better. "Where I come from, when people decide they want to spend their life with someone, they check to make sure the other person feels the same way first. You can't just treat me like one of your furry little groupies. I don't take orders from men who don't ask my opinion about important things."

"I have groupies?" he asked, then shook his head impatiently. "It doesn't matter what your opinion is. But what I'm trying to tell you," he continued, holding up both hands to forestall her heated interruption, "is that it doesn't matter what *my* opinion is, either. We're mates. It's a fact. Neither one of us gets to ask or negotiate or back out."

Missy stifled the urge to shriek. With moderate success.

"Look, there's a very big detail here that you just don't seem to be getting. What you're telling me is the way things happen in your world, but I don't live in that world. You may have to abide by these traditions of yours, but I don't. The only thing keeping me here is my willingness—up until now—to stay, but I can leave any time I want and pretend that your way of doing things doesn't even exist."

His eyes turned a smoky, eerie shade of golden green and he bared a set of fangs Missy felt fairly certain he hadn't sported a few seconds ago.

"Do you really think that?" he growled, and the sound held all the menace of Cujo on a bad-hair day. "Do you really think that I would stand back and let you leave when I know you are my mate? You can't be that naïve, Melissa."

"What I doubt is your sanity if you think that a few hours of sex makes us mates, because I don't. So. Get. Off. Of. Me!"

She used all her strength to break free and all he did was jerk his head back, his expression morphing from threatening to vaguely surprised.

"Is *that* what this is all about?"

The genuine shock in his voice pierced her determination, and she paused. "Is what what this is all about?"

He drew back until he knelt astride her with his hands still cuffing her wrists and a half-surprised, half-bemused look on his face. "You think this is all just about sex."

The accusation in his voice did not sit well with Missy.

"What else is it about? We haven't spent four out of every five minutes in each other's company naked because we're study buddies in an anatomy course. I mean, we're practically strangers. I don't even know if you have a family!"

His bemusement slid into a grin, the kind that could almost make her forget why she was mad at him.

"My parents are retired and living in Bermuda. No brothers or sisters. A slew of aunts, uncles, and cousins." He pulled her up until he could wrap her arms around his neck and tug her into his embrace. His green eyes caught hers and held them. "And one very sexy mate."

His lips descended toward her and almost made it before she jerked herself back to reality.

"Not so fast," she protested, turning away and pressing against his chest to hold him at bay. "You are not going to turn this into more sex, and you're not going to use sex to make me your mate by default."

He gave her a comical pout. "But we only have about thirty-six hours before it's Monday morning and our agreement to spend the weekend together is over. I figured we shouldn't waste it."

"And how is thirty-six more hours of sex going to prove to me that this mate thing is about more than sex?"

The new pout wasn't quite so comical. "I told you it isn't. You're not just a warm body. You're my mate. You and I were Fated for each other, but it's not like destiny provided us with corresponding ID cards, so how am I supposed to convince you? Do you want me to take a lie detector test?"

Missy looked—and felt—decidedly unsympathetic. "You might try explaining to me how you came to the conclusion that I was the girl for you based on having known me for"—she glanced at her watch—"twelve and a half hours."

With a disgruntled sigh, Graham pulled away and flopped back on the sofa, where he glared up at her from a lazy slouch. "I just know. It's a Lupine thing."

"And I wouldn't understand?" Her voice sounded

dry even to her own ears, but it didn't seem to affect Graham. He continued to scowl at her while his fingers drummed impatiently against the leather cushions.

"I didn't say that, but I'm not sure you'd believe me if I told you."

Missy folded her arms over her chest, crossed her legs at the knees, and raised her eyebrows. "You won't know until you try me."

CHAPTER TEN

Taking a deep breath, Graham wrapped a mental noose around his impatience and hauled on it hard. If Missy wanted an explanation, the least he could do was give her an explanation. Not only did she deserve that level of common courtesy as his mate, but if he was going to live with her for the next fifty or sixty years with all of his limbs intact, he'd do well to keep her in a good mood.

He opened his mouth to speak, but a signal from his brain stopped him before he uttered so much as a sound. His olfactory lobe was telling him something very important. Something that required more data.

Another sniff filled his head with the scent of Melissa, that warm, sweet, rich, utterly delectable odor that stirred every one of his appetites and sent them into overdrive. In fact, it seemed to have an even stronger effect on him than it had when he'd first woken to find her snuggled against his side.

The scent of her that had driven him wild this morning now verged on driving him insane. He'd been right about her fertility, too, because unless he'd gone nose-deaf in the past few hours, the subtle changes he detected in her scent now told him unequivocally that Missy was pregnant.

Pregnant.

Missy was going to have his cub.

Graham's beast gave a mental roar of triumph, and he had to fight not to echo it aloud. The swell of emotions generated by that knowledge threatened to choke him, no matter how hard he struggled to beat them back. The sense of pride and excitement, joy, and possessiveness that stirred to life inside him all but knocked him on his ass. But that was nothing compared to the surge of love.

Love.

God damn it! He had fallen in love with her!

Graham froze. What the hell was he supposed to do now? Wanting her was one thing. Lusting after her generously round ass and the soft swell of her belly was totally okay with him. All well and good. Even being charmed by her chimeric flashes of timidity and boldness didn't bother him. He didn't mind laughing at her jokes or valuing her opinion, but damn it, why did his stupid heart have to bring love into it? Why couldn't it be happy with lust, friendship, and respect?

She cleared her throat and pursed her lips, and Graham fought the urge to squirm like an eight-year-old before a parental firing squad.

"I'm waiting for you to explain it to me, Graham," she said. "And don't give me that bull about me not understanding. I want an answer."

He rubbed his hand absently against his chest, right over his heart, and knew he wasn't quite ready to tell her his big secret. Or her slowly expanding secret. If she still struggled to come to terms with the way they both burst into flames when they mated, no matter who was watching, then she damned sure wasn't ready to hear that he loved her and that he'd as good as deliberately made her pregnant when he'd known good and well he could have prevented it. Some things were better left unsaid. At least until he could be sure there was no turning back for either of them.

"You smell," he blurted out, then watched as her eyes widened before narrowing into thin little slits of pique.

"I *smell*?" she growled, doing a fairly good imitation of him in a mood. "You're telling me you want me to be your mate because I stink? Somehow, I'm missing your logic."

"Not stink. Smell," he clarified. "Smell wonderful."

Her lips were still thin and straight, so he pushed on and tried to explain something he'd never before tried to define.

"Lupines have acute senses of smell, thousands of times better than humans'. Even better than most dogs'. Everything around us has its own scent, and a lot of our social customs are built on the information we get that way. It's just ingrained. We're born smelling, even if it takes a few hours before we open our eyes."

Her mouth softened, just a fraction, but he saw it.

"It's only logical that we use that sense of smell when we mate. It tells us who we're attracted to and who we're not," he said. "The most beautiful female in the world won't appeal to a Lupine if she doesn't smell right."

"What smells right?" she asked. He could hear the reluctant curiosity in her voice, but it was still progress.

"You do."

"Clearly, I'm not the first woman who did. Did you tell any of them they were your mates?"

Damn it! Why couldn't he have found a stupid mate? It would have made his life a hell of a lot easier.

"No, because none of them were. You are," he said, as forcefully as he could without grabbing her and attempting to prove it to her graphically. "Lupines mate for life, which even wolves don't always do. But like humans, we don't always wait for our mates just to have sex."

"Which means you still have to explain how the way I smell makes me your mate."

He raked a frustrated hand through his hair and glared at her. "You're asking me to explain instinct here. That's like me asking you to explain why humans get all freaked out when they see us on full-moon nights."

"That might have something to do with the fur factor," she said, her tone wry. "See, some people cling to the crazy notion that werewolves aren't real. I hear it helps them sleep at night."

"What I mean is that the fear they feel is instinctual, not rational. You can't really explain something like that."

"At least I tried."

"You just smell *different*!" He was frustrated now, and it showed in his voice. He considered it a lucky stroke that it didn't show in him changing into something a little less human and tearing the stuffing out of his sofa. "Other women smell like sex. They smell . . . available. Like musk and perfume. You smell different. You're . . . fascinating. All rich sweetness, like honey and vanilla."

She rolled her eyes. "Great. I smell like vanilla. The most boring of all flavors. And this is supposed to convince me I'm irresistible to you?"

He shot forward so fast that he saw the surprise widen her eyes when she blinked to find him leaning so close to her that their noses almost kissed.

"You are anything but boring, Melissa Jane," he growled, meeting her brown eyes and holding their soft gaze with his own. "Remember, vanilla comes from orchids and was once paid as a high tribute to the Aztec emperors. If they could have smelled your scent the way I do, they would have demanded you, instead of a few orchid pods."

Her lips parted, drawing his eye like a beacon. Unable to resist, he leaned another fraction of an inch closer and traced the soft gap with the tip of his tongue. He felt the rush of air when she gasped, and closed his teeth delicately on her lower lip, nibbling and nipping and tugging at the sensitive flesh.

"No one else smells like you, Missy," he murmured, cupping his hand around the nape of her neck. "No one else ever has, and no one else ever could. You smell of honey and vanilla, and warm, sexy woman."

He saw the softness in her eyes, felt the tension sap out of her muscles until her arms uncrossed and her body melted closer to his. His hands closed on her, tight and possessive, and he drew a deep breath to drink in her scent.

"You smell damp and delicious and like I could devour every drop of you and still not be satisfied." He licked her lips, a slow, lapping taste that drew more of her scent into him and made hunger knot heavily in his stomach. "You smell like my mate."

He reached out to draw her closer, but the movement must have startled her, because she slipped away at the last minute and put the width of the coffee table between them.

"Okay, maybe you're right," she said, eying him warily. "Maybe the mate concept is a werewolf thing that I wouldn't understand, but I still need for you to take thirty seconds to look at this from my point of view, okay?"

Graham's first instinct was to dismiss her request and seduce her until she forgot why she was objecting to being his mate and melted all over him like warm honey; but as he reached for her, he saw the confusion and fear in her eyes and an unseen fist tightened around his heart.

Was this what it meant to be in love? Did it mean he would always feel like he'd be willing to ignore the laws of nature and physics and man and Lupine if only it would make her smile at him again?

If so, he predicted a short and volatile life together.

Instead of grabbing her by the arms and hauling her against his body, Graham closed his hands gently on the sides of her neck, cupping the slender column and rubbing his thumbs gently along the curving lines of her jaw.

"I'm willing to give it a shot," he told her, keeping his voice soft and even, "if you're willing to explain it to me."

She looked into his eyes, her wariness apparent. God, he must have come off to her so far like a steamroller with a penis if she trusted him this little. And over something so simple.

Impatience nudged him, but he pushed it aside and watched her. And waited.

"I'm not sure you can understand," she finally murmured.

Graham felt his mouth curve into a wry grin. "Now, where have I heard that before?"

Missy rolled her eyes and blew out a breath. "I mean, I don't know if you can really put yourself in my position. We're so different."

The tips of his thumbs flicked playfully, tenderly, against the softness of her bare earlobes. When their cub was born, he'd fasten diamonds there, he decided. "Being different is what makes us fit together so perfectly."

"I'm not just talking tab A and slot B. You're so much stronger than me. Not just the way any guy would be stronger than me; I mean, you could bench-press me one-handed for a month and not break a sweat. You could break any one of my bones with your little finger. Heck, you could probably do it just by staring at it hard enough."

"Are you afraid I'll hurt you?"

She answered with a laugh that nearly broke his heart. "Terrified. But not that you'll break one of my bones."

When she went silent, he waited for a dozen heartbeats before his fingers squeezed gently. "Melissa, tell me what you're afraid of."

Her lips parted on a shaking breath, and her lids fell over her warm brown eyes, almost as if she couldn't bear to look at him while she spoke.

"I'm not like you," she whispered miserably. "And I don't mean that I'm not Lupine. I'm sure you've figured that out by now. I mean I'm not like any of the other women you've been with before, either. They're all beautiful. *You're* beautiful."

Graham shook his head slowly. Maybe he couldn't understand her. Not unless she started making sense.

"I'm plain," she ground out, a silver liquid tear leaking out from beneath the sweep of sable lashes and etching a salty track over her rosy skin. "I'm average and boring and shy and awkward and I don't know anything about men or sex or—"

He swallowed her idiotic words, wiping them away with broad strokes of his tongue and nipping her lips to punish them for voicing her nonsense. When he felt her soften and sway against him, he lifted his head and sipped the tears from her skin.

"Melissa Jane Roper," he said in a voice husky and dark, "I can't decide whether to smack you upside your thick little skull or bend you over this sofa and prove to you exactly how beautiful and special and exciting and sexy you are."

Missy's eyes flew open to stare at him in dazed incomprehension.

Laughing and groaning, Graham shook her gently before pulling her against his chest and hugging her tight. Pillowing his cheek atop her hair, he felt her trembling with suppressed emotion.

"I sure as hell hope that these ridiculous notions of yours aren't why you think we might not be mates."

Small, determined hands pressed against his chest until he allowed enough space between them for her to frown up at him. "I don't see what gives you the right to call any notions of mine ridiculous."

"How about logic?"

"Wha—?"

"Sweetheart, I don't know what kind of tales Regina and Dmitri have been telling you about me, but if they made you think that I'm such a horny bastard I can't tell the difference between ugly and beautiful or a good time and a lifetime, I need to give each of them a piece of my mind."

"They never said either of those things. Not exactly."

"Oh? Then what did they say?"

Missy shrugged and stared at his shirt collar. "Well, it's hardly a secret that you've got a reputation for being the biggest playboy in the Other world."

"But that's just it, baby." He slid a finger under her chin and tilted her head back to meet his gaze. "That was before I met you. Now I'm not playing anymore."

She pushed him back another inch. "Yes. That *is* just it. You just can't seem to grasp the idea that I might question how a man who has spent his entire adult life chasing after and catching the most beautiful women in Manhattan could suddenly fall head over heels, irrevocably, fated-to-be-together in love with a woman like me!"

It *sounded* like English, Graham thought, and the words themselves made sense to him, but something about the way she strung them together made him seriously question whether or not he and his mate were actually speaking the same language. "Why do you make it sound like that's impossible?"

"Because it is!"

"Not for a Lupine."

"For anyone who has graduated past believing in fairy tales!"

This was probably not the best time to talk to her about Faerie and the royal court of the Fae, he reflected.

"You know what?" he asked instead. "I'm starting to think that this has very little to do with the fact that you're human and I'm Lupine. I think this is more about the fact that you have a whole bunch of monsters in your head that keep you from believing me when I tell you how I feel about you."

She pulled completely away from him and crossed her arms over her chest, hugging herself tightly. "That's not as hard as you make it sound. Especially since you've never told me how you feel about me."

"What are you talking about? Of course I've told you. That's how we ended up in this ridiculous fight."

"It's not ridiculous. And it started because you told me I'm your mate, not because you told me how you feel about me."

Graham's mouth opened, hung that way for a long moment, then snapped closed with a clatter of teeth.

She was right.

He hadn't told Melissa how he felt about her. Not ever. He supposed he could have made a case for the fact that they'd only really known each other for a day and a half, or for the fact that he hadn't realized how he felt until just a few minutes ago, but neither excuse would have held much water with him. Why should it do better with her? Why should she accept either as an excuse?

Then again, would she even accept his love as the truth?

Mother Moon, but humans could be confusing!

Grimly Graham stuffed down his impatience and tried to think like a human. Afterward, he'd treat himself to a big glass of scotch.

Humans, he reminded himself, were contrary beasts by nature. They wrote books and made films and told stories about the concept of love at first sight—what Lupines would call mating—and yet expressing a genuine belief in the concept often met with derision and scorn. Apparently, it was acceptable to fantasize about an instantaneous and lasting connection with a romantic partner but not to actually make one. If he told Missy how he felt about her, told her the full honest truth, would it reassure her or just make her run faster away from him?

Could he afford to take the chance of her running?

He struggled in silence for a minute, then ran an impatient hand through his hair and decided to walk a very fine line.

"I feel a lot of things for you," he said to her narrow, tense back. He watched her shoulders carefully, trying to read her mood in the lines of her body. "Some of them I haven't quite sorted out yet, but some of them I have. I know that you fascinate me. I know that you make me smile and you make me laugh and you sure as hell make me hard enough to split wood."

One soft shoulder sank a fraction of an inch, then the other.

Heartened, he continued. "I know that I've enjoyed every minute we've spent together and that I want to spend a lot more minutes with you. Whole hours. Days even. Maybe more. I know that I've spent most of last night and all day today trying to think up ways to convince you not to leave on Monday morning because I know I won't be as happy once you're gone as I have been while you're here."

Every single word he spoke was true, sincere, from his heart. And if his heart held a few more words that he hadn't managed to say yet, it wasn't so hard to convince himself that he was saving those for a special occasion.

Especially not when Missy hesitantly turned around to face him, her dark eyes shining with hope and warmth and too many doubts for his own good.

Her mouth curved into a lopsided smile and her shoulder hitched up in a small shrug. His heart melted and his tongue ached from biting it to hold back the final words.

"We've got thirty-five more hours," she offered, holding out a hand toward him. "We can be happy for those. And if you're really persuasive, maybe I can come back for dinner Monday night."

A wave of relief threatened to roll Graham into

the undertow. He grabbed her hand like a lifeline and towed her gently toward him.

"What if I'm really, *really* persuasive?" he murmured, lowering his mouth to hers. "Would you come back with a suitcase?"

She laughed and tangled her fingers in the hair at the back of his head.

"Give it your best shot," she breathed. "The worst I can do is say no."

CHAPTER ELEVEN

She said it a lot. Over and over and over again, as a matter of fact, and she still almost didn't make it out of Graham's house with her clothing intact. Only an emergency page from the club next door had given her enough time to refasten her buttons—for the second time that morning—and scoot out the front door before the Lupine Lothario succeeded in distracting her from her purpose. Yet again.

But after more than forty-eight hours of passionate togetherness, more than anything in the world Missy needed some time alone. Before she forgot everything she'd been working so hard to remember all weekend.

Like, her interlude with Graham was just that—a temporary interlude. And it would be a colossal mistake to let herself fall hopelessly in love with a man who would be bored with her inside of a month, provided his interest even lasted that long. No matter how sweet the words he used to promise her otherwise.

Men like Graham Winters didn't keep promises to women like Missy Roper.

Through the window of a cab, she contemplated the truth of that. She wasn't quite sure where she'd learned the lesson, since it wasn't as if she'd had her heart broken by some good-looking gigolo in the past. Her past featured no gigolos of any kind. And maybe that was the problem. Her past featured a grand total of two precious lovers, both nice enough boys around her own age and both refreshingly up-front about their feelings—or lack thereof—for little Melissa Jane.

Missy had never been the type of woman to attract men. She didn't repulse them, she didn't think; they just never seemed to notice her. She stood in a room next to Ava or Danice or Corinne or Reggie, and male eyes skimmed right over her to linger on one of her much more . . . vivid friends.

She didn't begrudge any of the women their appeal; she'd just wished occasionally that she had been able to share it. She didn't know if her career choice had left her with a tattoo on her forehead that read: "Kindergarten teacher: approach only if you require help learning the alphabet," or if all her clothes had fingerpaint stains that she just hadn't noticed. Either way, men tended to treat her as either another piece of furniture or their long-lost kid sister. Neither had given her a lot of experience in the love and romance department.

Yet here was Graham Winters, perhaps the sexiest man ever to walk the streets of Manhattan, and he claimed to be absolutely enthralled with her, body and soul.

Body especially.

Missy shook her head as she paid the cabbie and headed for the elevator to her apartment. She had always heard that it was easy for men to separate sex from emotional involvement, but if she hadn't known better, she might have sworn that Graham was using sex to try to convince her that he cared for her in addition to lusting after her. From what she had heard over the years, she'd assumed not even eighteen-year-olds could make do with as little recuperative time between intimate encounters as Graham had allowed himself over the past two days. He had reached for her so often that it had only been the liberal and repeated use of a miracle herbal salve that allowed her to walk this morning. Though even the salve had been unable to prevent her legs from feeling like rubber.

Old, brittle rubber that had been stretched too thin and run too hot over a long, long, bumpy highway.

Snorting at her own analogy, Missy pulled her keys out of her bag, shifted her bundle of ruined clothes beneath her other arm, and stepped out of the elevator.

Suffice it to say that she had needed to come back home, to take a few hours away from Graham, both physically and emotionally. She had enjoyed his company too much for her own good. It was past time for a reality check.

The first thing Missy saw when she unlocked the door to her apartment and pushed it open was a thin sheet of notepaper that looked as if it had been slid under the door and onto the parquet entry pad. The rest of the apartment—or at least the living room, which was all she could see—appeared deserted. Glancing down at the messy scrawl, she attempted to decipher the handwritten note. Judging by the script, Ava hadn't lied about the man being a doctor.

> *Dear Melissa,*
> *Sorry our evening didn't work out. Ava told me about your family emergency. Please give your mother my best, and let her know she should stay off that broken leg for at least two weeks before she gives crutches a try. I hope you and I can reschedule for another time. After everything Ava has told me about you, I can't wait to learn if you're actually too good to be true.*
>
> *Stephen*

Pursing her lips, Missy set the note aside on a small table and set the locks on the door, simultaneously flipping on the overhead lights to combat the dull, gray day. Stephen sounded like a decent fellow; it was too bad he'd let Ava set him up on a wild date.

Still, at least she'd had the decency to have him clear out. One could never precisely count on Ava for decency. Witty company and the burning hell-fire of vengeance, yes, but not decency.

Dropping her torn clothes in the small mending basket she kept beside the sofa, Missy toed her shoes off and placed them beside the front door so she would remember to bring them back to Graham so he could return them to Samantha.

Provided she saw Graham again.

Which was, of course, the crux of her problem two days after it had first come to her attention.

When would she see Graham again? And why? He had seemed just as eager to spend time with her when he'd woken her up just before dawn, but had that been a sign of his affection or a by-product of his morning erection? When he'd kissed her good-bye before dashing off to handle his club's crisis du jour, he'd whispered that he wanted to take her out to dinner tonight, somewhere special. Had he meant that, or had it been just one of the things he said to his women to leave them with a positive memory?

Could she possibly be overanalyzing this?

Missy sighed and padded into the kitchen for a tall glass of water. All the physical exercise she'd participated in over the weekend had made it difficult to stay hydrated. When she glanced at the phone on the wall opposite the refrigerator, the display window of her phone told her she had five messages in her voice mail. Statistics predicted that 4.7 of them would be from Ava.

Despite the screaming protests in her head, Missy activated the speakerphone and dialed the number to access her messages. After she plugged in her secret code, the machine repeated her number of messages and began to play them back.

"Answer your cell phone or die, Melissa Jane," Ava ordered. "Just because you managed to evade us doesn't mean you're off the hook for your fix. I expect a call within the hour."

"Did someone just tell me the greatest lie ever spoken, or did you leave this party over the shoulder of *Graham Winters*?! Since you won't answer your cell, you get to hear this same message in two voice mails. *Call me.*"

Ava again. "All right, Regina has managed to convince me Graham is not a threat to your life, so I know you're not dead, but if you're actually spending the weekend with that . . . wolf in man's clothing, I will be sorely tempted to make you wish you were. I sent your fix home, but that does not mean you won't be made to pay for this, Melissa Jane."

Missy rolled her eyes. Ava still hadn't quite come to grips with the idea that not only were vampires and werewolves and other assorted shape-shifters real, but also one of them had married her best friend, Regina. *Against her wishes.* And Ava tended to hold a grudge.

The fourth message was from Corinne. At least, it was spoken with Corinne's husky alto voice, but Missy didn't need to see the cue cards to know with certainty that the words were all Ava's.

The fifth message wasn't a message at all. Missy heard the brief pause that indicated her recorded greeting where she announced her name and number and invited people to leave a message for her had finished playing. After that, she heard only a few seconds of silence, followed by the click of a line disconnecting. Weird.

Idly she glanced at the caller ID display. The number read "UNAVAILABLE," but the call had come yesterday afternoon. On a Sunday, the only people likely to call her from unlisted numbers were telemarketers. And maybe Ava in disguise, but the day Ava declined to leave a threat on a convenient voice mail, Missy would sell all her possessions and join the French Foreign Legion.

A touch of a button erased all the messages and another disconnected the call and turned the speakerphone off. A moment later, Missy closed the door of her dishwasher after placing her glass neatly inside and looked around her with an odd sort of panic.

She had absolutely nothing to do.

It was spring break for her students, so there were no classes to teach, no assignments to evaluate, no reports to write. She didn't even have lesson plans to prepare, because the private school where she taught required all teachers to complete them at least one month in advance. Missy was caught up for another three weeks.

Wandering back into the living room, she glanced at the television and grimaced. The idea of vegging in front of the tube held little appeal. There was no way daytime television would ever occupy her mind enough to keep it from wandering back to Graham and speculating on what might happen after they had been apart for a few hours. It would take a diligent effort at decoding secret international communiqués to do that.

Missy pursed her lips and began to weigh the benefits of a nap or a long soak in a hot bath against the humiliation inherent in calling another cab and heading back toward Vircolac and the uncertain welcome of its sexy owner. Before her willpower could crumble at her feet like poorly made plaster, the intercom from the front desk buzzed.

She hurried over to the door and pressed the button to answer. "Yes?"

"Good morning, Ms. Roper," Clancy, the daytime security guard, greeted her with his customary mellow affability. "You've got a delivery down here. I checked the paperwork and it looks okay, so I'm going to send it up."

"Great. Thanks."

Frowning, Missy unlocked the door with a puzzled frown. She couldn't think of anything she'd ordered in the past couple of weeks, so she wasn't sure what she might be receiving, but security in her building was very good. If Clancy said the messenger was legitimate, you could bet he had some kind of package with Missy's correct name and address on it and a signed and dated order slip to go with it.

Curiosity had her opening the door in time to hear the elevator ding before the doors whooshed softly open. The man who stepped out was of average height and average weight and wore an instantly recognizable cap and uniform that proclaimed him an employee of one of the neighborhood's most popular florists. In one arm he carried an enormous bouquet of roses in every shade from white to deep red to yellow and deep violet. There must have been three dozen of the glorious flowers, and Missy could smell their fragrance from three doors away.

"Oh, my God, are those for me?" Mouth hanging wide, Missy stepped away from her open door and held out her hands greedily. "I can't imagine who would be sending me flowers. Especially flowers like this."

Graham! shouted an impertinent and imprudent voice in the back of her head. She shushed it ruthlessly. *It's just as likely to be from Ava's surgeon friend. She probably sent him detailed instructions. Heck, knowing Ava, she could have ordered them herself and had the florist make out the card. She must really want to see me date this guy.*

The messenger halted in front of her and consulted the clipboard he held in his free hand. "Are you . . . Melissa Roper? Apartment Seven F?"

Missy smiled. "That's me. Do you know if there's a card in here? I can't think—"

She couldn't finish her sentence, either. In fact, she couldn't do much of anything, not even scream when the clipboard and bouquet went crashing to the hallway carpet, sending sheets of paper and shards of wet glass in every direction. And the reason she couldn't make a sound was that the messenger had his hands wrapped around her throat and was dragging her toward the stair at the end of the hall with inhuman strength.

Strength that matched the glow in his distinctively Lupine-yellow eyes.

Terror and confusion warred briefly for supremacy in her mind before her adrenal gland cast the deciding vote and waved a victory flag over the field of battle. It didn't matter why a Lupine had attacked her, the hormone said. What mattered was that she get away alive. Her fight-or-flight response kicked in, and she decided in an instant that just because she couldn't scream did not mean that she couldn't express her feelings for the situation in other ways.

For instance, by abruptly ceasing to struggle and using her attacker's momentary surprise as an opportunity to slam her forehead into the bridge of his nose with all the considerable force she could muster. Which turned out to be a lot more than she would otherwise have predicted.

The Lupine moved fast, but the unexpected attack had given Missy an advantage. It wasn't much, but it meant that instead of missing her mark entirely, she managed to impact his cheekbone hard enough to result in an audible crack. Not as satisfying or as debilitating as a bloody broken nose, but it did send a fleeting warmth through the vicinity of her heart.

Her attacker roared something indistinct and used his grip around Missy's throat to swing her around and slam her head into the wall on the other side of what happened to be her favorite neighbor's favorite room.

Lincoln Kennedy Jones threw open his door and stormed out of his apartment with fury in his heart and a wooden spoon in his hand. He hated to be interrupted while he was cooking, but when he saw what was happening in the hallway, it became clear that the only thing he hated more was to see a man physically attack a smaller, weaker, softer individual. A woman, for example. A woman he considered a friend, like Missy, merely added insult to his injury.

"What in the name of all that's holy do you think you're doing, fool!" Lincoln roared in the voice that had served him well during his decade of bouncing for some of the roughest bars in the city. "You take your hands off that little girl before I rip your fingers off and use them to clean out your ears! 'Cause I know your mama must have taught you better than to hurt a woman, but you must not have heard her right. Maybe after I'm done with you, you'll listen a little better."

Any normal man would have taken one look at Lincoln's shining, ebony head; his fierce, tattooed face; his six feet, seven inches, and 375 pounds of muscle, and executed a strategic retreat. The Lupine, however, obviously thought of himself as far superior to a normal man, because he took one hand from Missy's throat—which was enough for her to draw a deep, grateful breath—and used it to take a swing at the side of Lincoln's jaw.

Unfortunately, the werewolf hadn't taken into account that Lincoln might be the son of an African savannah giant. Missy herself hadn't known until after Regina had become a vampire. That was when Missy had started to look at the world in a new light and to ask questions she'd never before thought to consider. Instead of sending the black man sprawling, all the punch succeeded in doing was knocking his head around and making him very cranky.

With his spoon-free hand, Lincoln grabbed the wrist of the hand the Lupine still had wrapped around Missy's neck and squeezed. It happened close enough to her ears that she could hear the distinct sound of each bone snapping under the pressure of her neighbor's huge, dark fingers. By the time she had counted the fourth snap, the Lupine's grip loosened and she was able to wrench herself free and stumble against the wall well out of reach of her attacker.

From the look of things, though, the werewolf had more pressing concerns than making another grab for Missy. From the sound of them, too. The man howled loud enough to raise the dead, but the rest of the doors in the hall remained firmly closed. Either everyone else in the building was at work at this hour or they had all lived in Manhattan long enough to know better than to stick their noses into the kind of business that sounded like this, even if it was happening right outside their doors.

Missy watched Lincoln raise his wooden spoon and bring it down over the Lupine's head so hard that the handle cracked with the force of an explosion. Shards of wood went flying around the hall, except for the ones she felt sure had embedded themselves in her attacker's skull.

The Lupine howled again, but the sound of Lincoln's rumbling voice nearly drowned him out.

"Look what you made me do," the half giant said, his fierce expression turning down in a scowl. "That was my favorite spoon and now all it's good for is being driven straight through your worthless heart. Just like this."

Lincoln raised his arm as if he intended to stab the Lupine exactly as he'd described, but the other man didn't give him a chance. With a twist and a growl and a blurring of space, the Lupine shifted his form, his broken wrist sliding free of Lincoln's grip as his body changed and morphed into that of a blondish brown wolf with yellow eyes and a red and black baseball cap perched incongruously atop his furry head.

Before Missy could do more than blink, the wolf spun around and threw himself at the door for the stairs, forcing the latch from its anchor and disappearing into the dim stairwell.

His wrist didn't appear to be quite so badly injured now that it was a paw, Missy noticed. He had barely limped as he raced away.

"Now, let me get a look at you, sugar," Lincoln said, drawing Missy's attention from her fleeing attacker to refocus it on Lincoln's expression of concern.

He hunkered down on the floor beside her and carefully tilted her head to the side so he could examine her throat.

"Son of a bitch left marks on you, sugar girl. I should have turned him into a winter coat."

Missy laughed, the sound rough and painful as it emerged from her bruised throat. "He was completely the wrong color for you, Linc. You need to set your sights on something in an arctic silver. Or maybe fox red."

The enormous man chuckled and lifted her gently to her feet. "I guess you're probably right, sugar. I'll make a note. Now come on into my kitchen and sit down for a while. You've had a shock and you could use a nice cup of my chamomile and rose-hip tea. With extra honey and lemon. And while you drink that up, I'll call one of those girlfriends of yours. You'll need someone to sit with for a while after a thing like that. You want Reggie or Corinne?"

Missy sighed. Lincoln was probably right. The attack hadn't really hurt her, but she could feel the shakes coming on as a result of the shock. She probably should have one of her friends come hang out with her for a while. Just until her nerves settled down.

Desperately she tried to stuff down the thought that the only person she wanted to call right now was Graham.

Forget it, she told herself. *You've known the man two days. That is not the kind of relationship you*

*call on in case of an emergency. It's way too soon.
This is why God created girlfriends.*

"What time is it?" she asked.

"Little bit before noon."

Missy shook her head. "Not Reggie, then. She's sound asleep at this hour. Call Corinne. If she's not out after a story, she can be here in twenty minutes."

Forty-five minutes later, Missy sat at Lincoln's kitchen table with a mug of tea in her hand, a plate of warm ginger-molasses cookies in front of her, and her cell phone against her ear. When her mind had blanked on Corinne's number, Lincoln had fetched it from her apartment for her to look it up in her contact list. Unfortunately, Corinne had been on a story and Lincoln had been forced to settle for leaving the reporter a voice-mail message. Half an hour later, the woman had finally called back.

"Don't worry about it. It's not important," Missy lied, ignoring the glower Lincoln had aimed in her direction. "I'm already feeling better. My neighbor has been taking great care of me."

"I don't care. I'll be there as soon as I can catch a cab." Corinne paused. "Well, actually, I'm in Wee-hawken at the moment, so first I have to take the ferry back to the city. But as soon as we dock, I'll hop in a cab and be right there."

"I said don't worry about it. I'll be fine."

"But you'll never be a good liar."

"Corinne—"

"Missy," the other woman echoed. "You need one of us with you. I thought about calling Ava, but I figured that even if you survived a mugging, seeing her right now might finish you off. But I did get ahold of Danice and I left a message on the machine for Reggie."

Missy winced at hearing her own lie repeated. Explaining that the attack had been more than a random mugging had seemed too complicated to go into over the phone. It would be so much easier to spell it out in person.

Wouldn't it?

"There's no need to cause all this trouble. You guys have jobs and lives and stuff. You don't need to come rushing over here to wrap me in blankies. I'm a big girl. I can take care of myself."

"Yes, but that's my job now," a voice said from somewhere above her, just before a large, familiar hand plucked the cell phone from her ear and folded it closed with a snap.

Startled, Missy spun around in her chair to see a much more welcome Lupine aiming a thunderous glare squarely at her head.

"Graham! What are you doing here?"

CHAPTER TWELVE

"What am I doing here? *What am I* doing *here*?" Besides stifling the urge to throttle her, Graham fumed.

"That's a very good question," an unfamiliar voice added, drawing Graham's attention to an enormous, muscular black man who stood at the kitchen counter, a huge knife in his hand and a furious expression on his face. He stepped forward until he hovered over Missy like a guardian angel. "What are you doing here and who the hell do you think you are? You think you can just walk into a man's apartment without an invitation? And how do you know Melissa?"

Graham blinked, unsure which question to answer first. He was also having a little trouble deciding whether to applaud the stranger's concern for Missy or to rip his throat out for presuming to stand between an alpha and his mate.

"When I hear that my mate has just been attacked outside her own home, where else do you suppose I would be?"

"Mate?"

Missy raised a hand and touched the man's arm. "It's okay, Lincoln. Graham is a-a . . . friend."

To Graham, the man appeared less than satisfied with her explanation, but at least he lowered the knife.

"From where I stand, man wants to be more than a friend, sugar girl."

"I already am." Graham bared his teeth in a possessive snarl. "And you'd better watch that sweet tooth, or I may have to knock it out."

A distressed sound from Missy yanked both men's attention back to her and averted an armed conflict. Graham had to wonder whether she'd made it deliberately.

Missy opened her mouth, and he could almost see her thinking twice about arguing her mate status with him again. It may very well have saved her life.

"How did you know I'd been attacked?" she asked instead.

"Your friend Corinne called and left a message for Regina," he bit out, his gaze scraping over her and lingering on the dark purple bruises emerging from the swollen flesh outside her throat. "Dmitri was screening the calls and thought I would want to know."

"Why would he think that?"

"For the moon's sake, Melissa, he's my best friend and his wife is your best friend. And in addition to that, the Other community is a metaphorically small one. I doubt there's a were-pigeon in Inwood who hasn't heard that you and I left that party together Friday night and didn't emerge from my house until this morning. He put two and two together."

She blushed and looked away. Any other time, Graham might have found the gesture charming, but at the moment he was too furious to notice. Not furious with Missy, but furious that anyone had dared to lay a hand on her, to harm what was his.

"You didn't need to come all the way over here," she said, her voice going quiet.

Graham knelt down beside her and brushed his fingertips as gently as a whisper over her bruised skin. When even that contact made her wince, he considered several primitive, gruesome, and exceedingly bloody forms of revenge on the man who had done this to her. All he had to do was find the bastard.

"Yes, I did," he soothed her, grasping one of her pale hands between his and feeling the slight trembling she couldn't control. "Wherever my mate is, that is where I need to be. Especially when she's hurt. Then I can't possibly be anywhere else."

She blinked at him, her dark eyes hazy with shock, and he felt a sharp stab of guilt to know he hadn't been with her when she had needed him the most. He hadn't been there to chase away all threats against her, and he should have been. He should have kept her with him, should have insisted that she stay at his house, where she would have him and at least forty members of his club staff no more than a shout away. She was the most precious thing in his world and he needed to take much better care of her.

With a decisive motion, he scooped her up in his arms and turned to leave the kitchen.

"Now wait just a minute there, Mac," the enormous cook said, stepping in Graham's path, the chef's knife once more grasped in his beefy hand. "Just where the hell do you think you're taking my sugar girl?"

Graham felt his eyes narrow. He glared up at the giant of a man—half giant, maybe?—and let loose a menacing growl. "Melissa is not your anything, *Mac*. And I'm taking her somewhere safe. So get the hell out of my way, or so help me, I will go through you."

"Graham," Missy murmured, and stirred restlessly in his arms. "Don't say things like that. Lincoln is just trying to look out for me. He doesn't mean anything by it."

"The hell he doesn't."

"The hell I don't."

"Lincoln, please," she scolded. "Don't antagonize him." She turned back to Graham. "And you can put me down now. I'm perfectly capable of walking back to my own apartment. It's just down the hall."

Graham opened his mouth to tell her he would be the one to decide what she was capable of. Then the lessons of the weekend came flooding back to him, and he decided to use his brain for a change, instead of his instincts.

"Hush, baby," he soothed. "It makes *me* feel better to carry you, so just humor me for a while here, okay?"

"Oh. Um, o-okay, then. I guess it's okay."

"Good. Now I have a suggestion."

That was a new word for him, but Graham hoped it would have a more positive effect than the orders he was used to giving.

"What kind of suggestion?"

"I could take you back to your apartment," he acknowledged, "but then you'd be alone again and I'd spend my whole afternoon worrying about you. Not because I don't think you can take care of yourself," he assured her when she would have interrupted, "but because I care about you and you've been hurt."

"It's just new bruises."

"Besides, it's only a few hours before I'd have to come back here to pick you up for dinner, anyway. That seems like a couple of wasted trips to me."

She turned wide, startled brown eyes on him, reminding him of nothing so much as a young doe caught by surprise at the edge of a stream. "You still want to have dinner with me?"

Tearing his mind from the memory of how much he enjoyed venison, Graham shook his mate very, very gently. "Of course I do, you little idiot." His words might have been harsh, but his tone was tender. "If I had my way, I'd have all my meals with you, and all my sleep, and all my spare time, too."

She frowned, but this time Graham thought she looked more thoughtful than dismissive. Thoughtful and increasingly sleepy. The adrenaline rush must be wearing off. In a few more minutes, she'd be ready for a nap.

He continued his suggestion. "Option number two is that instead of taking you back to your apartment, I take you back to my house. You can have peace and quiet there just as easily as here, but I wouldn't have to worry so much because I'd be able to be there in seconds if you needed me. Plus, help or company or whatever else you might need is only an intercom call away. What do you say?"

"I don't know. . . ."

He leaned in and touched his forehead to hers. "Please, Melissa," he murmured. "It would make me feel a lot better."

She sighed and nodded and let her head drop to his shoulder. "That's exactly what I'm afraid of," she said, sighing. "But I suppose it doesn't matter now. We can go back to your place."

Graham started to ask what she'd meant by that, but it was already too late. Missy had fallen asleep in his arms, her sweet lips parted on a sigh of exhaustion. Brow creased, he started toward the apartment door again. A flash of movement on his left stopped him.

The man called Lincoln set his knife carefully

aside on a wooden cutting board and fixed his eyes
on Graham's.

"I got to tell you one thing before you leave, Mr.
'Graham, Please,'" the half giant rumbled. "You
somehow managed to find yourself the sweetest
little girl this side of a fairy story, so you'd damned
sure better take good care of her. Because if you
don't . . ." Lincoln shook his head and rubbed his
meaty hands together. "If you don't, I don't care
how much she loves you. I will pound you into the
dirt until even the rain won't cry to see you. Understand?"

Graham raised an eyebrow and looked the black
man over with new respect. If their positions had
been reversed, he might have given Lincoln the
same advice.

"I understand," Graham agreed quietly. Then he
gathered Missy closer against his chest and turned
to take her back to his home. Where she belonged.

When Missy woke, the clock on the nightstand read:
8:00, but it failed to specify A.M. or P.M. She had to
glance toward the window to supply the missing information. P.M. The only light peeking through the
blinds had the dim wattage and the golden cast of
street lamps.

Though she had no trouble recognizing where
she was—she had become more than passingly familiar with Graham's bed over the course of the
weekend—it took Missy a minute to remember
exactly how she had gotten there. She seemed to

recall leaving that morning, making a concerted effort to separate herself from Graham and the crazy intimate spell he had woven over her with the clever use of sex and knock-knock jokes. Every time she'd been on the verge of running away, he had slipped in another ridiculously bad joke and made her laugh and groan simultaneously. The tactic had served to ease her tension and make him seem even more perfect all at the same time.

The man was devious.

Turning her head away from the window brought a whole host of memories from earlier in the day flooding back. There had been the trip home, the flowers, the attack . . .

Drinking tea in Lincoln's kitchen and feeling safe and drowsy in Graham's arms.

And that, she supposed, explained how she'd ended up back here. But it didn't explain what had happened to her host-cum-knight-errant.

Missy strained her ears to listen through the silence, but all she heard was the white noise of the quiet neighborhood outside and the faint rustle of her own breathing. If Graham was in the house, as opposed to in the club, he wasn't in the bedroom or even probably on the second floor. If she wanted to see him, she would have to go and find him.

So did she want to?

She remembered the last words they had said to each other before they fell asleep. Graham had been surprisingly restrained and reasonable and had asked her, rather than commanded her, to return to his house instead of to her apartment. And just like that, Missy had come to realize that it didn't matter how diligently she had been protecting her heart; it was already lost. It had been Graham's from the beginning. He had owned her heart when he'd still been an ill-defined fantasy trapped in the recesses of her most secret wishes. Getting to know him had only deepened her certainty that she would always love him.

If she had needed proof, her subconscious had provided it in the aftermath of her attack. The first thing she had thought of when the panic of the moment had faded was that she wished Graham had been with her. If he'd been with her before the attack, he would have protected her; and if he had appeared immediately afterward, he would have wrapped her up in his arms and made her feel safe and secure and cherished in a way no one else had ever made her feel. And in that moment after the crisis was past, all Missy had wanted was to feel Graham's arms around her.

If that wasn't love, she didn't know what was.

The problem with this sudden rush of self-awareness, Missy acknowledged, was that it did nothing to clarify the truth of Graham's feelings. He said he loved her, but was that his heart talking or a more southerly portion of his anatomy? And what would hurt more? Cutting her losses and running before she fell any deeper in love with him, or waiting to see whether or not he fell out of love with her as quickly as he had fallen in?

Missy sat up with a groan. She could spend all night dwelling on that question, but she had a feeling that in the end all she would have to show for it would be a headache and a bad temper. For a few hours maybe she would be better off just dealing with each moment as it happened.

Wow, I sound so Zen.

Snorting, Missy pushed away the blanket some-one—likely Graham—had tucked around her, and swung her legs over the side of the bed. To her surprise, she wore a pair of her own shortie pajamas in a soft pink, not the borrowed clothes she remembered going home in. Graham must have thought to pack her a bag this time.

Ten minutes in the bathroom left her with an empty bladder, clean teeth, and the kind of alertness that only came from many liberal splashes of cold water to a sleep-fogged face. So armed, she grabbed one of Graham's shirts from the closet to use as a robe and wrapped it around her before she padded down the stair and headed toward his study.

She ran into Logan in the downstairs hall and felt her face go so hot, she considered offering him an omelet.

Just crack a couple of eggs onto my cheeks and we're good to go.

The man didn't say anything about their last meeting, though. In fact, he didn't say anything at all. He also didn't look directly at her. He nodded politely, gestured for her to precede him into the study, and fixed his gaze on the doorjamb while she entered the room.

Once again she found Graham poring over a pile of paperwork, and again he looked up the moment she crossed the threshold.

"Hey," he greeted her, his expression softening into a warm smile. "How are you feeling?"

Missy reached to take the hand he held out to her and shrugged. "Not bad. My voice seems to have held up pretty well, so that's a benefit. The bruises look like heck, but they'll fade in a few days. All in all, I'd say it could have been worse."

Graham scowled and stepped out from behind his desk to draw her into his arms. "Don't say things like that. This was plenty bad enough."

Her heart fluttered inside her chest.

"Right," she murmured, unable to resist the temptation to lay her head on his shoulder and rub her cheek against the smooth cotton of his shirt. She could have leaned on him for the rest of the night. For the rest of her life. "Gotcha. No morbid speculation. I think I can handle that."

He pressed a kiss to the top of her head, his breath ruffling the fine strands of her hair. "That's my girl."

The expression had Missy pulling back and staring intently up at him. She didn't know what she was looking for. It wasn't as if she could read his intent behind every word on his face. But that didn't stop her from trying.

From the direction of the hallway came the sound of someone very politely clearing his throat.

Missy blushed. She had forgotten all about Logan.

Graham turned her until they both faced the door, and tucked her securely against his side.

"Logan," he greeted the other man. "I thought I told you I'd be taking the rest of the night off."

The pack beta nodded brusquely, his gaze fixed on Graham's right shoulder. The one farther away from Missy. "You did, but I've just gotten some news that I think you really need to hear."

Missy felt Graham stiffen beside her and glanced curiously from his face to Logan's and back again. Neither of them looked happy.

"What is it?" she heard Graham demand. "Is it the club?"

Somehow, Missy could tell by his tone of voice that he knew the answer to his question would be "no" even before he bothered to ask it.

Logan shook his head. "No. It's Curtis."

Graham swore with a creativity Missy might have admired under other circumstances, but the tension that filled him proved highly distracting. Then tension and a curious sense of foreboding filled her the instant Graham spoke the name of the cousin he'd explained earlier was attempting to take over the pack.

"Curtis again? Well, let him know that I'm not interested in anything he has to say. Unless he's come to admit his involvement in the attack on my mate that happened this morning."

Neither of the men so much as blinked, but Missy flinched as if she'd been struck. It had never occurred to her that Graham's troublesome cousin might be behind her attack. When it had happened, she hadn't had time to think at all, and since Lincoln's rescue she'd been either too shaken up or too asleep to speculate.

It didn't make any sense. Why would Curtis want to hurt Missy? She had no influence over Graham's position as Silverback Alpha. Harming her wouldn't undermine his position. In fact, based on what she had gathered about the general consensus among Lupines when it came to humans, getting rid of Missy might actually improve Graham's standing with the pack.

"You knew that wasn't going to happen," Logan said. "I'm sure he'll crow from the rooftops if his plan to seize control from you succeeds, but right now he knows that admitting his culpability would be a very bad move. So he's pulled something else entirely out of his bag of tricks."

"And what's that?"

"I'm not sure if it qualifies as overconfidence, hubris, or pure stupidity," Logan said, "but I'll admit that it's got balls. Curtis apparently wants to go into that Howl he called with new contenders for your place all lined up. Maybe he thinks that will make his own bid look more appropriate. Either way, he's already spread the word to the pack that Thursday night there will be a matehunt."

Missy heard Graham swear again, something soft and sibilant and extremely vile.

"He can't do that," Graham growled in a tone that would have sent most Navy SEALs running to their mothers. She could practically feel the anger vibrating through him, but she didn't fear it. Some part of her knew that no matter how angry he became, his fury would never be directed at her. "He's already called a Howl against every one of our customs. Now he thinks he can call the matehunt, as well? That little shit needs to be taught a lesson."

"You'll have to teach it at the hunt," Logan said. "The females are already arriving, and from what they tell me, the males who have been out of town are on their way back. There's not much we can do to keep it from happening now."

"Shit."

"Yeah. Pretty much."

There was a momentary silence during which Missy could feel Graham struggling for control. She knew he wanted to chew glass, but she also knew that he realized it wouldn't help. She hated to see him like this. Instinctively she raised the arm she had looped around his back and began to massage his shoulders with slow, soothing motions.

"Okay, so did you come in here just to ruin my day," he finally continued, "or do you have a suggestion for how we should deal with this?"

"I don't think we have much choice but to go along with it. If you call it off, it will look like you couldn't control Curtis well enough to keep him from issuing orders without your consent. And if you let it go but don't participate, you get the same problem, plus the pack will wonder if Curtis has a point and Breeder's Rights should be invoked."

"Translation: I'm fucked coming or going."

"Basically."

"Fine," Graham bit out even as he instinctively leaned back into Missy's stroking fingers. "We'll go ahead with the hunt. I don't see that at this point we really have much choice. I'll just have to make sure I catch the right prize. That should take care of most of Curtis's plans, right?"

"With luck," Logan said. "Anything that's still a concern can be answered at the Howl, I would think."

"Right. Is there anything else you need me for?"

"Why? You have plans?" The beta's question rang with a hint of amusement.

"You could say that, although the damn things have just changed, thanks to persons whose names I won't mention." Graham spoke wryly, his mouth twisting into the semblance of a smile. "Now it looks like I'll be giving lessons in cultural anthropology."

Missy frowned, confused.

"Well, you have fun with that, boss. Things look to be quiet at the club tonight, so I'll do my best to keep the idiot stuff off your desk."

"You couldn't have thought of that fifteen minutes ago?"

Logan just laughed and offered his alpha a salute as he turned and faded back down the hall.

"I think I missed about seven-eighths of that conversation," Missy murmured, her brow furrowed as she scowled up at the man beside her. "Was it supposed to be that way?"

Graham sighed. "Don't worry, baby. Whatever you missed, I can fill you in on now." Missy let him take her hand and tug her over to the sofa. She even sank down onto it without a hint of protest. "What parts didn't you get?"

"Well, they started with Logan having some news for you and ended with something about cultural anthropology. . . ."

He laughed. "You didn't get any of it?"

"No, I got some. At least, I got that your cousin Curtis is not only the one you think attacked me this morning, but he's also committed a serious Lupine faux pas of some kind by arranging a big shindig that you're supposed to be in charge of. Am I close?"

"Close enough. The problem, though, is less that Curtis arranged a couple of things without me and more what he arranged and why."

"Okay, I'm assuming that the way has to do with what you told me the other day, about Curtis wanting to take over leading the pack from you."

"Good assumption. I'm sure that's why he arranged your attack today. He knew that if he could take you out of the picture, it would only boost his own chances to be alpha."

"Why?"

"Because only mated Lupines are supposed to be alpha," he reminded her.

"Yeah, you told me that, but you've been alpha for, like, ten years, and you never had a mate."

"When I first took over, I was only twenty-five. It's not so unheard of for a male that age to be un-mated. Everyone assumed it would happen sooner or later. Unfortunately, I think they were all banking on the sooner."

"But where do I fit into this picture?"

"Right by my side," he told her promptly. "As my mate. Curtis just found out this weekend that I had found a mate. I didn't tell him your name, but it's impossible to keep secrets within the pack. Someone else must have let it slip, and he used it to track you down."

"I still don't understand what he gets out of kid-napping or killing me."

Graham gave her an incredulous look. "He gets to throw me back to being mateless. He gets to take away my woman, cause me intense pain, spoil any chance I had at future happiness, and he gets to step up with one child already as my logical successor."

Missy shook her head. "That makes no sense. Even if I am your mate, getting rid of me only hurts you temporarily. Once you find a new mate, you're back to being alpha and his murderous rampage is all for nothing."

"Have you listened to nothing I've told you about being a Lupine mate?" he demanded, half-laughing in obvious exasperation. "You are my mate. You're a part of me, and not an interchangeable one. We were *Fated* to be together. You think Fate offers a 'just in case' option? It doesn't work like that. You're it for me. You are my mate until the day I die. End of story."

"No," she protested, attempting to scramble off the sofa and away from him. "I'm not that. I can't be that. It's too much pressure. I mean, I was having enough trouble with the idea of being important to you. I can't handle being . . . *vital*."

He grabbed her arms and hauled her back down onto the cushions. "Well, that's too bad for you, because it's already a done deal. And if I were you, I'd work really hard on getting used to it. Otherwise I can't be responsible for what happens on Thursday night."

She opened her mouth for another tirade, but his words stopped her. She eyed him suspiciously. "Why? What happens Thursday night?"

"Was that one of the parts of the conversation you didn't quite get?"

She set her jaw at his sarcastic tone. "Let's say it was so you can feel all nice and superior while you explain it to me again. Then, if I like what I hear, maybe I'll decide to do you a favor and be your mate, in spite of the impossible job demands."

Graham's eyes narrowed, and she could almost

see the struggle for control going on inside him. "If you know what's good for you, you'll admit that we're mated and then you'll try very hard to convince me that you mean it, because that's going to be the only way you're likely to make it out of Thursday night with your dignity and sanity intact. We're going to a matehunt, sweetheart, and if you don't let everyone know you're already taken, you're going to get a lot closer acquainted to a lot more werewolves than just me."

His words made her eyes widen and her muscles stiffen. "What are you talking about? What's a matehunt?"

"A matehunt is what Logan came to tell me about. It's what Cousin Curtis is pulling next," Graham explained, running a weary hand through his hair before leaning forward and resting his elbows on his knees.

For a minute, Missy's compassion almost overwhelmed her uneasiness. He looked exhausted. Normally, he projected such an air of sex appeal and energy that it was easy to forget the kind of pressure he was under. Not only did he have a club to manage and a pack to run; he also had a power-hungry cousin looking to usurp his position, and now an almost-girlfriend who couldn't quite decide if that was what she really wanted to be.

"A matehunt is a traditional way for my kind to form breeding pairs," he explained. His voice was low and ominously rumbling. "It's where all the unmated members of the pack gather in the nearest wooded area, Central Park in our case, and the females get a thirty-second head start."

A head start? Oh, Lord, that did not sound good.

"F-for what?" she stammered, wondering if she really wanted to know the answer.

"For giving them a fighting chance," he replied. "Because after thirty seconds the males shift into their wereforms. And once they're turned loose, they go hunting."

Her eyes opened even wider. Her jaw dropped to her chin, and her breath stopped dead in her throat.

SO not good.

"And do you know what happens when a male catches a female, Missy?" he demanded. His tone was harsh, but underneath she could hear a faint, vibrating purr. Not the way a kitten purrs when it gets its belly rubbed, but the way a lion purrs when it's ripping through the tender belly of its prey.

She shook her head even though she was very much afraid she could guess.

"He takes her."

Missy had been so wrapped up in his words, she hadn't noticed the tension slowly building inside him. She had felt it building in herself, though. She hadn't recognized that as he explained the hunt to her, he might be picturing how it would be if it weren't an abstract concept featuring nameless "male" and "female." How it would be if it were Graham and Melissa and the full moon lighting the forest while he hunted for the other half of himself.

She hadn't realized he might be picturing that because she'd been too busy picturing it herself. Did it make her a big pervert, she wondered, that the idea of this man—and only this man—chasing her through a midnight forest with the sole intention of catching her and claiming her aroused her to an almost unbearable level?

Probably, she concluded.

Darting forward so quickly she couldn't have stopped him if she tried, Graham nipped her earlobe hard enough to sting. Missy yelped and jumped and tried to squirm away, but Graham was too fast. Before the command even traveled from her brain to her legs, he was on her, pushing her back on the sofa and pinning her there, crouching over her like a wolf over its prey.

"We pick the one we want for a mate," he told her, and now the glint in his green-gold eyes made it obvious exactly what he was picturing. Even if Missy hadn't already been picturing the same thing. "We chase her down. And we take her. There's no seduction, no asking what she wants. She knows what she's in for when she decides to run, and once she does, she can't back out. When the males give chase, they're in rut. Their instincts are in control, and there's no werewolf alive who can control his need to mate when he's in rut. If a hunt didn't end in sex, it would end in death. Which do you think is a better choice?"

Missy froze beneath him. The open savagery of what he was describing seemed so foreign, so incomprehensible, to her. It fascinated her even as it frightened her.

"But deaths are rare," he continued, voice harsh, eyes glinting. "They only happen occasionally, when more than one of us want the same woman. Do you know what happens then, Melissa Jane?"

Missy whimpered. He loomed over her until he blocked out the rest of the room, not that she would have been able to focus on anything but him. He filled her senses like air filled her lungs, and she was starting to believe he might be just as vital.

"If she's fast enough, she might run again until another male catches her. But if she's too hurt or too tired to run anymore, or if one of the males who caught her is the one she wants, she just lays there and watches while they fight over her. It's not usually to the death, but you can never tell. Some Lupines are just more . . . aggressive than others."

She trembled, trying not to picture the dark forest, the smell of rich soil and fresh blood, the sound of fangs biting and claws ripping, or growls and screams and the eerie silence of victory.

"Then whoever wins gets to take her again, only by that point, the winner is usually more beast than man, and he's not likely to care about his new mate's pleas for mercy. All he wants is to mate. To claim his woman and show her exactly how male and female were meant to fit together."

Missy swallowed hard, remembering exactly how

she and Graham fit together. If that weren't proof that they had been made for each other, nothing else in heaven or on earth would ever convince her.

"At that point, his beast is in control, not his man, and beasts aren't known to be tender lovers. They're rough and fast and frantic, and they claim her over and over until the sun comes up and dispels the hunt magic from the air. By that time she may or may not be able to walk, but it won't matter, because the winner will have her declared his mate, and he'll have as long as he wants to work off the residual hunt lust. I hear it only takes a week or two. On average."

She closed her eyes and shuddered. A week or two? She'd never make it. Two days had nearly landed her in the hospital, and he was talking weeks?

"Hmm. Was that fear, I wonder? Or arousal?" He nuzzled the tender hollow of her neck and rasped the sensitive skin with his tongue. "I wouldn't blame you for being afraid. Lupines, like wolves, are predators. They live for the hunt, and the only prey they won't go after is the kind that's already been picked clean. The only way to convince a Lupine that the prey isn't worth the chase is if someone else has already taken everything she has to offer."

His tongue licked a damp path across her throat to lave against the bite mark he'd left there. He scraped his teeth over it with exquisite delicacy before he lapped his way up to her ear. He tugged lightly at the plump lobe, swirled his tongue along the outer edge, and breathed quietly inside, "I have a feeling you'd be very sought after. If the hunters thought you were worth the chase."

Missy felt a powerful shudder rip through her, but she kept her eyes on his and spoke softly. "But what happens when a woman already has a mate? Isn't it his responsibility, his duty, to protect her? To make sure that no one else touches her, even if he has to chase her again like he did the first time?"

"Ah, does that mean you can see some advantages to being my mate?"

He smiled down at her and she found she didn't even mind the hint of smugness.

"We really have no choice but to join the hunt on Thursday," he explained, sounding almost as if he regretted it, regretted putting her through it. "Not only would sitting out give Curtis more ammunition for his challenge, but it would be an unforgiveable breach of tradition in the eyes of the pack. The alpha always participates in the hunt, but more important, he traditionally leads it."

"Even if he already has a mate?"

Graham nodded. "Even then. If he has a mate, his Luna leads the females into the forest and then runs for as long as she's in the mood for before she decides to let her alpha catch her again."

"And the alpha only hunts for his own mate?"

"Of course. Wolves mate for life."

Missy took a deep breath and let it out very slowly. "So if we're really mates, then we're in this together. If you run, I run."

Graham nodded. "But if you go as my mate, I can keep you safe."

She pulled a face. "Somehow I think I'd be safest of all if I didn't go in the first place."

"Maybe, but that's not an option," he said. "Not for either one of us."

"I'm not Lupine," she reminded him. "I'm human. Will you be allowed to hunt a human?"

He raised an eyebrow. "Why not? Lupines are predators. We'll hunt anything that runs away."

"And I really have to run from you? Even though I might not really mind so much getting caught?"

He smiled and eased himself down onto the sofa beside her until he no longer loomed menacingly over her. "Even then. Unfortunately, because we haven't made any kind of public announcement yet, I'm not officially mated, which means I have to participate in the hunt. And since you're my mate, you're the one I really want to be hunting."

She closed her eyes and groaned. "Lord! After what you just told me about these hunts, I would have to be completely out of my mind to go wandering out there alone in a park full of horny werewolves. You do understand that, don't you?"

He grinned and kissed her. "Absolutely certifiable."

Missy gazed up at him and sobered. "I need you to understand something for me, though."

"What's that?"

"Even if I am your mate, I'm still human, and the human part of me has a really hard time looking at this hunt thing as anything other than a glorified excuse for rape, so you're going to have to cut me some slack if I never express much enthusiasm for the tradition."

He grimaced. "It's not my favorite, either, and you're not going to hear a lot of regret in my voice when I tell you it's one that's been fading from use over the last few generations. Lupines might be traditional, but we don't live in a vacuum. Our females value their independence as much as the next human woman. Very few of them are much more enamored of the idea of the hunt than you are."

Missy gazed at him thoughtfully. "Does that mean it's something that we—" She stopped and blushed. "I mean, that you could work on changing? Could you relegate it permanently to the past?"

"I'm sure if *we* put our minds to it, *we* could accomplish just about anything."

Her lips curved as she lifted them to meet his. Their mouths fit together like puzzle pieces, clinging together as if shaped one for the other. After a few moments, though, Missy pulled away and snuggled closer against Graham's comforting warming, her head burrowing into his chest.

"What is it, baby girl?" he murmured, stroking the hair tenderly back from her face.

"If I tell you something, will you promise not to think less of me for it?"

Missy lifted her eyes to his and read only bafflement in the clear golden green depths.

"Why would I think less of you, you silly girl?"

"Because right now I'm so scared, I think I might hurl."

Graham heard the wry tone of the words, but he also heard the genuine fear underneath them. All at once, Graham looked down at her and saw not the bright, stubborn, vivid woman he'd come to know over the last few days but the shy and vulnerable wallflower he'd picked up in Dmitri's garden. He wrapped his arms around her and cuddled her close.

"Aw, baby. I'm sorry," he murmured. "I know you're scared, and I wish I could tell you not to be. I didn't mean to make you unhappy. I swear. Shh. . . . It's okay. I promise, it'll be okay. I'd never let anyone hurt you."

She lay rigid in his arms for all of two and a half seconds before she melted into him like sweet vanilla cream. Her arms wrapped around his neck, and she held him close, burying her face in his shoulder and trembling.

"I'm scared," Missy repeated, her voice whisper-soft now and choked with emotion, but at least half of that sounded like anger to him. "But the worst part is that I'm not even sure the matehunt ranks in the top three of my list of fears. In three days, you've managed to turn my entire world upside down."

She raised her head until he could see her expression, and the frustration and anxiety there made him want to kick his own ass for upsetting her. "Friday afternoon I taught a roomful of five-year-olds how to tie their shoes, and today you're telling me I'm going to have to run for my virtue through Central Park tonight, pursued by a pack of werewolves, one of whom thinks I'm his mate. I feel like I just got sucked into an alternate reality, and can't decide if it's based on dreams or nightmares."

Graham reached up and tucked a soft strand of hair behind her ear. "I'm sorry. I should have realized how hard I was pushing. It's not fair to you. I know."

She looked up at him with those big brown eyes, her lush, completely kissable lips trembling, and he cursed himself again, because as much as he regretted frightening her, there wasn't much he could do to make the fear go away. He had as little choice in the hunt as she did, and he'd be damned if he'd give her up in addition to his place in the pack. Those were two things he had no intention of living without. He brushed a kiss across her forehead and cradled her head in his hand, massaging her scalp with his fingertips.

"That's not the worst part, though," she told him solemnly. "The mate thing, the werewolf thing, the hunt thing . . . not one of those is as bone-chillingly terrifying as the idea that you might actually be the man I'm meant to spend my life with."

He frowned down at her, wondering if he could possibly look as baffled as he felt. "But that should make you happy. Why should knowing you've found the right person scare you?"

"Because there are so many ways I could ruin it."

Graham laughed. "Oh, baby, if you think I haven't had the exact same fear every minute of the time since I met you—"

She lifted her head and pulled back—the whole three or four inches he allowed her—to meet his gaze with a scowl. "Damn it, would you stop being all perfect for just a few minutes?"

Graham blinked. "Huh?"

"You have to stop it! You just keep doing and saying the right thing all the time, and it's driving me crazy! Where is the arrogant jerk I first met, the one who thought doing an impression of a bulldozer was the most effective way to win friends and influence people?"

The woman could change her moods so fast, she left him dizzy, Graham decided as the first squeezing knots of a headache began to form behind his eyes. *Shit.* She was actually causing him mental anguish! And this was his mate?

"Just tell me one thing," he groaned.

"What?"

"Was that supposed to make any kind of sense to me at all, because I really feel like that last sentence of yours was broadcast in Swahili and someone forgot to show me where the closed-captioning button is on this remote."

"Now you know how I've felt for the last three days!"

"And how did I confuse you?"

"You're the one who had to go and be a werewolf."

He gave a short bark of laughter. "Yeah, because God knows I did that just to piss you off."

"You know that's not what I meant. It's just this interspecies divide we keep running up against. It makes everything so bloody . . . complicated."

"Welcome to real life."

Missy gave an exhausted sigh and wriggled up into a sitting position.

"I suppose we'll each find some way to adjust," she offered. "I mean if you can try being more reasonable from time to time instead of always barking orders at me, I suppose I can run through the forest on Thursday night and let you chase me down. You know, since it will help save you from your evil, scheming cousin."

"Look on the bright side." He eased into a sitting position next to her and tried to look encouraging. "When I catch you, I'm going to throw you down and make you scream with pleasure."

"Sure, that's what they all say."

He sighed. "I'm sorry you have to go through this. I wish it wasn't a tradition, or I wish it had already become obsolete. But it is what it is, and I can't change it. And unfortunately, given the current situation, non-participation isn't really an option for us."

"Yeah. That's pretty much what I thought."

Graham felt her restlessness even before she stood, pulling out of his arms to cross the room. She stopped in front of the window, turning to stare out at the street outside below them, which annoyed Graham. He wanted to see her face, and it seemed like she was hiding it from him.

"So I guess I'm going to get to see a real-live Lupine matehunt," she mused. "Even if it kills me."

"I won't let anyone hurt you."

When she spoke, her words came so softly that he could barely hear her answer.

"I know."

CHAPTER THIRTEEN

Missy stared at the wall like a lobotomized inpatient and let the conversation drone on around her. The last few days had passed much too quickly, most of them thankfully full of laughter and sex and idle conversations and the kind of getting-to-know-you exercises most couples took months or years to get to. Yet in less than a week Missy felt as if she knew Graham better than she knew any other person in the world, maybe even including herself.

The only dark spot in an otherwise stellar experience had been the occasional feeling she had of being kept prisoner in a particularly luxurious jail cell. Since the attack at her apartment building and the declaration of the matehunt, Graham hadn't allowed her to spend a single minute unprotected. When she wasn't with Graham, he had Logan following her around like a big, furry shadow, and when neither of them was available, Samantha got drafted into guard duty.

Today, Graham and all of his most trusted male pack members were meeting to discuss the Curtis threat and their strategy for the coming matehunt. Half a minute ago, they had dumped Missy in this room full of women she didn't know, with the exception of Graham's secretary, and deserted her, hieing off to their secret clubhouse while she was condemned to endure the seeming equivalent of a werewolf tea party. Never mind that she'd been too dazed to protest, she still planned to blame everything on him.

She felt Samantha's hand tugging at her elbow and looked up at the other woman who had rushed over to greet her, the second Graham had left her at the door.

"Luna," the brunette murmured, urging her to face the crowd that had gathered around them. "Everyone's been waiting to meet you. Can I introduce them to you?"

There she went with that "Luna" thing again, even though Missy still didn't understand how she could be the alpha female when she wasn't even Lupine. Shouldn't they have rules about this kind of thing?

"Sure," she agreed, since she couldn't think of a way to disagree, and let Samantha lead her over to a large, almost throne-like chair and urge her to sit. The symbolism was not lost on her. She looked up at the Lupine who stood at her side like a sentinel and sighed. What the heck had she gotten herself into?

"This is Lucy Fallon," Samantha introduced as a tall, black-haired woman who looked capable of taking on Xena in a fair fight stepped up before the chair and looked down on Missy with an expression of obvious disapproval. "She's a police officer in Alphabet City."

Ah. That explained it. She probably worked the late, late shift, too. The one when all the bodies tended to be found.

"It's nice to meet you," Missy lied. She felt horrendously awkward, unsure if she should be shaking hands or nodding her head or letting people kiss her ring—not that she was wearing one. Instead, she just smiled and hoped this wouldn't take too long.

Lucy stared at her until Missy saw Samantha frown. When the silence stretched for another few seconds, Samantha started to growl, and Missy looked at her in shock. Missy got an even bigger shock when she saw the secretary's lips twist and bare her teeth in a snarl.

"I just introduced you to your Luna," Samantha snapped, her voice sounding a handful of octaves lower than it had just a few seconds ago. "Be careful you don't offend her with your bad manners."

Lucy narrowed her cop's eyes, dark, flat, and vaguely unsettling, and bared her own teeth in a sneer.

"My manners are fine for meeting a human," she hissed without looking away from Missy's face. "It takes more than you calling her by the title to make her my Luna. She's human. The fact that Graham is fucking her does not make her my alpha."

The woman turned her back on Missy and began to stalk away, and it didn't take a Lupine Emily Post to make the reluctant alpha realize she'd just been insulted. Big-time. It didn't matter that she'd never asked to be anyone's Luna. She still wasn't the type to stand back and let herself be insulted.

"You may be right. Sleeping with Graham probably doesn't make me alpha," she agreed, raising her voice so it echoed clearly among the quiet crowd that had gathered to watch the interplay. She waited until Lucy turned back to face her before she finished her statement. "After all, it obviously didn't do much for you."

She knew she'd scored a hit when she saw Lucy's face alternately pale and then fill with bright color. Great. Not only was the woman a cop with an attitude, she had to be a jealous, scorned lover, too? That might just make Missy's day. Still, she'd made her stand, and she couldn't back down now.

Casually she crossed one leg over the other and smoothed an invisible wrinkle in her ill-fitting jeans as if she wore yards of fine-woven silk. "But there's a difference between you and me, Lucy. Graham may have fucked you once upon a time." She flicked her eyes up and down over the woman's tall frame, clearly insinuating that she couldn't understand that piece of Graham's past folly. "But I'm the one he made his mate."

"Bitch!"

If the woman had sprung first and cast aspersions later, she might have been able to knock Missy into another dimension entirely, but as it was, all Lucy managed to do was hit the back of the chair and send it tumbling ass-over-end with herself on top of it. Missy had slid out of the seat before the "b" sound had fully formed on Lucy's lips, and by the time the Lupine realized her prey had escaped, Samantha and another woman had stepped between the would-be combatants and faced Lucy with their teeth bared.

"Back off!" Samantha snarled, and Missy had to blink twice before she convinced herself she was looking at the same brunette she'd accused of being timid earlier that morning. Funny how a little violence could change her opinion about someone.

Climbing to her feet, she dusted her hands off on her butt and peered out from behind two Lupine shoulders, which meant she really couldn't see a darned thing. Wedging her hands between her self-appointed bodyguards, she pried them apart and stepped forward until she could look her attacker in the eye.

"Be careful whom you call a bitch, Lucy," she warned, meeting the other woman's furious gaze with a level one of her own. So what if her knees were knocking on the inside? In this case, appearances were all that mattered. "Only one of us gets furry once a month, and believe me when I say, it ain't me."

Lucy growled and shifted her weight forward. The women standing just behind Missy started to step forward, but Missy held them back with upraised hands. If by some weird twist of fate she really was Graham's mate, she did not plan to spend the rest of her life letting someone else fight her battles and defend her from the big bad she-wolf.

"Let me make this perfectly clear, Lucy," she said, her voice firm despite her inner unease. "The fact that I'm not Lupine has not escaped anyone. Not me and certainly not Graham. If he doesn't mind that I'm human, then it damned sure isn't any of your business. Do you understand?"

"It's my business when he parades you in front of the pack like an equal," the Lupine snarled. "It's my business when you set yourself up as alpha female despite the fact that you couldn't win a tug-of-war with a newborn pup. You're weak, and in our world, a weak leader is a dead leader."

"But I don't have to be as strong as you." Missy held herself tall and steady and dared any one of the women in the room to challenge her, Lucy included. They might be able to kick her butt, but that didn't mean she had any intention of cowering in front of them. "I am the alpha's mate. That makes me alpha whether you like it or not. I don't care if I can't fight you and win, because if you lay one single hand on me, Graham will rip out your intestines and feast on them. So tell me again how I don't deserve to be alpha."

Lucy met her steady gaze for one heartbeat. Two. Three. Then Lucy visibly swallowed a very bitter pill and looked away. Missy felt her knees almost buckle with relief.

"Very good." She nodded, pretending to be confident and self-assured and powerful and a hundred other things she'd never been in her life. "I'm glad to have met you, Lucy. Now get out of my living room before I forget to be a gracious winner."

The other woman stalked out the door like she had a hot poker jammed up her rear, but at least she left. When the door closed behind her, Missy took a very deep breath and let it out on a sigh.

"Well," she said, turning to face Samantha. "That was fun. Why don't you introduce me to everyone else?"

Spending an entire afternoon with a roomful of unmated female werewolves turned out to be one of the most educational experiences of Missy's life. In between some of the most bloodcurdling and frankly terrifying descriptions of sex she'd ever heard, she managed to piece together the story of Lupine mating, matehunts, and being alpha in a much more coherent manner than Graham had been able to manage.

"So he was really serious about that," she said, sitting cross-legged on the floor beside the empty pizza boxes. It was now around dusk and she'd been "chatting with the girls" for most of the afternoon. "If Graham hadn't taken a mate, his cousin could honestly force him to step down from being alpha? Just because he didn't have a mate and pups? Isn't that a little insane?"

Annie, the woman who had formed the other half

of Missy's Lupine shield against Lucy, shrugged. "It's tradition. That's just sort of the way things work."

"Yeah, but that doesn't make it less insane."

"Well, you've got to realize that things weren't always so easy for Lupines as they are now," Samantha explained. "Now we're integrated into the rest of the world, even if we're still a great big secret. But a few hundred years ago, people used to burn us at the stake for being disciples of Satan."

"I thought stake burning was for witches."

"A fallacy, actually, since most witches were hung. Werewolves got burned. Or beheaded. Or shot with silver bullets, once gunpowder made its debut."

"Yay." Missy grimaced.

"Exactly." Annie nodded. "So you can see how making sure that each pack would have a successive generation to keep us from dying out became a pretty high priority. We might really be just legends, if it hadn't been for Breeder's Rights."

Missy guessed that was true, but she wasn't quite sure why it still applied in the twenty-first century. And she really wasn't sure why it applied to a human. She swirled her glass of soda and watched the ice cubes circle like racers on a NASCAR track.

"Do Breeder's Rights apply in this case?" she asked as she raised her head to meet Samantha's eyes. "I mean, no matter what Graham may say about me being his mate, it can't really be true. Can it?"

Annie looked slightly aghast. "Of course it's true! Lupines don't lie about mating. The bond is sacred."

"I didn't mean I thought Graham was lying," Missy soothed. "Just that he might be a little . . . confused. I mean, he's Lupine, but I'm not. I'm human. I don't even know if we're . . . compatible in the way he's hoping for. Are Lupines and humans the same species? Can we even have babies together?"

"Of course," Annie said. "Lupines and humans are related in much the same way as wolves and domestic dogs. They are biologically a different species; however, they share an identical number of chromosomes and such a large statistical percentage of mitochondrial DNA that they can and do mate and produce reproductively viable offspring. In fact, empirical evidence would seem to support the hypothesis that the offspring of a Lupine-human union may even have a more vigorous reproductive system than either of its respective parents, due to the introduction of new and varied forms of DNA into the genetic pool."

Missy blinked. "Oh."

Samantha leaned forward to murmur an explanation. "Annie is a biology professor at NYU. Genetic research."

Missy repeated, "Oh."

Sure she was. Why not? Why put limits on the surrealism that was fast coming to encompass Missy's life?

"Then you're saying that Graham could get me pregnant?"

Annie shrugged. "Sure."

"Has that happened before? I mean, are there lots of little hu-pines running around?"

Samantha grinned. "Not so much. I think Annie was giving you the theoretical data, not a case study. There are stories about it happening in the past, but I've never met anyone who was mated to a human. It's supposed to be a trip, though. The stories say that some of the pup's talents can leak into the mother. She can sort of borrow the quicker reflexes and better night-vision thing while she's pregnant. Isn't that wild?"

Missy's eyes widened. "Yeah, wild."

"Mind you, it's just conjecture," Annie said, "but due to the physical connection between mother and pup, it does make a sort of logical sense."

The repetitive use of the word "pup" leached the color out of Missy's face faster than the flu. "Would I have . . . puppies?"

Anne saw Samantha's grin and raised her a chuckle. "No, so you can calm down. Lupine pups look just like human babies. Shifting is something we have to learn how to do. Some precocious pups learn it as early as seven or eight, but most come into their abilities around puberty."

Relief made Missy sag against the legs of the armchair she'd been leaning on. "Okay. That's slightly less terrifying. Mind you, only slightly, because, hello? Horny teenagers are hard enough to

deal with, but a horny teenager who can turn him-
or herself into a werewolf?" She shuddered. "But
I'll take what I can get."

Samantha looked at her as if Missy had just
handed her the key to the city. "So you're okay with
it then? You don't mind being Graham's mate? You
don't mind having babies and staying with the
pack?"

When she put it that way, the speech made Missy
shift uncomfortably, so she hedged. "Well, I'm not
running away screaming, am I?"

"I think there's a bit of middle ground between
running away screaming and living happily ever after with our alpha."

Annie gave Missy a stern glance.

Missy squirmed. "Give me a break here. This is
a lot to adjust to, you know. Before last Friday, I
didn't even know Graham wanted to take me out
to dinner, let alone that he was going to pull this
mate thing on me. I need some time to get used to
this."

"You've got about three more hours." Samantha
glanced at the clock and back at Missy. "You might
want to hurry it up." The reminder of the time and
the hunt that would take place later that evening
made the knots in Missy's stomach pull tight.

"Yeah, right. The matehunt. About that . . ."

Samantha crossed her arms over her chest and
looked at Missy. "What about it?"

Fidgets overcame her, and Missy sighed. How
was she supposed to explain to someone who had

grown up with Lupine culture that the idea of being chased through the dark of Central Park by a pack of aroused werewolves didn't exactly get her juices flowing? In fact, it froze them as solid as a glacial crust.

"Look, I know this is a tradition for Lupines, but it's really not something I can even conceive of. I mean, the whole idea is half a step from terrifying. And by that, I mean half a step *more* than terrifying."

Annie nodded. "I'm sure it is, for a human. I mean, you're a woman to begin with, which makes you by definition weaker than a male, and then when you add the fact that you're human to the equation and our men are easily ten or twenty times stronger than a non-Lupine—"

Missy groaned and buried her face in her hands.

"Annie," Samantha snapped. "You are not helping."

The scientist blushed like a teenager. "Oops. Sorry."

"Luna, you have nothing to be afraid of. Our alpha will protect you. You'll never be in danger. There is no chance of one of the other males catching you. Graham would kill them before they touched you."

Somehow, Missy's nerves demanded a little more soothing than the other woman's hand patting her knee. "And what if something goes wrong? What if Graham gets hurt or distracted? What happens then?"

"It won't happen," Samantha repeated. "The alpha will not allow it."

Missy's laugh strangled on her frustration. "I don't think Fate particularly cares what Graham will 'allow.' Luck isn't something that's going to show its belly just because Graham plays big bad wolf."

Samantha blinked at that. Her brows furrowed, and she looked over at Annie, confusion plainly written on her face. Missy just shook her head to realize that these women honestly couldn't fathom the idea of a person, a being, or an idea that wouldn't bow its head before the Silverback Alpha.

Annie shrugged, as if to indicate she didn't know what the Luna was yammering on about, either, and turned back to Missy.

"But Luna," she explained, with the slow deliberation math teachers used when dealing with dense seven-year-olds, "the alpha will protect you. You just have to trust him."

Trust a man whose sanity she was beginning to doubt?

"Sure," Missy muttered. "Right. No problem."

CHAPTER FOURTEEN

Missy hurried across the street and kept her ass to the wall until Graham put a hand at her back to push her forward.

"Come on," he growled. "We're running late. The hunt will start any minute."

"Well, excuse me for trying not to flash the whole island," she muttered, letting him herd her down the empty path into the quiet park. "This outfit you gave me to wear is ridiculous."

"It offers ease of movement. Did you want to be running from the pack in heels and a miniskirt?"

"How much worse could that be than skintight spandex and biker boots?" Missy griped. "I feel like a cross between a Hell's Angel and a go-go dancer. What's wrong with jeans and a good pair of sneakers?"

"They don't give me nearly as good a view of your ass." He punctuated his comment with a theatrical leer and a light smack to her bottom. It wasn't enough to make her flinch, but when his hand lingered to cup and squeeze, she did shoot him a dirty look.

"Why am I not surprised that's the real answer?"

Graham grinned and continued to lead them deeper into the park while Missy tried to ignore the nervous fluttering in her stomach. She would have called it butterflies except that the damned things were breeding like rabbits, and no matter what clever pop psychology technique she used to try to calm them down, nothing worked. In the end, she just had to grit her teeth and bear it. After a few minutes, Graham led the way off the path altogether and pulled her through the trees into a thickly wooded area.

About the only thing she could see in the pitch-blackness was the glowing light of his eyes, and those didn't quite cast enough of a glare to light her path. She had to resort to clinging to Graham's side and stepping very carefully to avoid tripping over roots and rocks. For his part, Graham steadied her when she needed it, but he pushed her relentlessly forward all the while. She felt a little like the helpless blonde in a B movie, which didn't do much for her mood.

"Where the heck does this hunt happen?" she demanded after another ten minutes of scrambling over boulders and between tree trunks. She hadn't known there were this many trees on Manhattan, let alone that Graham would expect her to climb over them all. "We must be practically in Albany by now."

"Sh! Look."

Mr. Monosyllabic pointed through the next stretch of trees and urged Missy in that direction. At first she thought it was another werewolf thing, but after a couple of blinks and some furious staring, she thought she could make out a cluster of orange firelights in the distance.

"Is that it?"

Graham nodded and nudged her forward. "And they're almost ready to start. Hurry."

She decided not to mention she'd been hurrying for the last hour, ever since Graham pounded on the door to the bathroom where she'd been dressing and told her to move her sexy ass. Those were his words, not hers, and they'd been the only things to stop her from slamming the door on his toes. He did seem rather fond of her behind, after all, and Missy could appreciate a man with good taste.

As they strode forward and the trees began to thin in preparation for a clearing, Missy could make out the glow of some sort of lamps and a big ol' bonfire about thirty feet ahead of them. It was a wonder the FDNY hadn't swarmed all over the Lupines like bees at a flower show. When she and Graham got close to the tree line, he tugged her to a halt.

"Remember what we talked about?" he asked, his eyes green and glowing in his serious face.

"Of course." How could she have forgotten? Her "mate" had lectured her on the finer points of her behavior tonight for at least forty-five minutes. "I stay close to you and keep Samantha and Annie nearby just in case. I keep still until the hunt starts and don't stare directly into anyone's eyes but don't look down, either, or they'll think I'm submissive. Don't crowd anyone too close, and don't get offended if someone tries to sniff me. Remember that the wolves are people, too, and I should keep my mouth shut unless I have something of earth-shattering importance to relate. Oh, and when the hunt starts, I should run like hell directly north."

She finished the litany with her hands crossed primly in front of her and her eyebrows hovering somewhere around her hairline.

Graham stared at her for a few seconds, then gave a curt nod. "Good enough," he growled. "Let's go."

He tugged her wrist so hard she almost went flying. He muttered an apology, but Missy couldn't be sure how much attention he paid to it, since he never bothered to slow down.

As they got closer to the pack gathering, she could feel a new sort of tense energy building inside him. Every step seemed to make him wilder, more feral, less civilized. His body temperature shot up until the touch of his bare hand on her arm felt like a heating pad had been laid directly on her skin. It was bearable but decidedly hot. She shivered.

When they stepped out of the concealing shadows of the woods, she fought to keep that shiver from turning to a shudder. Everywhere she looked, the clearing was filled with werewolves, more Lupines than she had ever thought she'd see. The animal forms ranged in size and color from small, red-gray wolves the size of coyotes to some big, black monsters she swore were the size of Shetland ponies. Luckily for her nerves, not everyone was in wolf form.

Normal, human-looking pack members milled about the clearing or stood in groups, talking in a disconcerting mix of words and growls, yips and snarls. This went beyond *Twilight Zone* and straight to the Sci Fi Channel, especially when a small group stepped out of the tree line on the other side of the large bonfire. Missy had to blink three times before her eyes agreed to filter what she was seeing to her brain, which only grudgingly translated it into understandable terms.

These guys were werewolves.

Real werewolves. Not just Lupines, who looked like humans and could even behave like them when the situation warranted. Not even Lupines in wolf form, who looked like they could step right into an Animal Planet special and make themselves at home. These werewolves were about as hairy as wolf forms, but the resemblance ended there.

Four of them traveled in their own small pack, each walking on two legs that bent in the wrong direction. Their knees arched out behind them, making them look permanently coiled and ready to spring. Missy couldn't tell their colors until they stepped close enough to the bonfire for the flames to illuminate their fur, and then she was almost sorry they had.

One had a coat the mottled char gray color of wood ash that faded to dirty gray-white on his chest and belly. Fascinated, she followed the color changes until the fur shortened to a plush, velvety-looking pelt that covered but couldn't conceal the lycanthrope's heavy and very human genitalia. Her eyes shot back to his—he was very definitely male—face and stayed there, and she made darn sure not to look lower than the sternum on any of his friends.

Two of the others had the red-gray, coyote color she'd already noticed looked most common among the wolf forms present, and the last werewolf sported a light brown pelt flecked with black and gray, like the brindled greyhound Missy's downstairs neighbor had rescued from a racetrack last year. Judging by the snarl that curled the brown lycanthrope's muzzle, though, she doubted he had much in common with the friendly and mild-mannered Turtle.

Missy opened her mouth to ask a question but snapped it shut again when Graham dropped his grip on her arm and stepped forward out of the shadows that concealed them. Surprised, she scrambled after him. No way did she plan to be alone in this clearing, thank you very much.

Still looking more like a *GQ* cover model than the Terror of Central Park, Graham strode across the carpet of moss and leaves and into the bonfire light. Hurrying to keep pace with his ground-eating stride, Missy followed until he stopped near the same pile of jumbled boulders where the were-wolves had paused.

"Curtis," she heard him growl.

The brown lycanthrope stepped forward, and Missy got her first close-up view of a Lupine in wereform. He was covered from head to foot in a coat of coarse, thick fur, though it seemed to grow thicker at his back, neck, and upper chest, like the ruff of a real wolf. And as she'd noted on the gray werewolf, it shortened to a velvety pile on Curtis's abdomen and stomach. She made a point of skirting away from looking at his sex and moved right along to areas less likely to freak her out.

He stood upright like a man, but his legs were the hind legs of an enormous wolf, with feet like a dog's paws, only a whole lot bigger. His arms were long and thickly muscled, with vaguely human hands that were tipped with lethal, curving claws. His head looked almost completely canine, with neat triangular ears and a long, pointed muzzle full of razor-sharp teeth. Missy couldn't vouch for the sharpness of those teeth, but she decided to go with her instincts on that one. They certainly looked razor sharp.

She stood beside Graham, kept about a half step behind him, and decided she really didn't need to be any closer to any of the lycanthropes. Her view was fine from right where she was. In fact, it might be better from Nebraska. She stifled the urge to go see.

"You're being very impolite, Cousin," Graham

said, his voice low and rough and so menacing, Missy shivered even though he wasn't talking to her.

The brown lycanthrope swung his head in their direction and snarled. Muscles clenched to keep from recoiling; Missy blinked and almost missed the most amazing thing she'd ever seen. One minute she stood looking at the lycanthrope Graham called Cousin, and the next, reality shifted, leaving behind a man where the werewolf had been. The man had hair the same brindled-brown color of the werewolf's fur and eyes the same yellow-gold.

He also stood there stark naked.

"Not impolite," the lycanthrope said with a sneer, "just impatient. It's been too long since the last hunt."

"Hunts are a dying tradition. Our females seem to prefer to choose their mates in a more modern fashion."

"A more human fashion. I, for one, hardly call that progress."

"But then, it isn't your call to make."

Missy kept one ear on the conversation—if you could call their verbal sparring match a conversation—but both her eyes were locked on the other three lycanthropes. As she watched, that same shift happened. The three forms blurred around the edges. Their features and outlines faded and became indistinct.

She saw movement and a sort of rippling wave, and then everything came back into focus and the werewolves were suddenly men. Naked men. The transformation had her so fascinated, she barely stopped herself from demanding they do it again.

"If you don't want to lead our pack in the ways of our people, then don't be surprised if someone else does, Cousin," Curtis snapped, pulling Missy's attention back to the matter before her.

She heard the growl before she felt the movement and well before she saw anything, because there really wasn't anything to see. It all happened so fast, she doubted film could have caught it, but suddenly Graham wasn't just growling at his cousin; he had his hand wrapped around Curtis's throat while the other man's toes dangled three inches off the ground. Instead of shouting or struggling, Curtis laughed.

"I haven't challenged you," he pointed out, his voice hoarse and rasping but clear. "It wouldn't do much for your reputation if the Silverback Alpha killed a member of his own pack without provocation, would it?"

Missy saw Graham's jaw clench and saw the first hint of fang flash between his lips when he spoke.

"Oh, I've been provoked," he snarled, "and I know just who's behind it all, too. Did you think I wouldn't notice a gamma in my own pack calling a Howl in the Silverback name? Did you think I wouldn't care about an unscheduled and unauthorized matehunt in the middle of my territory?" Graham tossed his cousin aside as if touching the other man's skin had contaminated him. "I am still alpha of this clan, Cousin, and I know precisely what you're trying to do."

Curtis landed on his feet in a coiled crouch and sneered up at his clearly stronger cousin. "You may know, but you can't stop me," he taunted. "Not unless you can produce a cub before next week, Cousin. I thought I was doing you a favor. After all, if you can manage to catch a female tonight, you have an entire week to hope she comes into heat so you can fuck her for that pup you need so badly."

Missy snarled this time, before Graham even got the chance. She wasn't sure where the sound came from, just that it ripped out from between her lips as she took an instinctual step forward.

Curtis's head snapped around, his feral yellow eyes fixing on Missy and narrowing to menacing slits.

"Well, what have we here?" he growled, taking a prowling step toward her. "What's this, Cousin? Some new prey for us? She's pretty enough, in that totally ordinary way some women have, but she smells . . . human." His mouth twisted, and he reached for her but touched only air.

Graham leapt in front of Missy, forcing her back a few steps and facing his cousin with his lip curled and his fang-like teeth bared.

"Stay the fuck away from her," he ordered. "She's mine."

"Yours?"

Missy watched Curtis's expression twist and contort as if he'd scented something foul, and her own eyes narrowed.

The Lupine took a step toward her, and Graham snapped at him.

"Stay away," he commanded, his eyes flashing hot and angry in the near darkness. "I don't want you anywhere near her."

Curtis offered them a look of wounded innocence so insincere it appeared plastic. "But I don't mean anyone any harm, Cousin. I'm simply curious. It's not often a human is offered up to us on one of our hunts. I do hope she doesn't get too badly hurt. Some of our males can get a bit . . . rough, in all the excitement." He bared his teeth, but no one watching could have called it a smile. "I'd hate to see her pretty skin torn off."

"No one will touch her."

"Ah-ah. Now who's being rude?" Curtis chided. "You know the terms of the hunt as well as I do. She belongs to whoever is strong enough and fast enough to catch her."

Missy opened her mouth for a truly unladylike retort, but her attention strayed when a wave of excitement so intense even she could feel it rippled through the crowd. Samantha and Annie appeared on either side of her, each clad in a Cooper Union sweatshirt, comfortable jeans, and tennis shoes. Missy shot Graham a dirty look.

"The moon is almost up," Annie said. "When it breaks over the tree line, the hunt will be on."

"Stay close," Samantha murmured, leaning down a little to speak directly into Missy's ear. "That rat, Curtis, has something planned. I can feel it."

"I believe you. Trust me. I'm not about to go wandering off by myself. I promise."

Missy eyed Curtis suspiciously while he and Graham continued to snarl at each other, even though she no longer understood a word either one said. They'd gone from English to Lupine and now communicated with grunts, growls, snarls, yips, and barks. Samantha and Annie seemed to know what they were saying, but neither one bothered to fill Missy in. She couldn't decide whether or not she minded.

"I see he's got Larry, Moe, and Curly with him," Annie said, her disdain clear as she nodded at the three Lupines who had accompanied Curtis.

"Greg, Marco, and Paul," Samantha clarified, her eyes also fixing scornfully on the trio. "They're Curtis's right-hand idiots."

"Um, I think idiot number three heard that," Missy said as the man pointed them out to his friends. He detached himself from the small group and swaggered toward the women.

"And what are you supposed to be?" Paul sneered. "The human's bodyguards?"

In human form, he stood maybe five-ten, with an indifferent physique and strawberry blonde hair. Missy remembered his wereform had been at least six inches taller and about a hundred pounds of muscle more imposing. She raked a deliberately dismissive glance up and down his frame, pausing to give an extra sneer at his unimpressive, semi-erect cock. He snarled.

"She needs very little guarding," Samantha retorted. "Alpha keeps one eye on her all the time. And he hates to see worthless little pups annoying her."

"You shouldn't antagonize me, Samantha. It's a hunt night," he snarled. "It's bad strategy to piss off one of our males. He might decide to catch you and make you pay."

"You couldn't catch me with a baited hook," Samantha scoffed. "And you couldn't take me if you did. I'm beta female in this pack, Paul. I would never let myself be mated to a little gamma nothing like you."

Paul didn't appreciate that remark, and he demonstrated his feelings by springing full force across the ten feet separating them and attempting to drag Samantha to the ground beneath him. Missy jumped out of the way, and fortunately Samantha was quick enough to do the same. She spun neatly out of reach and snickered when Paul grabbed air and tumbled to the hard-packed ground.

"You see what I mean?" Samantha taunted, sneering down at the fallen male. "You're pathetic. Beneath me. I think even less of you than I do of your boss, and I think he's a worthless little nothing who disgraces the name of the pack. Don't think I'll ever let you touch me, because it's never going to happen."

The look of rage that contorted his face made Missy fear she was about to witness bloodshed, but before the fallen Lupine's muscles could do more than shift and bunch, a sharp command cut through the tension.

"Melissa. Come here. Now." Graham's hard tone matched his stony expression, but Missy quickly thought better of arguing.

In any other circumstances, she might have objected to the ring of dominance in his voice, but these circumstances fell far short of ordinary. She had stepped into his world the minute she followed him into the Ramble, and for the moment she had to live by his rules.

The rationalization worked long enough for her to hurry back to his side like an obedient little mate. She halted next to him and looked up at his granite profile. He didn't bother to look down, but she knew he was aware of where she stood, down to the very inch. His eyes remained on his cousin.

"She seems quite obedient," Curtis said in a tone of voice that made Missy's teeth clench and her knuckles itch to make contact with that snarky smile. "I wonder if she'll respond so quickly when I order her to spread her legs once I catch her."

Disgust spoke for Missy, because her common sense had obviously taken a vacation.

"I don't think that will be possible," she replied, letting her expression telegraph how loathsome she found him. "I find it's hard to come running when I'm doubled over vomiting at the thought of you touching me."

Curtis's arm twitched, as if it longed to strike

out at her, but Graham's menacing presence and warning growl kept him in check.

"I told you, you will never touch her. I'll kill you before you lay a single finger on her. She is my mate, and she will run to no one but me."

"Mate?" Curtis's question hissed out, soft and sibilant and full of icy rage. "She's no fit mate for one of the pack. She's human. They aren't worth the bite of our teeth."

A slow smile spread across Graham's chiseled mouth, making him look wicked and smug and too sexy for Missy's own good. Even in the midst of their dicey situation, just watching that little grin curve his lips made her want him. She tried to ignore the spark of lust, but it got tougher when she felt an answering surge of heat rush through him and saw his glowing green eyes light with that particular heat she recognized all too well. The intensely primitive animal energy she'd recognized coursing through the crowd had been building, winding tighter with each passing moment, and now, it seemed, even Graham couldn't contain the effect it had on him.

She shivered and forced her gaze away from his face so she could focus on the pack, but he trashed that idea by sliding a hot, rough hand around her waist to rest over her barely rounded tummy.

"Oh, I think this one is worth a lot," he finally said, replying to Curtis's taunt in a way that made the other man's eyes narrow. Graham rubbed his palm in slow, soft circles over Missy's stomach, and his gaze never wavered from his cousin's. "In fact, I'd say she's priceless, now that the next Silverback Alpha grows fast and strong inside her. Congratulate me, Curtis. Missy is going to make me a daddy."

If Curtis's expression displayed a sort of abject and angry shock, Missy figured her own wasn't too dissimilar. Did Graham mean what she thought he meant? Had he just told his cousin that she was pregnant? That she was even now carrying a little werewolf?

He had to be out of his mind! She couldn't be pregnant. And even if she was, the embryo would have to be less than one week old, and no one could know something like that so soon, so Graham had to be using the lie to taunt his already furious cousin.

"You lie!" Curtis hissed at them, sounding more like a reptile than a Lupine, but Missy felt inclined to agree with his accusation.

Not that she intended to contradict Graham in front of him. Whatever game the man was playing, he knew a lot more about it than she did, so she would cheerfully go along with whatever he said. She could rip him a new asshole later. When she wasn't facing a forest full of strange werewolves.

"Do I?" Graham drawled.

"It's a trick! A trick to buy yourself time, but you won't be able to lie to the Council. They'll know whether or not you really bred her—"

"I don't need to lie, Curtis. And if you weren't so blinded by greed and ambition, you'd realize I'm telling the truth."

Missy thought the man's head might explode, his rage was so blatant and so intense. She watched as his eyes narrowed to angry slits and his muscles tensed and his nostrils flared, and he turned that rage onto her.

"You bitch," he growled, his body coiling into a tight spring as he took the first threatening step toward her. "You think you can come into the middle of my pack and ruin all my plans? I'll rip that brat right out of your fucking stomach!"

Curtis lunged toward her, but Graham was faster. He picked her up around the waist and swung her out of the way, blocking his cousin's charge with his own body. Missy felt the shock wave of impact ripple through his muscles and into hers, but he held on long enough to get her out of Curtis's range. By the time he set her aside, Samantha and Annie had raced over, and he handed her to them.

"Keep her safe," he growled, and before her eyes, he began to change.

Missy watched, torn between awe and fear, while her lover began to transform from a normal, human-looking man to something much, much more dangerous. In a matter of seconds, his muscles and tendons stretched and reshaped themselves, growing larger, denser, harder, where they covered his elongated bones. He went from an intimidatingly large man to a terrifyingly huge beast.

In his wereform, Graham stood at least seven feet tall, every inch thick and ripped with muscle. His thighs looked as powerful as a Mack Truck, and his shoulders could have blocked out the sun. Thick, plush fur grew to cover his body, a dark, rich shade of chocolate black that faded to toffee on his belly and groin and bore a light frosting of silvery gray directly between his shoulder blades. Only his eyes looked familiar, even in the wolfish face with its long muzzle and sharp, jagged teeth. She saw those eyes fix on her, and she swallowed, instinctively taking a step backward.

He held her gaze and stepped toward her. "Don't be afraid of me. I would never hurt you, my mate."

Mate. The word had sounded weird and exotic when he'd used it before. Now it seemed almost frightening. Even though she'd known he was a werewolf from the first moment she'd met him, she'd never really known it before. Not until now. This instant, when he loomed before her looking like a creature from her nightmares and sounding like the man she loved.

It took several deep breaths and a whole lot of mental affirmations, but Missy finally squared her shoulders and stopped backing away from him.

"I'm not afraid," she lied, hoping no one would look too closely at her trembling knees and call her bluff. "I have no fear of my mate, or of any other member of his clan. The Luna of the Silverback Clan doesn't need to be afraid."

"Bitch!"

Graham spun around and threw himself in front of his mate just in time to foil Curtis's next attack. This time Missy got to see a transformation at high speed, because Curtis shifted even as he jumped. By the time he and Graham met, there in a tangle of fur, teeth, and rending claws, both were in were-form and neither had any intention of giving in.

The moon stopped them.

Before teeth could tear and claws could shred, a low, haunting noise filled the clearing and launched itself into the crystalline night sky. One lone wolf sounded the howl and everything else in the woods fell into silence. Even Graham and Curtis froze, turning as one with the rest of the pack to watch the bright, silver crescent slowly rise over the tree-tops like dawn over the eastern ocean.

"It's almost time," Samantha spoke into her ear, but when Missy turned to look at her, she saw the Lupine's eyes glued to the luminous night sky. "Be ready. When the moon is up and the howler goes quiet, run."

The woman's soft words made Missy's stomach clench, and she gritted her teeth against a wave of panic.

"I don't know if I can do this," she whispered. "I don't know if I can."

"You are Luna. You can do anything you need to do. And you need to do this."

The Lupine's words ended as the last quivering note of the howl died and the moon broke free of its woody veil. A single heartbeat of silence followed, and then the woods exploded in a fiery blaze of excitement.

Hard hands shoved against Missy's back as her

two Lupine guards leapt forward, propelling her along ahead of them.

"Run!"

And the hunt was on.

CHAPTER FIFTEEN

Her boots pounded against the hard earth of the forest floor as she ran to the north for all she was worth. Adrenaline drove her forward with Samantha and Annie bounding along, one at each side. They pushed hard through the dense brush, and Missy charged forward, ignoring the sharp sting of thin branches snapping against her and cutting into her exposed skin. She had never been much of a runner, and now she wished she'd run track in high school. The experience could have come in real handy.

"They're following us!" Annie shouted so they could hear her over the pounding of footsteps and the crunch of debris under their shoes. "Curtis's goons. They must be after Missy!"

"Tough shit! They can't have her!" Samantha crowded closer and Annie followed suit until Missy felt caged in by them. In these circumstances, being caged didn't seem like a bad thing.

I feel like I'm in an old episode of The Fugitive *or something,* Missy thought, feeling her legs already begin to deaden and become heavy from the unaccustomed demands she placed on them. *Only I'm even less anxious to be caught than Richard Kimble ever was. He didn't have sex-crazed werewolves after him!*

"Left!" Annie shouted, and veered in that direction, forcing Missy to follow. She saw why when a dark figure crashed out of the trees just a few feet from their path and sped toward them. "Sam, they planned this! It's a goddamned ambush!"

Samantha growled a response and darted in front of the approaching figure to cut him off. The ash-colored lycanthrope roared his displeasure and backhanded the brunette with enough force to send her flying several feet. Her head struck a tree trunk, and she slid to the ground in a heap. Greg, the gray werewolf, turned back to Missy and leapt forward.

"Come on! Faster!" Annie braced her shoulder against Missy's back as if she could force the human into even greater speed, but Missy's limited energy was already failing her.

"I can't!" she gasped, every breath painful as it rasped in and out of her abused lungs. They felt like they were on fire, burning from the inside out.

"You don't have a choice!"

Well, since she put it that way . . .

Missy tucked her chin to her chest and tapped into a store of energy she didn't know she had. A fresh surge of adrenaline spun her pumping legs even faster as she and Annie struggled to escape. Even with Missy's eyes resolutely trained on the ground in front of her, dimly lit by the heavy moon overhead, she could see Annie racing a few steps in front of her. The Lupine kept glancing back, a look of concern and unease on her face, and Missy knew the other woman was holding back for Missy's sake.

Without the human to worry about, Annie probably could have been at the state line by this point, but she kept her pace deliberately slow so she could stay close. If Missy didn't already feel like the most pathetic excuse for a Luna ever invented, this cinched it. She was so not cut out for this.

She figured that was pretty obvious a nanosecond later when she shrieked like a little girl. She had a good reason—what normal person wouldn't shriek to see a 250-pound werewolf jumping out of the trees at them?—but in present company she still felt like a scared little girl.

"Annie!" she shouted for her remaining body guard, and darted left just in time to evade a huge, grasping hand. "Annie!"

The woman was by her side so fast Missy barely saw her move. All Missy saw was a blur of cotton and denim, and then her attacker stumbled backward under the force of Annie's body weight slamming into his chest.

"Missy, run!"

Her head whipped around, and she saw the reason for Annie's cry. A familiar brindled brown form wove through the trees as it loped toward her with a frighteningly long stride. It was Curtis, and he was making a beeline for Missy. Spinning like a top, she threw herself forward again and ran as if her life depended on it. At this point, it probably did.

Her boots pounded against the uneven ground and her heart pounded against her rib cage, but she could feel Curtis gaining on her. She wasn't enough of a twit to look behind her so she could fall over a log like a horror movie scream queen, but she also knew she wasn't going to be able to outrun him. She was a five-foot, three-inch human, and he was a six-foot, seven-inch werewolf with the stamina of a freight train. All she could do was hope she could evade him until Annie or Graham or Samantha came to her rescue. Feminist though Missy was, the idea of rescue sounded more like a blessing than an insult.

"Bitch!"

When she heard Curtis's voice close enough behind her to whisper that kind of sweet nothing in her ear, she screamed—horror movie clichés be damned—and dodged sideways. Curtis moved faster.

He caught her by the arm and spun her around forcefully. His glowing yellow eyes sent distaste crawling through her, and the expression in them didn't do much to set her at ease. Hate radiated off him, so intense she could almost see it distort the air between them like heat waves. She saw his eyes narrow as his lip curled in a snarl. His mouth was open, tongue lolling out as he panted from his run and from his struggle with Graham. She didn't know how Curtis had gotten away, unless he'd bolted while Graham was distracted by the moonrise, but it didn't much matter how he'd gotten away, just that he had and that he'd come after her.

She recoiled when he leaned closer, but he followed the motion, his wolfish muzzle pressing close and scenting the air around her. She heard the quick sniffs as he drew in her scent, felt the rush of air against her skin when he pressed his snout close up against her neck and drew deeply. She gritted her teeth against the urge to scream and jerked her head away.

"Bitch," he growled again, rearing back just enough to meet her eyes with his own. "My cousin didn't lie about it. He did get himself a cub, on you. A filthy human."

He held her with one powerful paw/hand gripping each of her arms just above the elbow, but her instincts wouldn't allow Missy to stand still. She squirmed and struggled and tried not to think about the incongruity of watching that canine mouth move and hearing human sounds issue from it. She also tried not to think about what it meant that her scent had convinced Curtis she really was pregnant.

"He would shame our kind by letting a half-breed grow up to lead our pack!" Curtis ranted, shaking her in his fury. "Allowing human blood to taint the Silverback line. Well, I won't have it. I'll cut that brat from your belly before I let it play alpha over me!"

Missy snapped. She literally felt something give way inside her, and she knew she carried a child. She also knew she would kill anyone or anything who tried to harm him. Growling a pretty fierce sound of her own, she brought her booted foot down hard on Curtis's bare one, then followed it with a quick knee to the groin.

Unprepared for a struggle from the "pathetic human," he took the blow square to the balls, and his grip loosened. Doubled over in pain, he made the perfect target when Missy linked her hands into one giant fist and brought it down hard at the base of his skull. It would have felled a human, but in wereform the heavy ruff and thick muscle protected him, and Curtis remained standing, bent at the waist while he struggled for breath. Ripping free of his loosened grasp, Missy ran again and just hoped she was still heading north like Graham had ordered her to do.

An angry howl told her Curtis wouldn't be down for long, and she dug deep for the last of her reserve strength. She found it in her belly, where the baby she now knew she carried rested, tiny and warm inside her. Thinking of nothing else but protecting him so that she could flay the skin off his father's back when she saw him again, she fled deeper into the forest.

If she hadn't been running for her life, she might have taken time to wonder about how she saw so clearly in the heavy darkness, but she really had other things on her mind, like listening to her back trail for the sounds of Curtis's pursuit.

She concentrated so hard on what was behind her that she didn't see what was in front of her until she ran headfirst into it.

Missy bounced off something hard, resilient, and thick with soft, plush fur. She backpedaled quickly and looked up—way, way up—into Graham's wolfish features.

He stared down at her with the same eyes she'd come to recognize, though they now glowed bright and constant. The hands he reached out to steady her with were strong and gentle, despite their tips which gleamed lethally sharp. He was still covered in fur, still in the wereform she'd first glimpsed in the clearing right before he attacked Curtis, but when she looked into his eyes, all she saw was Graham. The same Graham she'd fallen wildly, irrationally, and irrevocably in love with.

"Stay put," he growled, picking her up and depositing her on the far side of a fallen tree a split second before Curtis leapt out of the shadows and launched himself at Graham's throat.

Graham countered, throwing himself into the battle. They met in midair, claws ripping, teeth tearing, before they even made it to solid ground. Missy had never seen a real fight, not between men, not between wolves, and certainly not between wolf men. They grappled a little like wrestlers, but mainly they fought like animals, each using teeth and claws and sheer physical might to try to force the other into submission. The moves were so fast and furious, so brutally contained, she could barely see what was going on. All she saw was the twisting shift of muscle and a few bits of red when one or the other landed a swiping blow of razor-sharp claws or tore through fur and flesh with strong, white teeth.

They fought for control, a struggle for the dominance of the alpha position just like it had been explained to her earlier in the day. While Graham, Annie, and Samantha had been explaining the nuances of werewolf etiquette to her, they'd mentioned dominance fights, since several inevitably broke out during a matehunt. Emotions and hormones ran high on these nights, and when two males wanted the same female, they settled the contest with a fight, the more dominant winner getting the girl. Fights in a matehunt usually ended with one Lupine giving in and submitting to his stronger opponent, showing his belly and averting his eyes to show his subordinate pack rank. The only problem was that this fight between Graham and Curtis wasn't really about her. It wasn't a matter of who got the girl, it was an alpha challenge, and those fights could and often did end only in the death of the subordinate were.

Missy knew Graham was stronger than Curtis and could easily handle his cousin in a fair fight, but in the short while she'd known Curtis Missy had begun to doubt Graham's cousin would offer a fair fight. She just hoped Graham wouldn't count on honor to keep their struggle weighted in his favor.

She fisted her hands into knots to keep from wading into the fray and helping Graham beat his cousin into a bloody pulp. She only held herself back because she knew she'd be in the way, which might prolong the fight, and she wanted this over with as soon as possible so she could beat up on Graham herself.

She winced every time she made out a blow that Curtis landed and bit her lip to keep from cheering every time Graham sank his teeth into his cousin's lousy hide. The struggle continued, fast and mostly silent, punctuated only by the occasional grunt or snarl as each of them tried to rip the other's throat out. The tangle of fur and teeth made it hard to tell where black ended and brindle began. Then she heard Graham howl and saw a dark red strip appear on his upper chest, and she jumped forward, not caring whose way she got in as long as she could get her hands around Curtis's neck and choke the life out of him for hurting her mate.

Lucky for her, she was still a slow human, because a hand on the back of her bodysuit pulled her to a halt before she got more than a foot closer to her goal. Her surprisingly sharp vision picked out Annie's form easily, and Missy's angry growl turned into a sigh of relief when she saw Samantha following close behind. Missy had been afraid Graham's secretary had been hurt badly, but Samantha looked completely conscious and relatively unharmed as she jogged to her Luna's side.

Missy's sigh turned into a blush when she saw Logan bringing up the rear of the arriving entourage. After this morning when he'd seen Graham fucking her in the front hall, Missy figured she'd probably keep blushing in Logan's presence for the rest of her life.

"What do you think you're doing?" Logan snapped as soon as he got close enough. He didn't bother to comment on her red cheeks and mortified expression. "That's an alpha challenge. You can't just go barreling in there like Joan of Bloody Arc. You could get hurt!"

Missy's blush faded in a rush of anger. "Don't tell me what I can't do," she snapped. "I'm Luna here, and that's my mate getting his hide torn to shreds!"

Logan scowled and straightened to his full height so that he towered over her by about a foot. He crossed his arms over his chest and dug in his heels like a mulish man. "You may be Luna, but I'm beta. Your authority is over the females, not over me. I will defer to you under normal circumstances as a sign of respect, but I will not and cannot let you place yourself in danger. You belong to the alpha, and I protect what's his."

Ignoring the difference in their heights, weights, ages, experience, physical strength, fighting ability, and species, Missy stalked the few steps it took until she stood toe-to-toe with the blustering male, tilted her head back, and stared him down through narrowed brown eyes.

"I'll place myself any damned place I want to, buddy," she bit out in a dangerously soft voice. "And instead of spouting off about how you're protecting me, why don't you do something useful, like protect the one who's currently getting his hide sliced off!"

By the time she finished yelling, she was standing on her tiptoes and leaning forward until Logan was practically bent over backward from trying not to touch her.

"Um, before you take my head off," he ventured, his expression changing from mulish to amused, "maybe you want to take a look at your mate and tell me if you still think he needs my help."

Surprised, she pulled back and turned in Graham's direction just in time to see him lift Curtis over his head and slam the smaller were to the ground before planting a foot on his chest to keep him down. Curtis lay belly-up, yelping while Graham crouched above him, one foot on his chest and one hand wrapped tight around his throat.

"Yield!" Graham growled in a voice so thick and savage and predatory it barely sounded like human English.

Curtis spat out a foul curse and then made a violent choking noise as the hand around his throat tightened.

"Yield," Graham repeated, and Curtis finally complied, hatred burning in his muddy yellow eyes. As Missy, Annie, Samantha, and Logan watched, the smaller lycanthrope went limp and relaxed beneath his foe and turned his head, averting his eyes from his cousin's harsh, triumphant features.

With a growl of satisfaction, Graham stood, keeping one foot on Curtis's chest as he turned and locked his eyes on the other people around him. Actually, his eyes locked specifically on Missy and sparked an even brighter green.

"You. Leave. Now."

Missy jumped at the tense, gravelly command, but Annie and Samantha were already turning away. More than happy to get away from the Mr. Hyde version of her lover, Missy took a step backward, freezing when Graham growled, the sound loud and deep and full of menace.

"Take him. Away. Go." Graham's eyes never left Missy, but Logan moved forward to obey the order. As soon as Graham lifted his foot, the beta grabbed Curtis and began dragging the bloody and battered lycanthrope back toward the clearing where the pack had gathered earlier.

Suddenly left alone with her mate, Missy took a deep, shaky breath and turned her gaze toward him.

Graham stood in the center of the small area where he and Curtis had fought, his chest heaving, his muscles tensed and bunched, ready to spring. He still wore his werewolf form, and his fur was matted and darkened with blood where Curtis had injured him. The worst wound looked like the one on his shoulder where his cousin's claws had bitten deep, but already the bleeding had stopped. Lupines healed at an amazing rate and Missy was getting to see that firsthand, but she still couldn't quite convince herself Graham was really well.

"Come here."

She heard him, but her feet seemed to be glued

to the ground. She was too busy fighting the conflicting instincts that urged her to go to him and run her hands over his magnificently furred body to assure herself he was really okay and to turn tail and run as fast as she could back toward civilization.

Instead of doing either, she remained locked in place, her eyes wide and fascinated as she ran her gaze over him from the tips of his pointy ears to the claws on his bare feet.

Except that she never got as far as his feet, because her gaze skidded to a halt when she saw his erection, long, thick, and jutting high above his tightly drawn balls. That was about when her mind turned to Jell-O.

"Here," he repeated, gesturing impatiently. "Now."

But the fear wouldn't let her. He was intimidating enough in human form, but the sight of him in wereform, tense and intent and aroused, bent her reality just a little too far. She recognized the light in his eyes, recognized his desire for her, but her mind couldn't get past his fur and his teeth and the frantic desire to get away.

She started to turn, to flee, but his growl stopped her, not to mention the fact that he leapt across the ten feet separating them in a single bound, landing between her and escape with the grace of a cat, or a wolf, and began herding her backward.

"Don't!" he growled. "Don't run."

She almost did. Her instincts almost took over, sending her hurtling through the dark forest, but then she looked into his eyes and her heart contracted.

He was in there. Her Graham. His eyes shone out at her from the face of the monster that terrified her, and she felt her fear begin to ease. His gaze, even sparking with raw hunger, was kind, reassuring, and familiar. She focused on it and found herself relaxing as a thought occurred to her. As she was growing up, her favorite fairy tale had always been "Beauty and the Beast," because her heart ached at the loneliness of the huge, terrible Beast and the unfairness that he had to change into something more human and more handsome just to give some spoiled beauty a happily ever after.

If Missy had been Beauty, she had thought, she would have wanted her beast to be her beast forever, not turn into some sappy prince just when she admitted she loved him.

Well, here was her fairy tale. Her beast stood before her, wild and fierce in appearance, but a better man inside than most human males could ever hope to be.

"Here," he said again. "Now."

Missy went.

She drew a deep breath, still a little shaky but effective, and crossed the small distance between them until she had to crane her neck to meet his gaze. She lifted a trembling hand to his chest, forcing her fingers to uncurl so she could lay them against his soft fur. She gasped, and he growled. Then he took two steps back and clenched his own hands into fists.

"Don't," he growled. "Too dangerous. Don't want to hurt you."

Feeling another layer of her fear melt away, Missy slid her hand down farther, over his flat nipple, and marveled at the similarities between his human form and this one. He might be so large now that she felt like an under-endowed Barbie doll next to him, but in either form, he trembled the minute her fingernail scraped over the tightly drawn flesh.

"You won't," she murmured, and she was beginning to believe it, too. "You won't hurt me."

He gasped, the air hissing through his clenched teeth. "Won't want to. Won't be able to stop."

That made her pause, both hands now pressed flat to the heavy muscles of his torso as she contemplated the implications of his lack of control. The things he'd explained to her the other night came flooding back. She could remember the chill fabric of the sofa pressing against her bare skin, the heat of his body looming over her. She could remember exactly what he'd said.

"We pick the one we want for a mate. We chase her down. And we take her. There's no seduction, no asking what she wants. . . . When the males give chase, they're in rut. Their instincts are in control, and there's no werewolf alive who can control his need to mate when he's in rut. If a hunt didn't end in sex, it would end in death. Which do you think is a better choice?"

He stepped back to evade her touch and hauled

in a deep breath. "Don't touch. Can't shift if you touch. Need control."

Even in rut, a state he'd said none of his kind could control, he was trying to protect her. He was afraid he would hurt her if he ended the hunt by taking her in his wereform, and Missy could see why. Even in human form, he was strong enough to crush her with his bare hands. In wereform he was more than a foot and a half taller than her, and probably two hundred pounds heavier. He overwhelmed her, standing completely still. But he was still her Graham, and he needed her.

She bit her lip, torn between fear and love, unsure if she could give him what he needed, sure she couldn't live with herself if she didn't. She hesitated for long heartbeats, debating and agonizing and finally saying a quick, fervent prayer.

Then she laid one hand back on his chest, meeting his eyes as she slid it down over his velvety pelt to curl around the shaft of his flagrant erection.

"You need me," she whispered, leaning forward until her tongue could dart out and caress his nipple. She felt the shudder wrack him and smiled. "And you can have me."

CHAPTER SIXTEEN

For one heartbeat he remained utterly still, and Missy wondered if she'd made a horrible mistake. Then his clawed hand curled around her wrist, prompting her to look up at him once more.

"Don't tease," he growled, his teeth bared in a feral expression, but his eyes still full of Graham. "Need you. Now."

Her other hand slipped between his legs and cuddled the soft weight she found there. "Then have me. Now."

He broke. The fierce tension binding him in place snapped like a rubber band. He reached for her, burying his hand in the neck of her bodysuit and ripping it from her with one rough tear. He fisted his hands around the tattered cloth and snarled.

"Last chance."

Fronting a defiance she hoped looked more convincing than it felt, she unzipped her boots and kicked them off into the underbrush. "It's about time."

She had about half a second to look tough and

feel terrified before he sprang, wrapping his arms around her and carrying her to the chilly earth under their feet. He rolled so she landed on top of him, and not the rough ground, but the move still took her breath away. Before she could so much as draw a breath, he lifted her and deposited her on her knees beside him.

She sat back on her heels, prepared to chew him out for continuing to try to save her, but before her mouth could even open, he planted a hand between her shoulder blades and tugged her gently forward until she knelt on all fours. When he got on his knees behind her, she curled her fingers in the rough carpet of pine needles and braced herself for a brutal entrance and a short, wild claiming. She got neither.

She heard him move behind her and tried to look around to see what he was doing, but he placed his hand on the back of her neck to pin her head in one position so that all she could see was the backs of her own hands. He held her there while he positioned himself behind her, bracketing her legs with his own so she could feel the heat of his muscle and the velvety pile of his fur against her bare skin. She expected to feel him pressing immediately against her entrance and burrowing inside, to feel his weight draping over her back and surrounding her while he claimed her as his mate.

Instead, she felt a stir of warm breath against the top of her buttock and then the hot, wet glide of his tongue sliding slowly along her spine, vertebra by vertebra until she wanted to scream. She managed to contain the sound, but she couldn't contain the shudder that rippled through her. Graham reached the nape of her neck and swirled his tongue in the little hollow at the base of her skull, and the sensation made her teeth clack together on another violent shiver.

She heard a low rumble, more a purr than a growl, and his tongue traced a damp path from her neck to her ear to flick the lobe and tease the sensitive shell. Her hands clenched in anticipation, and her back arched to press against his chest, needing the contact of his heat against her bare skin. He made another rumbling noise and nuzzled his way around to her other ear, treating it to the same arousing torture.

"Graham," she murmured, savoring his name like she savored the sensations of his touch. She shifted her weight to press her bottom against his groin, feeling the familiar contours of his arousal and the unique, heady sensation of fur caressing her.

She had looked on this mating as a chore or a favor, something she would do for him because he needed it, despite how it might frighten or unsettle her. Only she felt perfectly settled and not at all afraid. She felt eager and had the deep internal aching to prove it. Neither her body nor her heart cared what he looked like, because she knew this was Graham, and every time she got within fifty feet of him, she wanted him.

Suddenly empty and needy, Missy began to shift her hips in a languid thrusting motion, rubbing her bottom firmly against his erection and feeling it swell even harder against her.

"Graham," she repeated. "I want you."

She heard him growl, heard his breath rush out in a hiss, and felt it feather against her skin. He let his weight drop above her until he covered her like a blanket and his hands rested palms-down on the earth beside hers. His head fell until he rested his velvety chin against her shoulder. He surrounded her, and she shook with excitement.

"Can't go slow," he bit out. His voice sounded loud and rasping in her ear. "Can't be gentle. Sorry."

She hitched her ass up high so his hard cock nestled between the round cheeks, and wiggled her hips so they rubbed teasingly against his length.

"I don't need slow, or gentle," she hissed. "I just need you."

This time, she felt him shudder, and then his hands were gripping her hips with bruising force and his weight lifted off her.

"Sorry," he repeated, poised for one heartbeat at her twitching entrance, before he thrust his pelvis forward and buried himself deep within her.

The long, high howl that tore from Missy's throat sounded more Lupine than human, and she wondered at it for a heartbeat before the feel of Graham's shaft impaling her tender flesh drove every thought from her mind except the need to get closer to him. She braced her clenched fists against the forest floor and locked her elbows, using the leverage to force her hips higher and harder against him.

Graham grunted his appreciation and pulled back until just the tip of his length remained inside her. She bucked, trying to force him deep again, but he held her in place with his powerful hands.

"Mine," he snarled, teasing her with a shallow thrust that moved no more than an inch or two against her sensitive opening.

Missy moaned and tried another thrust. Again he held back. If this was his idea of fast and rough, they needed to have a serious talk. Right after he got on with it and took her!

"Mine!" His growl was more forceful that time, but his thrust was not, and Missy decided he had developed a fondness for torture.

"God, Graham, please!" she gasped, shaking and shivering beneath him, her pussy clenching hard around the meager number of inches he allowed her, trying desperately to lure him deeper. But he resisted.

"Mine!" More force this time, along with one blessedly hard thrust that sent him driving deep inside her, nudging her womb before he drew back and paused again just beyond her entrance.

Her entire body clenched and shook under his merciless teasing. Her breath panted out in shivering sobs, and she had to clench her teeth hard to keep them from chattering. He reduced her to practically begging, and she would do it gladly if it meant she would feel him driving her hard and fast toward orgasm. "Graham!"

"Mine!" His hands clenched on her flesh hard enough to bruise, and he began to ease out before her muddled mind finally grasped what he wanted.

"Wait!" Half gasp, half scream, the word tumbled from her in a rush, and she just prayed she'd spoken clearly enough for him to understand. It must have been enough, because he paused, the thick, plum tip of his erection barely breaching her entrance, but he wasn't pulling away anymore and that was important. Now she just needed to get him back inside her and she could die a happy woman. She drew a deep, shuddering breath, licked her lips, and gave him everything.

"I'm yours, Graham. Your lover, your mate. Whatever you want me to be. Yours!"

"Mine!" And he thrust forward so hard, Missy thought she'd died. He pierced her to the core, his thick shaft tunneling through her moisture until he filled every aching bit, and when he started moving, she thought she'd been reborn.

After that thrust, he kept his promise. He rode her hard and fast, moving forcefully within her, his hips thudding against her bottom with the raw, slapping sound of sex. Every forward motion drove the air out of her lungs and every withdrawal made her sob for more. It was fast, hot, and primal, and it made Missy understand what it meant to be claimed as his mate.

Every time he filled her, she felt as if a brand of

ownership burned deeper into her skin, and every time he pulled away, she wanted to beg him to mark her more indelibly. He had hunted her and fought for her and now he was making her his. The logic of it resonated on an instinctual level, and she gloried in it.

Graham tightened his hands on her hips and jerked her back to meet his thrusts. She cried out, a sound of pure excitement, and he lunged into her with even greater force. She felt the tension in her belly knot harder, felt her thighs clench and her heartbeat race double time in her chest. Her climax approached like a tornado, quick and powerful, and she reached toward it, wanting nothing more than to be swept up in the force of her mate's fierce sexuality.

She threw herself back against him, pressing every possible inch of her skin into his hard frame, but when he leaned forward and caught her shoulder between his dangerous jaws, she fell forward into the storm, her entire body clenching with the force of her pleasure. The orgasm ripped through her, and she came with a howl at the very instant that his teeth cut through her flesh, marking her forever as his one true mate.

In the haze of her pleasure, she heard his growl, felt him pull away and lap at the small wound he had made. She felt him thrust deep within her and stop, holding himself high and hard inside her, and then she felt him swelling. She felt his erection twitch and throb and grow impossibly thicker, stretching her tender flesh until she cried out and threw her head back on a wild moan. Graham echoed the sound with a roar, gave one last mighty lunge, and began coming apart within her.

The force of his final thrust knocked Missy's legs out from under her, and she sprawled in an inelegant mess on the cold ground. Graham followed her, collapsing on top of her and blanketing her with his heat. While she felt boneless with contentment, she felt his presence still hard and thick inside her while he emptied himself against her womb. She lay still, struggling to catch her breath, content to have him in her forever, loving the feel of him finishing inside her.

But he wasn't finished.

He tensed appreciably within her, then relaxed, the tension fading from his muscles even while his arousal stayed rock hard inside her.

Missy frowned and turned her head until she could rub her cheek against his plush fur. "Are you okay?" she murmured sleepily. "Aren't you . . . ?"

"I'm not finished," he growled back, though the sound lacked any sort of ferocity and sounded more like the natural gravel of his wolf form's voice. "Not nearly finished."

Then she felt him twitch inside her and another warm rush fill her, and her eyes opened so wide she thought they would pop out of their sockets. Her pussy twitched at the fresh stimulus, and she gasped. "What are you—ah!"

His tongue slipped out to caress her cheek, followed by a gentle nibble to her earlobe. "Lupines have a few other things in common with wolves," he rumbled as his erection stopped throbbing to rest inside her again. "In our wereforms, the males orgasm like wolves, staying inside the female and climaxing in lots of short bursts over an extended period of time."

Missy's thighs clenched involuntarily, sending another shiver coursing through her. She noticed that he felt just as hard as he had before he began to climax.

"How extended a period?" she managed to gasp while she struggled to bring her rioting nerves under some semblance of control. It wasn't working.

"Well, it varies," he drawled, and if he'd been in human form, Missy was willing to bet she'd see one of those wicked grins curving his mouth. "But it's usually around twenty minutes or so."

"Twenty minutes?!" Her voice squeaked out like a rusty hinge, and her body clenched while he made a sound in her ear that sounded suspiciously like a chuckle.

"About that. Sometimes a little more." He brushed the hair away from the side of her neck and gave a nibble. "I hope you're comfortable. This could take a while."

CHAPTER SEVENTEEN

They didn't make it back to his house until shortly after dawn. It would have been even longer if Logan hadn't been an extremely efficient beta and left a duffel bag with a change of clothes for each of them along with Graham's cell phone at the base of a tree a few yards from where they'd spent the night.

If Missy tried really hard, she could almost keep herself from thinking about the sounds the Lupine must have heard coming from their part of the forest. The man just knew way too much about her sex life.

Some things it didn't pay to dwell on, so she let Graham bundle her into some clothes and call a cab, and she didn't even protest when he carried her swiftly out of the Ramble and to the nearest park entrance. The cab was already waiting for them. Graham loaded her inside, slid in after her, and gave the cabbie his address. Then he cuddled her in his lap all the way home, where he swept her right up the stairs and into bed. When she tried to protest and mumble something about talking, he shushed her and told her there would be time for that when she woke up.

She woke up just after one, sore, hungry, and determined to have that talk. Pushing up into a sitting position, she tucked the bed's only covering—a mismatched sheet obviously added just for her benefit—under her arms and looked around. Graham was nowhere to be found. She was debating whether or not to waste her energy by working herself into a good mad when the door opened and he stepped inside carrying a breakfast tray, looking quite human and decidedly gorgeous. His eyes fixed on her, and she blushed.

"Good morning, sleepyhead." He smiled, kicking the door shut behind him and carrying the tray to the bed. "How are you feeling?"

He set the tray over her lap and took a seat next to her, taking care not to upset her breakfast when the mattress shifted under his weight.

"Fine." She shrugged, picking up a piece of buttered toast and trying not to blush harder.

"Good." He reached out to tuck a strand of hair behind her ear. "You did a fantastic job last night, but I wanted to make sure nothing that happened gave you any bad moments."

Ignoring the twinge of sympathy for a man who walked so blindly into a trap of his own making, Missy set down her toast and raised an eyebrow.

"Bad moments?" She pretended to think about it. "You mean like when your cousin sent his goons chasing after me and they hurt one of my new friends trying to get to me? Or were you talking about when Curtis grabbed me and threatened to kill me for daring to be chosen as your mate? Because no. Neither of those caused me any real problems."

He started to relax, but he must have taken a closer look at her face, because the tension flooded back into his body.

Smart man, she thought. *Occasionally.*

"Of course, I suppose you could have been referring to the part where I had to stand by and watch someone try to kill you because of me. Or when I saw him slice your chest open so that you bled all over yourself. Was that what you meant?"

He shook his head and opened his mouth, but Missy wasn't quite finished.

"No, neither of those bothered me, really. But thanks for asking."

He forced an uncomfortable smile and reached for her, but Missy pulled away to glare at him. He winced.

"Now that I think about it, though, there was one part of the night that did really upset me, and now that you mention it, I'm not sure I've really dealt with it yet."

"Baby, I'm sorry," he began, his green eyes dark with regret. "I know I hurt you. I should have been more gentle. I should have waited until I shifted back before I ever laid a hand on—"

Missy brushed off his apology with a negligent wave. "I wasn't talking about the sex," she said, clearly dismissive. "That was fine. No, I'm upset about something else entirely."

Now Graham looked confused, which was just how she wanted him. "I don't understand."

"Oh, I'll tell you," she said, her tone so sweet it made him shift uneasily. "It's just a little thing. You might not even remember it. It's the part where I found out I'm pregnant, you twit!!!"

She shouted so loudly the silverware clanked together, and Graham winced like he'd been hit with hurricane-force winds. Missy figured Category 4 had nothing on her.

"Missy, I—"

"How could you do that to me?" she demanded, slapping her hands against his chest so hard that when she lifted them from his skin she left perfect impressions of them in flaming red detail.

"Sweetheart—"

"How could you treat me like that? I thought you were supposed to be my perfect man?" She drew back her fist and pounded it hard against his stomach. Then she did it again for good measure. "Some perfect you turned out to be! Humiliating me like that!"

"I never meant to—"

"And to have the nerve to act casual about it!" Her eyes dropped to the knife on the breakfast tray and he turned an interesting shade of gray. "I just can't believe your nerve."

"Baby, if you'd just let me—"

"Were you ever planning on telling me?" she

demanded, rising up on her knees and planting one hand on her hip while the other clenched the sheet across her bare breasts. "Did you think I might like to know about something like that before you announced it to a bloody stranger? Huh? Did that ever occur to you, Mr. High-and-Mighty Alpha?"

"I didn't mean—"

"Well, I don't really care what you meant," she shouted, far from finished. "That was a lousy thing to do! You treated me like some sort of secret weapon, like this whole thing was a plot to knock up the first bimbo who came along just so you could rub your cousin's nose in it, and that sucks. It's my uterus, damn it! I deserved to be the first one to know it was growing something."

Her anger dissolved on a sniffle, and she cursed whatever hormones were already hard at work turning her into a blubbering idiot. Then she cursed whatever ones made her glad when Graham wrapped his traitorous male arms around her and snuggled her close.

"Aw, baby, I'm sorry," he murmured, letting her bury her face in his shoulder while he drew her into his lap and rocked her like a child. "I know it was lousy, and I apologize. I should never have treated you like that, but my cousin had me trapped. Telling him about the baby was the only way I could think of to keep you safe. I was hoping that if he knew about the cub, he'd realize his plan was futile and he'd give it up."

Missy snorted. "Yeah, and that strategy worked really well."

"I noticed." He hugged her close and pressed a warm kiss to the top of her head. "I almost died when he went after you, and letting him live after he touched you was the hardest thing I've ever done. I never wanted to put you or the baby in any danger. You have to believe that."

She did believe that, just like she believed the big moron was in love with her, but she still intended to make him say it.

"I do," she whispered, nuzzling his throat and letting her arms snake around his chest. "I believe it. But I'm still hurt that you told him before I knew, and I don't understand how you did know."

"Your scent," he explained, kneading her back with soft, affectionate circles. "Like I told you, I recognized you as my mate the minute I smelled you. When you got pregnant, your hormones started to change, and that changed your scent. Pregnant women all have a similar sort of scent. It's hard to describe, but it's a little bit like . . . pumpkin."

She pulled back to frown at him. "Pumpkin?"

"Like pumpkin pie," he clarified. "Rich. Spicy."

She took a second to digest that. "And is that a good thing?"

He grinned. "Am I happy you're pregnant? Sweetheart, I'm ecstatic. I can't think of a single thing that could make me happier."

Missy could think of a single, very important thing that would make her happy, but they were getting closer. She could sense it building in him, but it would require a few well-placed digs before she finally uncovered it. "Does that mean you didn't deliberately get me pregnant? That you want me and the baby for ourselves instead of to satisfy some weird Lupine laws?"

Graham drew a deep breath and opened his mouth to answer. Then he snapped it shut and frowned. Missy felt her stomach knot.

"Are you saying you did just want the baby because of your damned Breeder's Rights thing?"

"God, no!" he assured her, his arms tightening around her to keep her from escaping. "That's not the part I hesitated over. I don't give a shit about Breeder's Rights. The elders can decide whatever they want, but anyone who wants to take over the alpha position of my clan will have to kill me first. I'm not giving in just because of an archaic tradition."

Missy felt her eyes widen and her jaw drop open. "Then . . . are you—are you saying you deliberately got me pregnant?"

"You make it sound like I had it planned," he protested, looking grumpy and uncomfortable and very sweet. "It wasn't like that at all. It's not something I had in mind, but when you came into heat—"

"When I what?"

"Ovulated," he corrected quickly. "When you ovulated, I knew what would happen if I came inside you, and I did it anyway. As soon as I pictured you having my baby, I knew I wanted that. I knew exactly what would happen, but I did it anyway. So yeah, I guess it was deliberate."

How had this conversation spun so far out of her control? The man created more questions than he answered.

"Okay, first, how did you know I was ovulating?"

He gave her a look that said it should be obvious. "If I can smell when you're a few hours pregnant, I can certainly smell when you're fertile. It doesn't take a rocket scientist, just a good nose."

"So you really want this baby."

He hugged her. "I'm over the moon, honey. Like I told you, you couldn't make me any happier."

Unable to pull free to hunt up a blunt object to knock some sense into him, Missy had to resort to point-blank bluntness. "Is it only the baby that makes you happy? Do I have anything to do with it?"

He jerked back to stare at her with an expression of abject confusion. "What? Baby, of course! I love you, just like I love the baby. How can you not know that?"

"Because you've never told me so, you hairy twit!"

Frustration made her yell and curved her mouth into a pout, but she could feel her tension melting away. "Remember, I'm the human here. I have no magical powers. No mind reading, no wonder nose, nothing. If you feel something for me, you need to tell me, okay?"

His lips twitched into a slow smile, and he leaned

down to press a kiss on the end of her nose. "Okay," he agreed, and snuggled her close against his chest.

They sat that way for a few more minutes until Graham brushed her hair away from her face and pressed a kiss to her temple.

"You know, for all our strength and speed and heightened senses," he said, smoothing his hands over her back with lazy strokes, "werewolves are really different from vampires. We're not just humans who've been infected with the virus and had our DNA mutated. We're an entirely different species. Closely related, yeah, but still different from humans."

Missy lifted her head and frowned up at him. "What?"

"It's actually lucky that we share enough common DNA with humans to make reproducing fertile offspring possible," he continued, ignoring her question. "A few more separations in our genetic code and we'd be like oil and water. We're really lucky."

She pushed away from his chest to stare at him in confusion. "What are you yammering on about?"

Again he ignored her. "Because some people just sort of assume that because we're both different, werewolves and vampires must have a lot in common. But it's just not true. Other than being faster and stronger and those kinds of surface things, vampires and Lupines are as different as night and day."

"And your point is?" By now, Missy's spine had straightened like a poker and her arms rested in a fold against her chest.

"I just made it. My point is that Lupines and vampires are really very different from each other."

"Well, I knew that," she said, exasperated. "What I want to know is why you're bringing this up now."

He gave her an entirely, suspiciously innocent look. "Well, I just thought that since you're such good friends with Regina, and you know Dmitri and all, that you might be a little confused."

She rolled her eyes. "Yeah, well, I think that even with my human senses, I can tell the difference between fangy and furry, Einstein. You can relax."

His green eyes opened wide, and she could swear he actually batted his eyelashes at her. "Oh, so then you haven't assumed I can read your mind?"

His sledgehammer subtlety finally got his meaning across, and Missy groaned. "Oh, for heaven's sake. Yes, I love you! Are you happy now? I really don't think that elaborate torture session was quite necessary."

Graham shrugged, grinning his wicked grin. "Maybe not. But it was fun." She reached out to thump him in the chest, but he caught her hand easily and brought it to his lips. "I need the words just as much as you do, honey."

Missy humphed, but she knew he was right, and frankly, she was still in a fairly charitable mood after hearing him declare himself. Blame it on the hormones.

Letting her head drop back to his shoulder, she rested a hand on her unchanged tummy and sighed.

"It doesn't seem quite real," she murmured. "What if we're wrong and I'm not really pregnant?"

"Well, I certainly would be willing to put my all into trying again," Graham said with a grin, "but we're not wrong. He's in there, honey, growing up quick."

She looked up at Graham. "Do Lupines grow that much faster than humans?"

"Not once they're born, but a standard Lupine pregnancy is only about five months."

Missy's eyebrows shot up and her lips parted in surprise. "Five months? I'll only be pregnant for five months?"

"More like six, in your case," he said. "I called an obstetrician—a Lupine to ask her if she knew anything about mixed pregnancies, and she said when a human woman has a Lupine baby, her pregnancy is usually about six months long. Longer than Lupine, shorter than human."

"Usually? I thought this didn't happen a lot. Lupines and humans together."

Graham shook his head and shifted his grip, one arm still supporting her back with his hand resting on her bare hip. The other reached out to tug away her sheet and bare her to his appreciative gaze. "Not often, but it's not entirely unheard of, either. Dr. Howell knows enough about it to take good care of you. In fact, she told me to bring you to her office this week for an exam, just to make sure everything's normal with you and the pup."

Missy gave up the sheet after a brief struggle. Graham was simply too strong, and she was simply too easy. He traced little circles around her nipples to watch them pucker. She shivered. Then she registered what he said, and she tensed.

"The pup?" She swallowed hard. "Um, Graham, Annie and Samantha told me I wasn't going to have a puppy. Please don't tell me our baby will be born with a tail."

He laughed out loud and hugged her. "Sorry, didn't mean to scare you. 'Pup' is just an expression. We tend to call our children 'pups' or 'cubs,' but they're normal babies. Unless you were Lupine, which you're not, and you happened to be in wolf form when you went into labor, which you won't be, you don't have to worry about whelping anything but a normal baby."

She gave a sigh of relief. "Maybe I should make an appointment to see that doctor. I think I'll have a lot of questions to ask her."

"We'll call tomorrow. I'd like to go with you, if you don't mind."

"Of course not," she assured him, shifting in his arms and pressing the breasts he'd been teasing against his broad chest. "I'd like to have my mate with me. After all, this is your baby, too."

He smiled and leaned down to kiss her. It started out as a sweet, affectionate gesture, but Missy took care of that by reaching down between them and unfastening his jeans. When she slipped her hands inside to curl around his already erect cock, he groaned into her mouth. Smiling against his lips, she freed one hand to yank his T-shirt up over his taut stomach.

He took the hint, jerking his T-shirt over his head and tossing it to the floor before returning to devour her mouth in a deep, hungry kiss. She matched him for a moment before pulling away and pressing a hand to his chest to urge him back onto the mattress. He got rid of the tray first, then stretched out on the cool silk sheet and opened his arms as if to offer himself to her. Missy was not about to refuse.

Smiling a smile that even felt wicked on her lips, she reached for the waistband of his jeans and tugged them off. Dropping them on the floor, or maybe on top of the breakfast tray, she knelt astride his thighs and leaned back to get a good look.

Lordy, but the man got her hot every time she looked at him, and when he was naked, looking at him got her wet, too. As if her body were drooling for him. Heaven knew her mouth was.

She watched him run his gaze over her and blushed but didn't make a move to cover herself. An entire weekend with him convinced her that Graham really did love the way she looked, which made the feeling mutual. She certainly had a hard time resisting the lure of his beautifully muscled chest.

"You're gorgeous," he growled, reaching up to cup her breasts in his large hands, cuddling their petite curves and rubbing the nipples with callused thumbs. "I love you, baby."

The words felt even better than his hands and

made Missy shiver. Smiling, she leaned down and set her mouth against the hot, steady pulse at the base of his throat. Her tongue dipped out to taste the salty, musky flavor of his skin, lapping at the small hollow before beginning a slow, teasing descent.

She worked her way down his body with an excruciating lack of haste, pausing for long moments at each of his nipples, tracing the contours of his muscles, the crisp hair and smooth silk of his skin. She spent a few tense minutes investigating his belly button just so she could savor the rough, purring sound of his moans, but when he rolled his hips against her, she took pity on him and resumed her trek south.

His body rose to greet her, his erection already thick and hard and begging for attention. How could a girl resist? Missy didn't even put up a fight. She leaned down, rubbing her cheek against the surprisingly smooth flesh like a kitten begging to be stroked. She felt his hands bury themselves in her hair and his fingers massage her scalp as she parted her lips and drew him in.

He slid easily past her lips, a warm, welcome presence that filled her mouth and made her hum with pleasure. She swirled her tongue around the head and heard him moan. The sound did as much for her as a well-placed caress, sending warmth shooting through her body to pool as moisture between her legs. Loving him was almost as good as being loved by him, and it gave her a sense of power and control that she relished. Especially after last night.

His hands continued to cup the back of her head, cradling it gently as she settled into a lazy rhythm of licks, nibbles, and gentle pulls that made him harden even further in her warm mouth. Her fingers rubbed the tender skin at the crease of his hips while she sucked him, one straying farther and farther toward the inside of his thigh with every caress. When it finally reached its destination, it feathered lightly across the drawn skin before curving to cup the weight in her palm. Softly she kneaded the sensitive globes, timing her squeeze and release to coincide with her suckling.

In minutes his hips began to rock gently, sending his cock gliding between her lips in a restless motion.

Missy drew back, placing a soft kiss on his thigh before she crawled up to kneel, straddling his hips with her palms braced flat against his chest. She felt his thick length pressing against her inner thigh and smiled.

"I love you, too," she murmured, then slowly began to join their bodies together.

Graham growled, the sound familiar and exciting, softer than the growls of last night but sounding no less aroused for coming from a human throat. It still made Missy shiver, which made her muscles clench tight around his shaft, which made him growl again. Life couldn't get any better.

She let gravity pull her slowly down his length

until her bottom rested against his hips and his arousal rested to the hilt inside her. The feel of him made her want to howl, but she restrained herself. Not out of embarrassment, but because she wanted to conserve her breath for better things. Like a hard, fast ride to the edge.

Dragging her hips up, she pulled almost entirely free of him before plunging back, savoring the feel of him stretching her and filling her and making her burn. She settled into a rapid rhythm of lift and fall that he echoed with powerful upward thrusts.

Within minutes, Missy was panting, her lungs straining to grab enough oxygen while her body strained to keep Graham lodged deep inside her. She felt torn, wanting to continue making love with him forever but needing the intense climax she could sense building on the horizon. She slowed her movements, unable to choose, until Graham took the decision out of her hands.

Strong fingers closed around her hips, anchoring her in place while he flipped their bodies, settling her on her back and himself firmly between her thighs.

"Wrap your legs around me," he growled, and she complied, lifting them high to curl around his waist and locking her ankles together in the small of his back.

The move seemed to drive him deeper, and she cried out, "Now. More."

He gave her more. Bracing his hands against the mattress, he bowed his back to press deeper inside her, pausing as if he were savoring the fullness of their connection. Then he drew back and began a hard driving rhythm that had her clutching at his shoulders and digging her heels into his spine to try to pull him deeper. He filled her until she wasn't sure she could take any more, but she wanted more and demanded it.

His thrusts became shorter, harder, digging inside her with frantic force. She welcomed every second of it, letting him drive her higher and higher up the peak until he sent her hurtling over the edge in a climax that curled her toes and clamped her internal muscles around him with enough force to drag him along with her. He emptied himself with a roar before collapsing in a hot, boneless heap on top of her.

He must have dredged up a last little bit of energy from somewhere, because he had enough to nuzzle her neck and plant a soft kiss on the damp skin there. Missy couldn't offer much more than a breathless sigh in return, but she felt his lips curve in what she was sure would be a self-satisfied grin, if she had enough energy to turn her head and look. Which she didn't.

"I've changed my mind about using earth-shattering sex to convince you to move in with me," he murmured after a brief pause, presumably to work up the energy for speech.

"Hmm?" Missy hadn't built up enough reserve yet for anything so complex.

"I'm not going to do it. I've got another plan."

Her eyelids felt weighted down with lead as she drifted in a state of utterly sated contentment, but she managed to work up a burst of energy to communicate, "Huh?"

"It still involves plenty of sex," he assured her, and she smiled through her haze, "but this time I'm going to use it to convince you to marry me. What do you think?"

The smile that lit Missy's face didn't require energy. It was the kind that came from her soul, and she couldn't have stopped it if she'd tried. That left her one last thread of energy, which she used to give the only answer that mattered.

"Yes."

Visit stmartins.com/ChristineWarren

and sign up to receive

HEART OF THE SEA—

a never-before-released FREE short story from Christine Warren's *The Others* series.